FAKING IT

CHRISTINA ROSS

CHRISTINA ROSS

INTRODUCTION

Faking It is the first book in a three-book series that focuses on the entertainment industry. Next up is *Making It*, and then comes *Killing It*. Each book is a stand-alone novel with a guaranteed HEA, plenty of drama, hot sex, humor, angst, and characters you'll come to love—and never forget. Characters from *Faking It* will be showcased in minor roles in *Making It*, and the same will be true for *Killing It*, which will feature characters from the previous two books. In other words, welcome to my new book family—and three sexy new book boyfriends!

For my friends and my family,
and especially for my readers, who mean the world to me.

Also to my best friend, Erika Rhys,
who was indispensable to writing Faking It.

ABOUT THE AUTHOR

Many readers have asked, so! ;-)
Here is the reading order for the Annihilate Me series:

Annihilate Me, Vol. 1
Annihilate Me, Vol. 2
Annihilate Me, Vol. 3
Annihilate Me, Vol. 4
Annihilate Me, Holiday

Unleash Me, Vol. 1
Unleash Me, Vol. 2
Unleash Me, Vol. 3

Annihilate Him, Vol. 1
Annihilate Him, Vol. 2
Annihilate Him, Vol. 3

Ignite Me

Annihilate Him: Holiday

A Dangerous Widow

Annihilate Them
Annihilate Them: Holiday

Unleash Me: Wedding

1

New York City
June

THE MORNING after I arrived home from a whirlwind trip to the Cannes Film Festival—where my first movie, *Lion*, won the Palme d'Or and where I somehow also won the coveted Un Certain Regard prize for best actress—my agent, Harper Carmichael, was on the phone first thing.

"Sienna, darling, it's Harper," she said in that breezy voice of hers. "Are you awake? It's seven o'clock, so I need you to be awake. Because everything is blowing up right now."

"I'm awake now," I said as I sat up in bed and shielded my eyes from the sun pouring through the window in front of me. I'd arrived in New York last night, just before midnight. By the time I'd gotten to my apartment, taken a shower, and crawled into bed, it had been past two in the morning. Apparently I'd forgotten to close the curtains.

"What's blowing up?" I asked as I got out of bed and shut the curtains. "Has there been another terrorist attack?"

"You really are out of it, aren't you?"

"I've only had a few hours of sleep."

"Cry me a river," she said. "Because what's blowing up is *you*. After your win at Cannes, things are finally happening. People are talking. My phones are on fire. And I probably should get another e-mail account dedicated solely for you. Because right now, *everyone* is hungry to get a piece of Sienna Jones. And because of that alone, you need to be in my office by ten, because we have plenty to discuss. And later in the day, you're scheduled for an audition."

"An audition?" I said. "With whom?"

"Naturally I know, but since I want to see your face when I tell you, I'm keeping my mouth shut. But I will tell you this: it's as big as it gets. It's with a major A-list actor—and I mean huge. As in action-star huge. If they like your audition and you snag the part, we're talking total career game changer here, so I need you to show up looking your best. Full hair and makeup. Wear a summery dress that makes you feel pretty—and also a little bit sexy."

"Harper, I'm not sure I can do pretty or sexy right now. Cannes was intense. I barely got any sleep. Those parties you told me to go to were nonstop. So, as for giving you pretty, let alone sexy, let me just say this: I'm pretty sure that right now the only thing I can pull off is a hot, sexy mess."

"Spare me the lies," she said. "Those parties—paired with your charm and your superb performance in *Lion*—are the very reasons you won that award, Sienna. So, I need you to do this—not for me, but for you. Have your coffee. Get into your zone. And then take a long, hot shower before you pull yourself together and come here looking like the star that you are."

"*Lion* isn't even out in theaters yet," I said. "I'm no star, Harper."

"You're about to become one, sugar, because after your win, you're also about to do a shitload of interviews. *Vogue* wants you to be the face of their September issue."

"Come again?"

"You heard me."

"Are you serious? Their September issue? But that's—"

"*Their biggest and most important issue of the year*," she said. "And then there's the *Times*, which wants to do a sit-down with you stat. *Variety* and the *Hollywood Reporter* are eager to tell your story—which is critical, because they're the trads. And the list goes on. When it comes to interviews alone, I've got you booked for the next two weeks. So, I need you to listen to me very closely, because this is something I've seen happen only a few times before, and I know what it can do to a career."

"All right," I said, feeling as if a part of my body were separating from itself. "I'll do it—whatever I need to do. I'll pull it together and be in your office by ten."

"Good to hear," she said, "because lightning can't strike if you aren't standing out in the rain, my dear girl. And for you? Right now it's pouring, and my job is to make sure you get soaked so that lightning can strike time and again. I'll see you at ten. And don't disappoint me. Come here looking like the knockout I know you can be."

"WELL," Harper said when I entered her office at ten. "Look at you! Not such a hot mess after all."

"Consider it the miracle of a hot shower and two strong cups of coffee," I said after I'd given her a hug. She hugged me back in the way a mother would, said it was good to see me, and then took a step back to assess me with a sweeping glance.

"More like the miracle of youth and the luck of having good genes."

At fifty-four, Harper Carmichael was a force to be reckoned with. She was a self-proclaimed lipstick lesbian who was part of an elite few who led the careers of some of the world's finest talent.

For her age, she was also smoking hot.

She was the complete package—a beautiful, well-preserved blonde who was smart, quick, driven, connected, and successful. She was as tall as I was, which allowed her access to the kind of fashion that wasn't accessible to most women. Today she was wearing a white Gucci embroidered cluny lace dress with a jeweled back bow that showed off her toned legs. On her feet glimmered a pair of Jimmy Choo fearne patent crisscross wedge sandals in black, which I knew for a fact had set her back a cool grand. She wore her hair raked away from her face in a way that I thought accentuated her fine bone structure.

We were in her expansive office on Lexington Avenue in the Chrysler Building, where the all-powerful and all-important Creative Artists Agency held its offices on three separate floors. Anyone who was anyone in Hollywood was either signed now by CAA or had once been signed by it. Among its current clients were Meryl Streep, Will Smith, Sarah Jessica Parker, George Clooney, Lupita Nyong'o, Julia Roberts, Johnny Depp, Nicole Kidman, and beyond.

When I was nineteen and had first come to the city from Dubuque, Iowa, Harper was the only person out of the dozens of agents I'd met with who had seen my potential. When we'd first met, I'd told her that my dream was to work as an actress on Broadway—or if I had to, maybe even in film or in television. Broadway was my first choice, which is why I'd come to New York, but really I just wanted to act. When Harper asked me pointedly how much money I had in the bank, she had other ideas.

"You'll model," she'd said. "Because if you're going to live in this city, you also need to make quick money just so you can eat and pay the rent. You're a beautiful girl, Sienna, and modeling will do that for you. On the side, you'll take acting classes. And one day—if we're lucky—things might come together for you. Here's what I suggest: we get your face out there, you become known as a professional who is easy to work with, and when I feel the moment is right, I'll work my contacts and get you auditions. But before we go any further, I need you to understand a few things first."

"What things?" I'd asked.

"Over the years, too many people sitting where you are now have come to me with the perception that stardom comes quickly, swiftly, *easily*. But the harsh reality for most is that it takes years of hard work, talent, and a hell of a lot of luck to make it in this business. If you want to succeed as an actress, I need you to know that we're likely looking at a marathon here, not a sprint. If by chance you do happen to make it, you also need to know that it won't be without a major fight and much sacrifice on your part—because this business is hard, Sienna. It's not for the faint of heart. It's fraught with frustration and crushing disappointments. So, before I agree to sign you, I need to believe that you're up for that kind of a challenge, because my time is valuable, and I don't take a chance on just anyone. If I don't believe you're truly committed to this—and can handle this—know that I'll wish you the best going forward."

"Ms. Carmichael, I came here to make it," I'd said with

unexpected passion in my voice. "I came here to win. I've wanted this ever since I was a little girl. I grew up on a working farm, and believe me when I say that I know what hard work looks like. If I can shovel steaming piles of cow and chicken shit at four o'clock in the morning—as I did for years before I had to head off for school—then I can take whatever bullshit this business has to throw at me. This is my dream. If it turns out to be a marathon, let it be a marathon."

At that, she'd raised an eyebrow at me.

"Do you have a good support system around you?" she'd then asked. "People you can rely on who will help you through the difficult times?"

"I have an excellent relationship with my parents," I said. "And I have several close girlfriends I can always count on."

"How well do you handle disappointment?"

"Generally I take the hit and move on."

"Even when it gets personal?"

"I'm no robot," I said. "I'm not going to lie to you and say that I don't have feelings. What I can say truthfully is that I'm a fighter. And I'm especially ready to fight for this."

"Well," she'd said after a moment. "That's good to hear. I'm also glad to hear about your relationships, particularly the one you share with your parents, because going into this, you're going to need them, Sienna."

And then she'd signed me—and my God, had she been right. This journey of ours had been one mother of a marathon.

But we'd made it.

After eight years of modeling and taking bit parts in movies and television shows, last year I'd finally landed the lead role in *Lion*. As difficult and as challenging as everything leading up to that moment had been, in hindsight, all the hard work had been worth it—despite the fact that during most of those years, I'd barely made enough money to support myself in this ridiculously expensive city.

But here Harper and I were now—finally on the cusp of realizing all that we'd worked so hard for. And since she was nothing if not a silo of energy when things were going well, it was that silo that faced me now.

"Your dress," she said as she stood back to appraise me. "Love it. Who are you wearing?"

I was wearing a bright-yellow Lela Rose floral *fil coupé* dress with a jeweled neckline, half sleeves, and an A-line silhouette, which complimented my height. At five foot eleven, I was a tall, slender, stacked, and leggy brunette, which was pretty much coveted in the modeling world. After all these years, my wardrobe outbanked my personal bank account due to the sheer kindness of the designers I'd worked for. Many of whom—like Lela—had been nice enough to gift me something of theirs that I'd worn on the runway.

"It's a Lela Rose," I said to her. "Since I have no idea whom I'm auditioning for, I hope I chose well."

"You did. Let's sit down, have a cup of coffee, and talk. Because after Cannes, I don't know even where to begin when it comes to you."

"Can't we begin with this mysterious audition?"

"That will come in time. First, you and I need to decide who has access to you and who doesn't. Because not everyone should, Sienna. We need to choose carefully. Over-exposure is a career killer. When it comes to you, we need to leave the masses with a sense of mystery that turns into a hunger, so that's what we'll aim for."

She turned away from me and walked toward her glass desk, on which sat an iMac, two telephones, her own cell phone, a pad of paper, and a pen. "Sit," she said, pointing to the chair opposite her desk. "I'll call Julia and ask her to bring us coffee."

Julia Jacobs was Harper's personal assistant and also my best friend. Just hearing her name made me smile. When she'd arrived with two cups of coffee, shooting me a discreet wink before she left, Harper and I got down to it.

"Obviously you're doing *Vogue*'s September issue," she said. "I've already told them to count you in. That's a done deal."

"I still can't believe it," I said. "I mean, how exciting is that?"

"Pretty fucking exciting," she admitted. "And congratulations, Sienna. They called me right after all your buzz at Cannes, not the other way around. And since we're talking Anna Wintour here—and given the influence *she* and *that* magazine wield—this opportunity is indeed huge. Now, since the trads target the industry, we need you in *Variety* and the *Reporter*. I want to position you as the next It Girl so that all the studio execs come to think of you that way—and thus start sending you scripts. I'll schedule interviews and photo shoots with both of them, and I'll also ask if they will give us the covers for each—yes?"

"Yes, please."

We strategized about publicity for another thirty minutes before Harper leaned back in her chair, kicked her heels up on her desk, and narrowed her eyes at me. "Now for the good stuff," she said.

"I assume this is about the audition?"

"It is. But before we go there, I have to ask you a serious question. Because what's been proposed to me by a colleague here at CAA is something that will radically change your life, likely by the end of this week if you get the job."

"How will landing one job change my life by the end of the week?" I asked.

"Let's consider this a unique audition," she said. "Sorry to be vague, but I have no choice. When I was approached about this opportunity, I was asked to sign a nondisclosure agreement before I was told anything. And before you know what this is about, you'll be asked to do the same."

"That sounds kind of ominous..."

"Not in this business, it isn't. You can't even imagine how many NDAs I've signed over the years. Frankly, they aren't a big deal—as long as you take them seriously. Because if you don't, and if you get caught breaking the NDA, I can guarantee you that you'll be sued. Worse, when it comes to this business, your career likely will be over."

"I'm already not liking this," I said. "I've worked my ass off to get to where I am today. You know that, Harper."

"I do know that, and trust me, I've taken several days to consider whether to even bring this to your attention. But in the end, I came to the conclusion that this will be a major win for you—professionally and financially. Because if they do agree to go with you, you'll be paid handsomely."

"How handsomely?"

Her eyes sparkled at me.

"Ten million dollars for eight months' work," she said.

A chill ran down my spine.

"Harper, don't play me," I said. "You know I don't have much money. You know that kind of money would change my life."

"I'm not *playing* you, Sienna—and yes, ten million dollars would change your life. And I *want* that for you. What you should also know is that their opening offer to me was two million dollars. I got them to come up to ten, because there's a goddamned good reason you should be paid that much when it comes to *this* job."

"What job? Harper, you have to give me *something* —come on!"

"Here's what I can tell you," she said after glancing at her watch. "In ten minutes, we'll leave for a meeting with the action star I told you about earlier...and also his miserable bitch of an agent. What you need to know is that if they want you for the job—and if you take it—your private life as you know it now will officially be dead."

"What does that mean?"

"That you can send it your condolences. And roses— white, never red."

"Would you please just be straight with me?"

She swung her heels off her desk and leaned toward me. "You'll be targeted by the paparazzi. They will hunt you. They will stalk you. And they will place you firmly in the public eye. What concerns me is that you haven't experienced that kind of fame yet, and it can be daunting, sometimes crippling. But after all our years together, I know you, Sienna. And I believe you are tough enough to see this through to the end. As we tend to building your career, I see no quicker or more powerful way of doing so than what's about to be proposed to you. Because if you're chosen for the job, and if you agree to do what's asked of you, you will indeed become Hollywood's new It Girl. You just need to understand that in the process, you will be forfeiting your privacy, and your life will be lived out in the tabloids for eight straight months—and likely a month or so after that, when all is said and done."

"After what is said and done?"

"Are you willing to sign that NDA?" she asked me.

"To find out what this is about? Of course I am."

Satisfied, she stood. "Then, let's go," she said as she smoothed down her dress and came around the table to offer her hands to me. When she did, I took them and stood in front of her. "Signing the NDA doesn't commit you to anything more than silence. If they sense the kind of chemistry they're looking for and do want to sign you, you can still walk away from this if it doesn't feel like a good fit for you."

"So, this is about chemistry?"

"Oh, my love, it's *all* about chemistry," Harper said. "This whole *thing* is about chemistry."

"Now I'm really intrigued."

"Intrigued," Harper said almost whimsically as we moved toward the door. "Actually, your mind is about to be blown. So, do your best to keep this in mind before we go into that meeting: be the excellent actress you've become, maintain a poker face throughout all of it, and don't you dare let any surprise or emotion show until you and I are alone again. Got it?"

"Got it," I said.

"Good," she said. "Now, follow me..."

2

———————

"So," Harper said as we took the stairs from the twentieth floor down to the nineteenth. "Here's something else I probably should tell you, even though a part of me wants to die inside that I even have to."

"What's that?" I asked.

"The actor in question happens to be repped by a former lover of mine—Mimi Kennedy."

"Mimi Kennedy?" I echoed. "You two were a couple? We've been together for eight years, and you're just telling me this now? My God—she's almost as big as you are."

"Almost, but not quite, so let's not overdo it. Because when it comes to *that* one, I will always have the edge over her."

"How long were you together?"

"I don't know—four years? Something like that."

"That's a long time."

"Trust me, toward the end...it felt like a lifetime. And then another lifetime. And then another on top of that."

"How long since you broke it off?"

"Nine years, which is likely why I never mentioned it to you. Let the past be the past, I say."

"Are you on bad terms?"

Harper shrugged. "At this point? Not really. For the most part, she and I try our best to keep things professional between us. But since we're both fiercely competitive— which is what drove us apart in the end—you might catch us tossing a few zingers at one another, which is par for the course when it comes to us. Sometimes it can get personal, but for the most part, we don't allow it to go too far. That said, if jabs are taken, try your best to overlook them."

"Got it."

"Or dodge them."

"Got that, too."

When we stepped out onto the nineteenth floor, we walked down a busy hallway thrumming with a host of slim, sleek, well-heeled people striding this way and that. At the end of the hall, we hooked a right, and Harper greeted a pretty young woman seated behind a large desk.

"Andrea," she said, "so good to see you. Please meet Sienna Jones."

"It's a pleasure," Andrea said, looking up at me as we shook hands. "I loved you in *Lion*. You were amazing in it, Sienna. And huge congrats on your win at Cannes. That must have been so exciting for you."

"Thank you," I said, a bit taken aback by her enthusiasm but grateful for it just the same. "It was unexpected, that's for sure."

"Is Mimi ready for us?" Harper asked in a bored tone.

"She is," Andrea said. "Let me give her a quick call to let her know you and Sienna are here."

"Mimi is big on announcements," Harper said to me

with a roll of her eyes. "It's all about showbiz when it comes to that one."

When Andrea had made the call, she stood, showed us to a tall, mahogany-paneled door, and swung it open. Harper went in first. I followed.

"Mimi!" Harper said as the door clicked shut behind us. "Good to see you. Trim and terrific as always."

"As are you, Harper—always so on point," said the raven-haired beauty who stood before us. Mimi Kennedy was wearing a black power suit, straight hair that fell just to her shoulders in a brisk cut, and a bold red lip. I couldn't tell if she was younger or older than Harper, but after a swift assessment, I had a feeling they were close to the same age. And that her presence was just as formidable as Harper's.

"Sienna has agreed to the terms," Harper said. "She'll sign the NDA."

"Smart girl," Mimi said as she came over to shake my hand. "It's nice to meet you, Sienna."

"It's nice to meet you, Mimi," I said.

"Well done on your big win," she said to me. "I loved your performance in *Lion*. It was as perfect as it was profound. Don't be surprised if you see an Academy Award nomination coming your way."

"Thank you," I said. "But that's probably a long shot."

"I disagree," came a deep male voice to my left. "You were brilliant in that movie, Sienna. Both you and it won for a reason. I think Mimi might be right. You're going to get a nomination. We think you're about to become the next big thing."

I turned to see who it was—and for the life of me, I couldn't *believe* who it was. *It was fucking Jackson Cruise*, and he was seated in the middle of the room on one of two sofas that faced each other. When he blistered me with that famous, sexy smile of his—the one with the irresistible dimples dented deep into his cheeks, which had won women's hearts all around the globe for years, including mine—I felt as if my body was being lifted off the ground. This meeting had to do with *him*? Seriously? I was here to audition for one of the hottest-looking and most successful men in the business?

God, help me.

Keep your cool. Be polite. Wear your poker face.

"Thank you, Mr. Cruise," I said.

"It's Jackson," he said as he stood. "And it's nice to meet you, Sienna. You're even more beautiful in person."

And you seriously are better looking in person, I thought as he strode toward me. He was wearing tight, faded jeans and a white T-shirt that did nothing to conceal his muscular frame, and his dark hair gleamed in the office's natural lighting. When he held out his hand to me, I noted the expensive-looking silver watch on his wrist and felt the smoothness of his skin as we shook hands.

"I'm such a fan," I said to him. "It's an honor to meet you."

"Likewise," he said. "Consider me a new fan of yours, Sienna."

How can this be happening? Am I really here right now? How can it possibly be that I'm about to have an audition with Jackson Cruise? And why all the secrecy? Why the NDA? What's about to transpire here?

"Sienna, Jackson and I are thrilled that you agreed to come today," Mimi said. "And we're also grateful that you've agreed to sign the NDA so we can move forward with the *real* reason you're here today. I'm afraid we put Harper in a difficult place, because I know she was unable to answer the many questions you likely had for her before arriving here.

That must have been frustrating for each of you, and I want to personally apologize for any duress it might have caused you."

"Thanks a million, Mimi," Harper said as she looked at her nails. "I appreciate the sentiment."

"I'm sure you do, Harper."

In response, Harper simply blew her a kiss.

"Sienna," Mimi said. "If you'd come over to my desk and sign the NDA, we can begin."

When I walked over to her desk and saw how thick the document was, I looked blankly at Harper. "This might take a while for me to read," I said.

"*Read*?" Mimi said. "I just need your signature, dear."

"She's new to this, Mimi. Allow me to walk her through it."

"Of course…"

"It's all aboveboard," Harper said to me as she flipped through the document, quickly skimming each page. "This is the standard NDA document CAA uses, and it's exactly what I signed to bring us all together today. All you need to know, Sienna, is that after you sign it, everything that's about to be said in this room stays in this room. And whether or not you land the job in question, you must never speak about what is said here today. If you do, you likely will be sued. Do you agree to those terms?"

"I do," I said.

"Then, sign." She looked up at Mimi and snapped her fingers at her. "A pen would help, Mimi."

"Right, right," Mimi said as she reached for one next to her MacBook Pro. "Here, Sienna. Use this." She handed me a pen, took the document from Harper, and pointed out the three separate places where I needed to sign and date, which I did.

"This is now officially binding," Mimi said to me. "Congratulations. Now, the four of us can talk freely. *Quel soulagement!*"

I trusted Harper to my core, but frankly all this sounded kind of sketchy to me. Why did I need to sign that document just to speak freely in front of Jackson Cruise?

"We can," I said to her with a smile I didn't feel.

"Good," she said. "And thank goodness! Because this is officially behind us now, isn't it, Jackson?"

"It is," he said quietly.

She motioned to Harper.

"How about if Sienna and Jackson sit on that couch and you and I sit opposite them on that couch?"

"Works for me, Mimi. This is your show to run, so...you know—run it."

After we took our seats, Mimi clocked me with a glance.

"Sienna, do you follow the gossip rags?" she asked.

"Sometimes," I said, looking over at Jackson, who appeared weirdly uncomfortable to me right now. "But not for the past couple of weeks. It was only late last night that I returned home from Cannes. It was so crazy there. I've been out of the loop."

"Then...you haven't read or heard anything unusual about Jackson recently?"

"No," I said. "Should I have?" I turned to him. "I'm sorry if I missed something big. It's probably about a major deal you've signed, right? I should have been paying closer attention."

"Yeah," he said wistfully. "If only if it were about that, Sienna."

Confused, I shot Harper and Mimi a few glances. "I'm afraid I don't understand."

"This is rather delicate," Mimi said.

And then a frustrated Jackson Cruise looked directly at me. "Actually, it isn't," he said. "I'm gay, Sienna. Last week, the *National Enquirer* photographed me kissing another man. It's all over the news, and my career is about to go into the shitter because of it."

"Not if I can help it," Mimi said. "Because you and I have a plan."

Jackson Cruise is gay? I thought incredulously. *Seriously? I've been surrounded by gay male models, actors, and my own gay friends for years. Everyone knows my gaydar is legendary, and yet I somehow missed this? How is that even possible? Never once would I have pegged Jackson Cruise as a gay man. I've lusted after him for years, for God's sake, as has every other straight woman in the world.*

When I looked at him, I saw vulnerability in his eyes—and I felt for him. With this out in the media right now, I could only imagine the hell he was going through—particularly since the public and his fans viewed him as this big, butch action star. In my opinion, he still was, but stereotypes could affect that perception, which also could affect his career.

And so, without thinking, I instinctively reached over and grasped his hand. At first, he seemed surprised by the act, but when our eyes met, I knew he only saw my compassion for the situation he was in and not judgment—which is likely why I felt him relax when he squeezed my hand in return.

"I'm sorry," I said to him.

"It's my fault," he said. "Even though I was getting on my own private plane when the photographs were taken, I should have known better than to kiss this guy I've been seeing over the past several months when he greeted me on the tarmac. I should have waited until we were inside the plane, where it would have been private. But I was so caught up in the moment, it felt right to kiss him there. And when I did? I fucked up big time, because the photographs don't lie, and I'm about to lose everything I've built for myself over the past thirteen years. The media is trying to tear me down as we speak."

"But that doesn't mean they'll *win*," Mimi said. "The photographs that were taken of you were shot at such a great distance that all of them are blurry. In every one of them, it could be interpreted that you were simply kissing your friend on the cheek before you stepped onto that plane."

At that, Jackson groaned.

"Anyway, all of this is why Sienna is here," Mimi said quickly. "We've talked about this, Jackson. You aren't the first actor to face this kind of crisis. It can be managed. We've discussed how the system handled Rock Hudson back in the day—and how well it worked not only for him but also for the likes of James Dean, Tab Hunter, and Montgomery Clift. And just look at the rumors that have long beleaguered Hugh Jackman and John Travolta, for God's sake. Travolta's career might be on life support because he just keeps getting stranger and creepier, but Jackman's career is thriving despite the speculation surrounding his sexuality."

"Hugh Jackman doesn't have a photograph of him kissing the man who pilots his private plane, Mimi," Jackson said. "He just has an older wife and sings and dances in Broadway shows, which people can't wrap their heads around since he's best known for playing Wolverine."

It was slowly dawning on me where this was leading...

"All right," Mimi said tentatively. "Would you prefer if we just cut to the chase?"

"I would. I don't want to waste Sienna's time any more than I want to waste my own."

"That's fine," Mimi said. "And I agree. Now look—Harper and I just saw how Sienna reached out to you. We witnessed your connection, especially when you responded to her touch. It was real, and it was honest. Do you think we even need to go through with an audition at this point?"

"I don't know," he said. "In fact, I don't know anything right now." He looked over at me when he said that, and I could literally feel his embarrassment, which saddened me. Nobody should feel ashamed or be shamed for their sexuality, but Jackson Cruise clearly felt differently. He was suffering because of this. "Sienna, when you took my hand a moment ago, you were very kind. Whatever happens between us going forward, I want to thank you for that, because it meant something."

"Signed documents or not, your secret will always be safe with me, Jackson," I said. "I'm sorry that you're going through this. I don't mean this to sound trite given the world we live in, but you should be allowed to live your life freely, not one that suits a mold meant to be sold to the masses. It infuriates me that you aren't able to do that, even though I understand why you don't want to risk the consequences. The idea that your sexuality is even an issue in this day and age enrages me. I'm angry for you. So, tell me, Jackson—what do you need from me today? There's a reason I'm here."

Before he could speak, Mimi leaned toward me.

"What we need is a distraction," she said. "And we'd like it if *you* were that distraction."

"Go on," I said.

"You're a gorgeous woman, Sienna. You're fresh on the scene, and people are starting to talk about you. And then there's Jackson himself. Even before this happened to him, he mentioned to me in passing that he loved your performance in *Lion*. And then, just a day or two later, when the crisis hit and we were trying to figure a way out of the speculation surrounding his sexuality, I reminded him about you. And what I suggested to him has been done countless times before in Hollywood."

"And what's that?" I asked, already knowing what it was but nevertheless wanting to hear Mimi say it.

"What we're proposing is that you enter into a fake relationship with Jackson as of today. If we play this right—if we really show off your budding romance in front of the world's eyes—we think eight months will be enough time for this nightmare to be behind us before you two publicly decide to go your separate ways. But before that happens, you must know this: you will be seen everywhere together—at popular restaurants, movie premieres, parties, and just out and about on the streets of New York—especially since Jackson is about to start shooting his next movie here in the city tomorrow. What we're seeking are plenty of PDAs."

"What's a PDA?" I asked.

"A public display of affection," Harper said.

"Exactly," Mimi agreed. "We need the paps to see you two holding hands, kissing each other, and looking into each other's eyes as you fall in love with one another. At first, people will speculate, because people in general are risible human beings ripe for the sewer. But given your combined acting chops, and because this agreement means that you will be exclusive to each other for the duration of the contract, I believe your relationship will look real and that it will eventually shift the attention away from those unfortunate photos and Jackson's true sexuality. After eight months, each of you will be free again to see whomever you want."

Since I hadn't been with anyone since I'd ended my relationship with Eric two years ago—when that motherfucker had cheated on me—eight months of forced celibacy really didn't bother me, if only because of the deep scars Eric had left in his wake. I didn't want to be involved with anyone right now, so eight months of being in a fake relationship meant nothing to me, especially since I planned on seeing nobody anytime soon.

"Sienna," Harper said, "what's in this for you is exposure. Being romantically linked with Jackson Cruise will only funnel more interest to you. As I said earlier in my office, the next stage of your career is all about exposure. The interviews I'll line up for you will help, as will snagging the cover of *Vogue*'s September issue. But if you do agree to do this, which I think you should, it will only amplify everything. It will do amazing things for your career."

"And mine," Jackson said. " I'm not going to pretend that it won't."

"True enough," Harper said. "So, if you two agree to this, Mimi and I are also in agreement. Even though you'll be faking it, we know you can pull this off, because each of you is an excellent actor. What all this comes down to is simple: Sienna, do *you* want to do this? Because if you don't, Mimi and Jackson can find somebody else, and we can all part friends. Beyond the NDA you signed, there is no pressure on you. After all, you have your own career to tend to. And all of us in this room respect that."

"We do," Mimi said.

"I sure as hell do," Jackson said. "Because I remember what it was like back when people were first talking about me like they're now talking about Sienna. It was thrilling. Thirteen years ago, I was the new guy on the block. I was just eighteen at the time, and it was a shitload of fun. I had the time of my life back then, and as you are just being discovered, Sienna, I don't want to rob you of experiencing what I experienced. That wouldn't be right. I only want you to do this if you feel it's something you *want* to do. And I mean that."

He wasn't acting for me now. As I looked him in the eyes, I knew in my gut that he wasn't. Because no one was *that* good an actor. Jackson Cruise really did care how this might affect me.

And so I made my decision.

"I'm in," I said to him. "You can start wooing me now."

"Kiss her, Jackson," Mimi said in earnest. "Let Harper and I judge for ourselves if you two can make it believable before you try to sell your lust and love for one another to the world."

"Jesus," he said. "Mimi, sometimes I think you missed your calling as an actress."

"I've always been theatrical," she said. "But you love that about me."

Harper coughed when she said that and then sharply cleared her throat.

"You can kiss me," I said to Jackson. "In fact, I wouldn't mind if you did. You know...if only to have one of my fantasies met."

"Your fantasies?" he asked. "Doesn't the fact that I'm gay crush that?"

"Not when you look the way you do, Jackson."

"Lean in for the kill," Mimi demanded.

"Are you sure?" he asked me.

"Just think of me as one of the hottest men you've ever seen," I said. "Kiss me the way you'd kiss him."

When I said that, Jackson Cruise gave me a mischievous smile, took me into his arms, and planted one mother of a kiss on my lips. He kissed me in ways that were so heated, sexy, and yet somehow tender that I felt my stomach do a little flip-flop. I'd just been kissed by one of my idols, and I couldn't give a damn that he was gay.

"That was hot," I said when our lips parted.

"Really?" he said. "I don't get it."

"Let's just put it all down to technique," I said, "because you've got that in spades."

He laughed when I said that, and in that moment, I could sense the tension lifting off him, which made me happy. I hated that he was being smeared for his sexuality. If I could make a difference for him, I would.

"Look, Jackson," I said. "I only hope that whatever man you kissed before you boarded that plane of yours experienced what I just experienced. Because that was something. You seriously know how to kiss."

"So, this is done?" Mimi asked. "Jackson, do you want to work with Sienna?"

"Totally."

"Sienna, you're certain about this?" Harper asked.

"I am," I said. "As long as *you're* sure."

"I am," she said. "I think this will be a good move for you."

Harper had never lied to me, so that was that. "Then... let's do it," I said. "I'm officially here with my new beau." I looked at Jackson when I said that, and I addressed him seriously. "I'll have your back," I said to him. "Let's do our best to turn this around for you, OK? Let's romance the hell out of each other before we break things off. What do you say?"

"That I'm grateful. And that you're an amazingly kind woman, Sienna. Not many would be at my side at this point in my career. Don't think I don't know that, especially since you're on the cusp of taking Hollywood and the world by the balls."

"We'll fix it," I said. "Because after that kiss, I'm fairly certain we could do a few more of those to appease the paparazzi—and likely to get people talking." I looked at Harper and Mimi. "Do I need to sign anything else so we can get this going?"

"You do," Harper said as she and Mimi stood. "Mimi has the contract detailing the terms of your fake eight-month affair."

"I do," Mimi said. "It's on my desk—let's go to it now."

While Jackson remained on the sofa, Harper, Mimi, and I walked over to Mimi's desk, where she removed the contract from a folder next to her computer.

"Harper, you've read this?" I asked.

"About a dozen times."

I hated to ask about how payment would be handled in front of Jackson and Mimi, but since money was so tight for me, I needed to know the answer. "What are the terms of payment?" I asked. "Am I just looking at the full amount at the end of the eight months?"

"No," she said. "Since you won't be able to work elsewhere for the duration of the contract, today you'll receive two hundred and fifty thousand upon signing, and then Jackson will pay you the remaining proceeds in one lump sum at the end of the contract—provided you've successfully completed it."

"What does 'successfully completed it' mean?" I asked.

"Well, my goodness," Mimi said. "She certainly is thorough, isn't she?"

"As she should be," Harper said. Then she looked at me. "All you need to do is show up for your daily public outings with Jackson, behave as if you two are falling in love, and remain exclusive to him. If for any reason you get sick, the contract allows for ten sick days, with room for more if for some reason you become seriously ill."

She held up a finger of warning to me.

"But if you make the mistake of breaking exclusivity and get caught seeing another man on the sly—which would break the illusion we're trying to create here—then you would need to pay back your signing bonus and forfeit the ten million dollars that's being offered to you, the contract would end, and you would be open to a lawsuit should Jackson decide to pursue one with you."

Since I had zero plans of seeing anyone, I was perfectly fine with all that. But I still had to wonder...

"What are Jackson's terms?" I asked.

"Stricter than yours," Harper said. "If for any reason he breaches the contract by being caught with another man, for instance, the contract ends, and you would receive the full ten million, which would be paid to you at once."

"That seems more than fair," I said.

"Any other questions?"

"No," I said. "And I promise that I'll meet my obligations."

"I know you will," Harper said to me in a soft voice. "When haven't you?"

"So...am I good to go?"

She motioned toward the contract on Mimi's desk. "If you want this, the contract is there. If you don't, we simply part ways as friends."

I signed the contract. And when I did, I felt proud of myself, because for me, it was more than just about the money and how being linked to Jackson might potentially lift my career. Now that I knew I was being treated fairly by Mimi and Jackson, what also mattered to me was how

Jackson was being treated by the press. I was a fierce advocate for the LGBTQ community, and that man sitting over there on that sofa—the one who hadn't challenged any of the questions I'd had about the contract—he needed me right now, and I planned to come through for him.

"So, what happens next?" I asked. "Harper is scheduling a lot of interviews for me. Is this going to get in the way of them?"

"Not at all," Harper said. "As Mimi noted, Jackson starts shooting his new movie, *Annihilate Them*, tomorrow in Manhattan. While he's busy at work, I'll schedule your interviews and photo shoots in ways that won't compete with his work. It'll be seamless. I'll make sure of it, because two careers need to be propelled forward here—not just one."

"They're like our mothers," I said to Jackson as he came over and wrapped an appreciative arm around my shoulders. As tall as I was, he literally towered over me, which was rare for me. Not many men were as tall as Jackson Cruise, at least in my experience.

"They are," he said. "We're lucky to have them on our side, Sienna."

"To say the least."

"Thanks for doing this," he said. "Thanks for helping me out. It means a lot to me. I need you to know that, Sienna."

"Just sweep me properly off my feet, OK? I want the world to think that I'm the luckiest girl in the world."

"Will do."

I looked over at Harper. "If we're starting this today, what's the plan?"

"Per se is the plan," Mimi said. "You both will be dining there later tonight. It's a hot spot for celebs. Now that you've signed the contract, Sienna, I can get to work on leaking the news to the paps that Jackson will be seen there with you tonight."

"Sienna," Harper said. "You need to brace yourself for that, because every bit of this is designed to make front-page news. As early as later tonight, your dinner with Jackson will be all over the web, Facebook, and Twitter. In the wake of Jackson's crisis, be prepared for that."

"You've given me plenty of warning," I said. "Now that I know what this audition was really about, I get it. The attention on Jackson and me is about to get hot—and fast. That's going to be new for me, but I promise everyone in this room that I'll do my very best to adjust to it as quickly as I can." I looked up at Jackson. "So, what do you say, Jackson? Do you think I have what it takes to catch your eye?"

"As long as I think of you as a hot cowboy," he joked.

"Then that's what I am," I said with a laugh. "A hot cowboy with a bulge big enough to shut down a bus stop. What time is dinner?"

"Eight," Mimi said. "Jackson will pick you up at your apartment at seven thirty. Turn yourself into a siren, Sienna, because with the sheer number of photographs that will be taken of each of you, you'll want to look your very best in an effort to assist your own career."

"Mimi's right," Harper said. "But there's also this: tonight, questions will be hurled at each of you, and when they are, I suggest that each of you say nothing. Don't give them a word. Instead, when you step out of the limousine, just make sure that you're holding hands as you make your way toward the doors. Let your chemistry speak for itself."

"Couldn't have said it better," Mimi said, placing her hand on Harper's shoulder. "And just look at how well we worked together today! How could it be that you and I ever broke apart?"

"To be discussed as in...never," Harper said.

"And there you go again," Mimi said. "Off your meds, as usual."

"Mimi, would you call Austin?" Jackson said. "No offense to Sienna, but I'm feeling kind of stressed out about all this. Hitting the gym before tonight would help."

"Of course," she said, picking up her phone and hitting a button. "Audrey, would you please ask Austin to come in? Yes? Thank you, darling."

"Who's Austin?" I asked.

"His name is Austin Black," Jackson said. "He leads my security detail. And because of that, he knows everything there is to know about me—sometimes a little more than he should know. We've worked together for years. At this point, he's kind of like a brother to me."

There was a rap on the door, and Mimi called out for Austin to come in. When the door swung open, it was literally filled with one of the tallest, most muscular, and most handsome man I'd ever seen.

Oh, my God, I thought as I soaked him in. *And...hello. How are you, Austin?*

"Austin," Mimi said, "come and meet Sienna Jones. Sienna, this is Austin Black."

As he strode toward me in his fitted gray suit, which strained to contain just how rock solid and muscular he was —and spectacularly failed to do so—I could feel a raw sense of confidence in him. As hot as Jackson was, Austin was way hotter. With his coal-black hair, chiseled face, full lips, and piercing blue eyes, Austin Black was the one in this room who should have been the A-list action star, not Jackson.

"Pleasure to meet you, Sienna," he said as his hand engulfed mine.

"It's vice to meet you, Austin."

"Vice?" Harper repeated.

"Sorry?"

"You just said, 'vice to meet you,' Sienna."

"Is that what I said?"

She lifted a brow at me. "In fact, it is..."

"Well," I said. "Slip of the tongue. Super busy day! All sorts of things happening at once! It's *nice* to meet you, Austin. And I mean that. It's really nice to meet you."

"The pleasure is mine, Sienna."

Could his voice be any deeper?

I saw him glance down at his hand, which I was still shaking.

Oh, girl, you need to get yourself together—as in now.

I released his hand and thought I caught amusement in his eyes before he turned to Jackson. "What's up?" he asked.

"I need to hit the gym."

"Want me to join you?"

"If you're up for it," he said. He nodded at me just as I caught Austin's gaze roaming over me. "She and I are about to fall in love," Jackson said. "And because of that, I need you to spot me, because tonight...tonight I need to look my best for her. And I plan to. When it comes to my life, shit changes *now*."

3

AFTER MIMI TOLD me that Audrey would deliver my first check to Harper by the end of the day, Harper and I thanked her, and we took the stairs to Harper's office—and I couldn't help but pepper her with questions.

"First of all, tell me that Austin's straight," I said.

"He's straight," she said. "And looking the way he does, I'm sure he's enjoyed his fair share of women—just as I'm sure that you have a job to focus on right now. I saw what happened back there. I've seen that look in your eyes before. The last thing we need is for you to become distracted by the head of Jackson's security detail when you've just signed a contract to be exclusive to Jackson himself."

"I understand what I signed, but a girl can still look," I said. "But come *on*—did you even see him back there?"

"Just because I'm a turbocharged lesbian doesn't mean I don't get why you're wetting your pants over him right now. Obviously, he's gorgeous. And also off-limits to you."

"Just for curiosity's sake, does he have a girlfriend or something? A wife? I didn't see a ring on his finger. And trust me—I checked."

We started to walk down the hall toward her office.

"Austin is single, and you've just entered into a fake relationship with one of the world's most sought-after men. I suggest you start acting the part."

"Look, my little crush is just between us," I said in a low voice as we passed a sea of smiling faces. I smiled cheerfully back at them, suddenly feeling light-headed and fluttery inside. "I tell you everything."

"It's 'vice' that you do." She opened the door to her office and motioned for me to step inside. "I'd ask you to have a seat, but I don't have any plastic wrap to keep the cushions dry."

"Give me a break," I said, taking the seat opposite her desk.

She looked at me when I sat down and then let out one mother of a long-assed sigh. "What the hell," she remarked. "It was time to have the furniture steam cleaned, anyway."

"Hilarious," I said. "So, what's his story? Strong, silent type? A romantic at heart? I need details."

"What you need is to have your ovaries yanked, because clearly there are way too many hormones flooding through your system right now. Listen to me, Sienna. If you want, you can try to tap Austin Black eight months from now. You know, when you're out of your contract with Jackson and can focus on someone new. But right now, you need to listen to me, because I'm very serious when it comes to the deal you signed today. Yes, Austin is a good-looking man, but you need to get him out of your head. You have a job to do, and I expect you to do it well. Do you even realize that you stammered when you met him?"

"I know I did," I said in embarrassment. "It was humiliating. Do you think anyone else noticed?"

"*Everyone* noticed. I mean, you literally turned red when

Austin shook your hand. And then you were suddenly speaking in tongues. It was beyond apparent that you were attracted to him."

"I'm sorry," I said. "It won't happen again."

"Look, what's done is done," she said. "Just forget about him for now. You and Jackson both need to get into character tonight. If Jackson thinks you're thinking about Austin, that's just going to throw him off his game. He deserves better than that."

"Got it," I said.

"Good. Now, what do you think you'll wear tonight?"

"God knows I have a closet full of clothes thanks to the kindness of designers. What do you think would be appropriate?"

"Something sexy, on-trend, and black."

"When I modeled for Carolina Herrera last fall for her spring collection, she knew I was so smitten with the sleeveless black cocktail dress I wore for her that she gave it to me."

"I know exactly the one you're referring to—and it is perfect. Wear that, couple it with some high heels, and style your hair down in loose waves. It always looks best that way. Then paint your face, and you're good."

"I'll do that," I said. "And I won't disappoint you."

"Actually, the person you really don't want to disappoint is *you*, Sienna, because you are finally on the cusp of real stardom. If you play this right with Jackson—and when solid roles start to come your way, which they will—I do see you hitting the A-list. I mean that, because you're that good. But you'll only get there if you remain focused."

"I will," I said.

She checked her watch. "Off you go, then," she said. "It's already past three, which means you only have a few hours to get home and get yourself ready for the evening. Shine tonight," she added. "Make the world believe in you and Jackson."

"I can do that," I said. "I mean, Jackson isn't exactly hard on the eyes, Harper."

"Exactly," she said. "Now, go and do it. Make me proud. We'll touch base in the morning."

I'd already stood up to leave when Harper stopped me with a look.

"And...Sienna," she said, "as RuPaul would say, don't fuck it up."

DUE TO HEAVY TRAFFIC, it was a good thirty minutes before I scrambled out of my return cab in front of my one-bedroom apartment on West Twenty-Second Street—which was rent-controlled and the only reason I'd been able to live in Chelsea since I'd first arrived in the city. After I climbed the three sets of stairs to my apartment, which was sweltering in the June heat, I switched on the air-conditioning as soon as I stepped inside—and got to work.

Inside my wardrobe, I found the dress I'd mentioned earlier to Harper, which was still fresh, neatly pressed, and ready to wear in its dry-cleaning bag. To complement it, I chose a killer pair of Jimmy Choo Mary Jane leather pumps in black with a four-inch heel and two straps with ties that would wrap around my ankles and lower calves. And even though Jackson would never see them, I chose a pretty lace bra and panties—each in black.

As time passed, it passed quickly—too quickly.

I worked on my face, which meant beating it with a

whole host of creams, exfoliators, and potent elixirs before I took a shower and tried to relax, which didn't happen.

I was so nervous about how things would go tonight that the only thing that could have relaxed me was a martini, but since I needed to focus, I chose to forgo having one. Instead, I ended the shower with a blast of freezing cold water, which I stood beneath until I couldn't stand it anymore.

After I'd toweled off, I put on my robe and checked my pores in the mirror. The cold water, exfoliator, creams, and elixirs had done their trick, because my skin looked tight and bright. With time running against me, I blew out my hair, which naturally dried in soft waves, and then I did my makeup, the lot of which took me over an hour before I could even start to get dressed.

You're going to be late! I panicked when I looked at the clock on my bedside table. *You've only got five minutes left before Jackson arrives—move it!*

But I didn't move fast enough, because I had just zipped up my dress when my buzzer rang.

Jackson was here.

Shit, I thought as I hurried into the foyer and buzzed him through. *I don't even have my shoes on yet!*

Moments later, when the inevitable knock came at my door, I was still struggling to lace up my heels. I had no choice but to give up on them. Jackson would have to help me into them, because the straps were more difficult to buckle than I'd remembered.

"Coming!" I called as I hurried out of the bedroom and into the foyer. Unlocking my door, I swung it open.

There stood Austin Black.

"Oh," I said in surprise. "I thought you'd be Jackson."

"He's waiting for you in the limousine," Austin said, "which is double-parked. We need to leave now."

He'd since changed into a black suit and tie. The sexy haze of a five-o'clock shadow graced his face, and he wore his thick black hair parted on the side, raked away from his face. He looked more handsome now than he had when we'd first met. Earlier, he'd worked out with Jackson, and it showed. His chest in particular looked massive to me.

And then I realized I was staring at it.

"My shoes," I said as I shot back into myself. "The buckles are a bitch. I'm ready to go, but I can't seem to get into them."

"May I come in?"

"What for?"

"To help you into your shoes, Sienna."

"You want to help me into my shoes?"

"We need to get out of here. Let me help."

"You're a lifesaver," I said, trying not to think of his hands on my feet. "Thank you."

"No problem," he said as he stepped inside. "Where are the shoes in question?"

"In my bedroom," I said. "And please don't judge me when you see it, Austin. Today has been so insane that my bedroom is a mess."

He looked patiently at me. "I'm not here to judge you, Sienna, but I *am* here going to get you to Per Se on time. We can't afford to keep the press waiting, because they'll leave if they think Jackson isn't coming. So, let me help you into your shoes." He paused for a moment and looked directly at me. "Because shoes are kind of my thing."

Because shoes are kind of your thing? I thought as I looked at him. *What does that mean? Are you a master at putting shoes on women, Austin? And if that's the case, how many shoes have you tied and untied? How many shoes have you had wrapped around that thick neck of yours? How many shoes have you licked and tasted before you ripped them off in a feverish blaze?*

Doesn't matter. Be professional. Get on with it.

"They're just in here," I said as I turned and started to walk toward my bedroom. "I've only worn them once, and now I remember why. They're hell to get into."

"I can take care of that," he said, following me.

I literally can feel him at my back. And I literally can't handle it!

"Here they are," I said, sitting on the edge of my bed. "I love them because they're sexy, but it's like bondage when it comes to putting them on."

"Like bondage?" he asked as he kneeled in front of me. "Is that it?"

"In fact, it *is* it," I said. "I mean, just look at them. Look at all those buckles and straps. Who in their right mind could ever navigate them?"

"I can," he said with authority. "Hold out your right foot for me."

I did, and when I did, his hands touched my heel, which sent a jolt of desire through me.

What is it about him? I thought. *Why am I behaving like this? I never behave like this. This city is filled with hot men. Ever since I left Eric, I've wanted nothing to do with men. So, why am I so attracted to him? It makes no sense.*

"You're tense," he said.

"And for good reason. Just look at what I'm about to walk into—the press, flashing cameras, people shouting questions at Jackson and me. Austin, this is all very new to me. And I'm not going to lie to you. I'm pretty stressed out right now."

"How about if you take a deep breath," he said as he gently massaged my foot. "Try to relax. Because I've been told that for the next eight months, I'm not only here for Jackson, Sienna. I'm also here for you."

"I don't know what that means," I said.

He looked up at me with a glimmer in his eyes. "I'm also here to protect you. So, how about if you just lean back a bit and let me release some of the tension you're feeling? Then I have a good feeling the shoes won't be an issue."

As he massaged my feet and kneaded them in ways that were undeniably erotic, soon my shoes were on, buckled, and fastened.

"You're a genius," I said to him as I kicked out my legs and admired my shoes. "Thank you."

"The pleasure was mine, Sienna."

Actually, it was mine.

I popped off my bed.

"How do I look?" I asked before we left.

"You look nice," he said.

"Just 'nice'? I was hoping for 'hot,' because Harper told me I needed to look hot tonight."

A moment passed before he seemed to come to a decision.

"You look beautiful, Sienna. And yes, you also look hot. You are someone any man would want to be with tonight."

When he said that, I was aware of his eyes glancing over my body before he checked himself. And when he did, the desire I'd seen a moment ago was quickly swept away. "We've been too long," he said. "We need to leave. We need to get you and Jackson to Per Se before it's too late."

4

"HOW ARE YOU?" I asked Jackson after Austin opened my door and I'd slid in next to Jackson on the limo's back seat. The sun might have set behind the Manhattan skyline, but it was still light out. "You certainly look handsome. I love your navy suit. It brings out the blue in your eyes."

"Sienna, you're almost ten minutes late," he said to me. "What held you up? Mimi has leaked to the press that we'll be arriving at Per Se at eight. If we aren't there on time—and if the paps have left by the time we get there—I'm laying that on you."

"I'm sorry," I said, startled by his angry tone. "I had trouble getting into my shoes."

"What grown woman has trouble getting into her own shoes?"

"Someone who chooses to wear something like these," I said, lifting up my shoes for him to see. "They're complicated to get into, but I thought they were right for tonight. Do you like them?"

"They're fine," he said dismissively.

"Jackson," Austin said, "we'll get there on time."

"I hope so," he said, "because at least *you* understand how important tonight is to me."

"Don't worry about it," Austin said. "If I have to bust a few lights, I will."

"All right," Jackson said. "Thanks for having my back."

Was Jackson Cruise a diva in disguise? He certainly was behaving like one. Gone was the warm and welcoming person I'd met just hours ago. In his stead was someone who had gone to a darker place and who was being so cold to me now that I almost asked Austin to turn off the air-conditioning because it was chilly enough in the car. While I got it that I shouldn't have been late, I also felt this had less to do with me and more to do with something else.

And then it occurred to me.

Maybe he's as nervous as I am, I thought. *He's about to step out into the public with a new woman on his arm—someone most people have never heard of before. And he's about to be faced with a hell of a lot of speculation when it comes to that, particularly after he was caught kissing another man. Of course he's on edge. Who wouldn't be?*

Let him cool off...

"How was your workout?" I asked.

"It was a workout," he said, not looking at me.

"Jackson," I said, "I'm sorry I was late. But you have to understand the lengths I went to to pull myself together properly for you. This will be our first time out together, and I had to look my best. Getting ready is different for men than it is for women. If you'd only look at me, you'd see that I've given it my all."

He was silent for a moment, and then he turned to me.

"Who designed your dress?" he asked.

"Carolina Herrera."

"And your shoes—the ones that gave you so much trouble?"

"Jimmy Choo, that motherfucker. He's clearly a sadist."

He cocked his head at me when I said that, and finally he smiled, reached for my hand, and held it in his lap.

"I'm sorry," he said. "I don't mean to be difficult. It's just that I don't know what the paps are going to say to us when we arrive at the restaurant. Because the moment they see me with you, it's only going to fuel more speculation around my sexuality. That's the last thing I want, even though I know that to get to the other side of this, I'm going to work hard to convince them that this relationship of ours is real."

"We can do it," I said. "I know we can. And I'm sorry, Jackson. I hate that you're going through this."

"Thanks again for helping me out, Sienna."

"We'll get through it together," I said. "We'll turn things around for you."

"That's the thing," he said. "I feel as if it's already too late for that."

"Almost there," Austin said. "The traffic lights are working in our favor. We won't be late."

"Thanks, man," Jackson said.

"Thank you, Austin," I said. "Again, I apologize for the trouble."

And for one heated moment, Austin Black lifted his eyes and looked at me in the rearview mirror, nodding silently at me. We continued to race across the city.

PER SE WAS LOCATED on the fourth floor of the Time Warner Center on Manhattan's Upper West Side. It was at Sixtieth Street, where CNN had its New York headquarters.

Harper and Mimi had chosen this particular restaurant for a reason. Not only was it smack in the middle of where Manhattan thrived, it also was one of the finest restaurants in the city. Thomas Keller—the renowned chef who had three Micheline stars to his name—owned it. If you could somehow snag a table here, I'd heard from friends that it was one of *the* places to go for fine dining in this city.

But if you were Jackson Cruise, getting a table here naturally wasn't an issue.

"We're here," Austin said as we approached the towering skyscraper and stopped in front of it. "And so is the press. Several dozen of them—and they've just spotted us. They're hurrying over, so get into character now, because photos are about to be taken."

"Kiss me," I said to Jackson. "Think of me as your hot cowboy..."

He must have done that, because when he swept me into his arms and laid one on me as the limousine's interior was suddenly illuminated with explosions of light, his tongue plunged into my mouth. I met his brazenness with my own, tugging at his bottom lip with my teeth. And then Austin opened Jackson's door.

As our lips parted, what I saw outside was a mob scene.

"Everybody, stand back!" I heard Austin shout above the roar as his hands swept out at his sides. "Give them room!"

The only time I'd experienced this kind of hunger and energy was when I'd won my acting award at Cannes. My photograph had been taken by hundreds of entertainment photographers and reporters from around the world while people cheered me on and whistled at me.

Only this time they weren't cheering or whistling. Instead, as predicted, the paparazzi immediately started lobbing questions at us.

"Jackson!" one man called out. "TMZ. Your fans want to know the truth—are you gay? Is the man you kissed before you got on your plane someone who is important to you? Is he your boyfriend? Or was he just a fling?"

With our heads lowered and Jackson's arm lodged tightly around my waist, we leaned into each other and pressed toward the building's main entrance as Austin cleared a path for us through the explosion of lights.

"You owe it to your fans to tell the truth, Jackson!" one woman called out. "And also to the gay community! You can come out. Your fans will accept you for who you are. Are you gay or not?"

His grip tightened around me, and my heart went out to him as the paparazzi surrounded us. This had to be hell for him.

"Jackson, who are you with?" a man called out. "Is she your beard?"

Seriously? I thought as rage sparked through me. *That's how you're going to label me? Over my dead fucking body, buddy.*

Unable to contain myself, I stopped, turned, and looked out at the sea of reporters as I was flooded with rapid successions of lights. I didn't know who had asked that question, but it didn't matter, because I had a message to deliver to all of them.

"My name is Sienna Jones," I said to them. "If you don't know who I am, Google it. Also, I'm far from being Jackson Cruise's 'beard,' as one of you had the nerve to suggest. If you'd been doing your jobs, you'd know that Jackson and I have been seeing each other for the past six weeks."

That wasn't part of the script, but it was now—and so be it.

"Who are you, again?" someone called out.

"Figure it out," I said.

"Six weeks?" I heard somebody say. "What the hell?"

"Who is Sienna Jones?" a woman asked.

"We're supposed to Google it," someone else joked.

"This way," Austin said, opening one of the building's doors for us.

I placed my hand against Jackson's lower back just as he impulsively leaned down and kissed me on the lips. I kissed him back with everything I had as the press swept in to capture the moment for all the world to see. In the blizzard of flashing lights and clicking cameras that sought to overwhelm us, our kiss nevertheless lingered before we broke away and followed Austin into the building—just as a rising chorus of questions about our relationship slammed against our backs.

"THEY'RE BUYING NONE OF IT," Jackson said in a low, irritated voice after the three of us crossed the lobby to one of two escalators that led to the center's restaurant and bar collection. The famed Porter House restaurant was one of them, as was Per Se. Best of all? The press weren't allowed on this level, which took the pressure off each of us—at least for the moment.

"They already know this is bullshit," he said. "And that's what I'm going to face tomorrow in print."

"This is going to take time," I said quietly to him as we followed Austin off the escalator. "But soon they will believe it, Jackson. We'll make them believe it."

"We can't make them believe shit, Sienna," he said, turning to me. And when he did, I saw that he looked at once furious, vulnerable, and unhinged. "They'll believe whatever sells papers or drives traffic to their websites."

"Let's not have this conversation here," I said. "Someone could overhear us. The press are gone for now. You and I need to see tonight through."

"Easy for you to say," he said. "You're not the one whose career is on the line."

"Jackson," Austin said, "I think you need to have a good look at what Sienna just did for you. The reporters questioned your sexuality—just as we all knew they would—and when they took things too far, Sienna got in front of the situation and challenged them. That took balls."

"Yeah, well, she has her own career to protect, doesn't she?"

I blinked when he said that but decided not to take it personally.

He's upset. He's angry. And he has good reason to be.

But at least Austin had come to my defense.

"That isn't fair to Sienna," he said. "And you know it."

"Whatever," Jackson said. "Look, I need a drink. I'll text you ten minutes before we leave, OK?"

"When you do, I'll let you know if the press is outside waiting for you two to emerge. If they are, I'll handle the situation."

"Everyone seems to be handling my situation," Jackson said.

"That's because it needs handling," Austin said in a firm voice. "Now, get yourself together. At dinner, you two need to sell yourselves to everyone in that restaurant, because the waiters who are about to serve you are going to be listening to you two. You and I both know full well that many of them are paid on the sly by the paps to get inside information, so my best advice is to let go of whatever doubt you're feeling, because Sienna is right. It's going to take time to turn the tables in your favor, and I believe that you will—if you don't fuck it up in the meantime."

Clearly these two are close, I thought, *because there's no way in hell Jackson would allow Austin to talk like that to him if they weren't.*

"I'm sorry if I'm being a dick," Jackson said. "I don't mean to be."

"Look, we get it," Austin said. "You're under a lot of pressure. You're upset. This is a lot for anyone to handle. But if you're going to get beyond this, you seriously need to chill, Jackson. Listen to me on this."

When Jackson took my hand, I could feel frustration coming off him in waves.

"I'll text you," he said to Austin as we started to move toward the restaurant. "Give us a few hours, and then get us the hell out of here."

5

THIRTY MINUTES LATER, after Jackson and I had been seated at a table that overlooked Columbus Circle—which was one of the prime seats at Per Se—Jackson was already two bourbons down with a third one on the way. He was drinking so quickly it was starting to concern me. I was still working on my first martini, for God's sake.

How well can he handle his booze? I wondered, looking at him nervously. *Because if he keeps drinking like this, I'm going to have to say something just to spare him from himself...*

Each of us had ordered the chef's elaborate tasting menu, which included a host of small bites designed to underscore why Thomas Keller reigned as one of the world's best chefs.

On the menu, some of the dishes had been given names, such as "Oysters and Pearls," "Peas and Carrots," "Bread and Butter," and "Gougère," which was a delicate cheese puff that I knew would be no simple cheese puff. And there were many other samplings that would just keep coming until we arrived at an assortment of desserts that included fruit, ice cream, chocolate, and candies.

Over the top didn't even come close to describing this place, which was beautifully lit with ambient lighting that gave the space a romantic glow, particularly with the city glimmering beyond the windows at Jackson's back. On some level Austin must have gotten through to him, because Jackson was holding my right hand and stroking the back of it with his thumb when his third bourbon arrived.

"Another martini for you, miss?" our waiter asked me.

"Maybe later," I said. "Once we're well into the meal."

"Of course. Now that you've had time to relax and enjoy your drinks, the tasting will begin."

"Thank you," I said as the man stepped away.

And when he did, Jackson let go of my hand, leaned back in his chair, and took a sip of his drink. "Tell me about you," he said. "Is Sienna your real name? Or your stage name?"

"No, it's my real name," I said, trying to keep my voice light and engaged. "But maybe I should have been more creative, because 'Jones' isn't exactly memorable, is it?"

"It could be worse," he said. "Hell, you could be 'Jackson Cruise.'" He took another pull from his drink. "Where were you born?"

"Dubuque, Iowa. How about you? Where did you grow up?"

"Here," he said. "In the city."

"You grew up in Manhattan?"

"I did."

"That must have been exciting," I said. "You had access to all the things I used to crave when I was growing up. Culture, the best concerts, city life, nightclubs, interesting restaurants, interesting people. I can't imagine what it must have been like to grow up here."

"Oh, it was great," he said sarcastically. "My father is one of the city's best brain surgeons. My mother is a best-selling, prize-winning novelist of *literature*. And since my two sisters decided to follow in my father's footsteps in ways that *I* never did, they also are doctors. They have two terrific husbands and two terrific children each. As for me...I'm the disappointment who failed to carry on the family name. So," he said after he'd tossed back his drink, finishing it, "there's that."

"But you're so successful," I said. "What you've achieved has to mean something to your family, Jackson. You're an international super star. And you're only thirty-five! You've been in twenty-five movies already, and pretty much all of them have been box-office smashes."

He was far from being drunk—which surprised me considering all he'd had to drink in the past forty minutes— but when he leaned toward me, I did notice him wavering a bit. This concerned me, since I knew that aside from the waitstaff, the diners eating near us had recognized him. And whenever a major celebrity of Jackson's stature was spied in a public space such as this, I also knew that word of his presence had already spread and that everyone in this restaurant knew he was here.

He starts work on a new movie tomorrow, I thought as I assessed him. *I need to make sure he doesn't make a fool of himself. But how do I do so without offending him?*

"Sienna, when it comes to my family, what I really am is an international fraud," he said, lifting his empty glass above his head and motioning for another drink before looking at me again.

"Your family really thinks that about you?" I asked.

"Let me clarify. My sisters are fine with the thing that shall not be named in public, but my parents express their disappointment in all sorts of ways—sometimes directly.

Like when my name appeared in the tabloids this week. I rarely hear from them, but I sure as hell heard from them then."

"What did they say?"

"In a nutshell? That I was an embarrassment. And that they'd raised me to behave better than that."

"By showing affection toward another person?"

"Toward another *man*," he said in a low voice.

"About him," I said, "is he anyone special to you?"

"He could be," he said. "But because of who I am, he can't be."

"Who is he?"

"My pilot. We've been seeing each other for a few months. It's not serious, because it can't be serious. He tells me he understands, but I have to wonder whether he really does."

"I'm sorry," I said as his fourth bourbon arrived. When our server left, Jackson lifted the drink in my direction and toasted me before he took a sip.

"So, you like him?" I asked.

"It's deeper than that...not that he knows. But let's not talk about him, OK? I'd really rather not."

"That's fine, Jackson."

"'Jackson,'" he said with a laugh. "That isn't my real name, Sienna, which you've probably figured out by now. I mean, who calls their kid 'Jackson Cruise'? No one. Certainly not my uptight parents. My real name is Mike Fleming. How's that one for you? My last name literally sounds like phlegm. Something that gets caught in the back of your throat that you want to spit out onto the street."

The alcohol is starting to affect him, I thought, getting worried as our first course arrived. It was the "Oysters and Pearls," which was a single oyster topped with tapioca and white sturgeon caviar. Since I wanted to encourage him to eat before he drank even more, I lifted up my shell to him and said, "Here's to us. And also to your new movie. Let's try the food."

"Why are you deflecting?" he said. "Is my life too much for you to handle?"

Time to take him on before he does more damage than good...

"Nothing is too much for me to handle, Jackson," I said quietly as I met his eyes with my own. "Because I've gone through my own share of shit ever since I moved to Manhattan—things nobody knows about. Dark times I never want to talk about. So, please, don't believe for one minute that I haven't had bleak moments of my own in my life, because that isn't the case. But that's enough of that. I'm hungry. And both of us need to eat."

When I said that, he picked up his oyster, tossed it back, and washed it down with another sip of bourbon. "Fantastic," he said. "To die for."

After I'd eaten mine, I looked hard at him.

"Jackson," I whispered, "you need to keep your voice down. If you don't, the people at the next table will hear you, which you don't want."

"I can handle my booze, Sienna."

"I'm thinking otherwise," I said, pushing the bread basket toward him. "Eat some bread. Get something on your stomach."

"Before I embarrass you, too?"

"Before you embarrass yourself."

"Fine—I'll eat some bread."

"And drink some water before you regret having too many drinks."

"Look at me, drinking water for the lady."

"Keep drinking it, because you need to."

"And look at that—I just finished my water," he said.

"Give me your drink," I said. "You've had enough."

"Nobody tells me when I've had enough, Sienna."

"Jackson, I understand that you've been through hell this past week, but you are in public now. We arrived here to offer up a smoke screen. You can't blow that. It's only our first day out in public together."

"Then take the bourbon," he said, pushing it toward me.

Thank God.

I swept it away from him.

"Let me ask you a question," he said after he'd torn off a piece of bread and started to eat it. "Have you ever been in love, Sienna?"

"Once," I said, not wanting to discuss it.

"Just once?"

"Yes, just once."

"How can that be? You're hot. And you're, like...what? Twenty-seven or something?"

"That's right. Twenty-seven."

"And you've only fallen in love once?"

"Unfortunately. In the meantime, I've been focusing on my career."

"Who was the lucky guy?"

"Neither of us was lucky, Jackson. Certainly not me."

"Jesus," he said. "And the mystery deepens."

"I'd rather not make light of it."

"What was he? Some kind of asshole?"

Yes, Jackson. The worst kind...

"Are you finished?" our server asked, materializing at our side.

"We are," I said with a bright smile I didn't feel. "They were delicious."

Without a word, the man took away our plates and left.

Moments later, he returned with the "Peas and Carrots" part of our serving course, which was delivered to us in shallow dishes with a small serving of sugar snap peas, carrots, and turnips topped with what I remembered from the menu to be a black winter truffle crème fraîche. Looking at the beautiful presentation was almost enough to distract me from the sheer ugliness that was unfolding in front of me.

"Thank you," I said to the waiter as he left. I looked over at Jackson, who had just stolen the bourbon I'd taken away from him and slugged it down. "Focus on dinner," I said to him. "The way you're going, the sooner we're out of here, the better."

"I am starting to feel a bit woozy," he said.

"I don't doubt it. Eat your peas and carrots."

"Now you sound like the nanny who raised me."

"You were raised by a nanny?"

"I was," he said, tapping his finger against his chest. "Because I'm what they call a mistake, Sienna. By the time I came along, my parents were fully vested in their careers— and not in me. They didn't have the same kind of time for me they had given my two older sisters. So, I was pretty much shoveled off to Nanny Grace, which is a pretty fitting name for a woman who became the mother I never had. A few years ago, when she needed to go into assisted living, I made certain to put her in the best facility this city has. I pay for all of it, and I'm happy to do so. Because without that woman, I'd be seriously fucked up."

My heart went out to him when he said that, and then I watched him look down at his plate.

"These are peas and carrots?" he asked.

"They are. You can see the peas. The orange mousse is the carrots."

"I think I need another drink."

"I don't think you do, Jackson."

"That's because you're not going through what I'm going through right now, Sienna."

"I understand that," I said in a low voice. "But here isn't the place to get drunk. If you want to do that, I suggest—for you and your career alone—that you do so at home. So, why don't we just call Austin now and bail on this dinner so you can drink in private? In fact, if we do leave now, we'd probably fool the paps, who likely think we're going to be here for several hours and have probably left to cover other stories before coming back here."

"I don't want to leave, because I like being here with you," he said, reaching out to hold my hand. "I feel comfortable with you, which is kind of weird, right? I mean, we only just met today. What am I to make of that?"

"People meet for a reason," I said. "And as far as I'm concerned, tonight that reason is for me to get you out of here before it's too late for you."

"Too late for me?"

"You're drunk," I said.

"I'm not *that* drunk."

"Yes, you are. And I'm concerned."

"What's to be concerned about?"

"Your making a fool of yourself. Call Austin. Tonight, I'll pay the bill. We need to get you out of here before those four bourbons you just drank in record time hit you harder than they already have."

6

WHEN AUSTIN CONFIRMED that he was waiting for us in front of the Time Warner Center, I looked over at Jackson as he turned off his phone. His eyes had become hooded. His cheeks were flushed.

"Austin's at the curb," he said, "waiting for us."

"Tell him to come inside and meet us at the restaurant."

"Why?"

"Just do it."

With a confused shake of his head, he squinted at his phone, turned it on, and started to text something, but God only knows what that was—or how coherent it would be. Why hadn't they given me Austin's number? I should be the one texting him, not Jackson.

I'd already told our server that I wasn't feeling well—and had paid the bill with my nearly maxed-out credit card. Thank God I had enough room left on it, because even though we were leaving early without finishing our meals, I'd nevertheless been asked to pay the full price for the tasting menu as well as our cocktails, which had cost me over a grand.

But at least we were getting out of here, which was nothing short of grand. Given Jackson's drunken, emotional state, I couldn't allow any of this to be mentioned in tomorrow's news.

His cell phone dinged, and he looked unsteadily at the screen.

"Austin's on his way up now."

"I need you to be as steady as you can for me," I said before we stood up from the table. "Everyone in this restaurant is aware that you're here tonight. They have their cell phones at the ready."

"How do you know that?"

"Because when I paid the bill, I casually glanced around and saw that some of those phones are trained on us as I speak. I need you to take hold of my hand as you stand, I need you to stand right at my side when we leave, and if we're lucky, we'll get you out of this place without causing a scene."

But we weren't lucky. Because when Jackson stood, he wavered a bit on his feet before his eyes crossed and he pitched forward. He slammed onto the table and took it down with him as I rushed back. Everyone looking on gave a collective gasp.

I heard Jackson's name being mentioned all around me.

And since I was acutely aware that photos and videos were being taken of us, I instinctively said—in a voice everyone around us could hear—"It's food poisoning—that oyster made you sick!"

Immediately, our server was at our side, helping me get Jackson to his feet, which was a sad state of affairs if there ever was one. Jackson had become a wobbling drunk who was so deep in the tank that he'd become his own horror show.

"It's clearly food poisoning," I said out loud, knowing this moment would inevitably be posted on YouTube. And when it was, I wanted people to wonder whether Jackson was drunk or if an oyster had made him so sick. "It was the shellfish," I said as I seized his arm. "You said it didn't taste right. You said it was off. We need to get you home."

He glanced at me. "Get me out of here before I throw up."

With every ounce of strength I could muster, I led him out of Per Se as people looked on in a mixture of excitement, disbelief, and horror. When I saw Austin waiting for us as we left the restaurant, he rushed toward us, which was a great relief to me.

"He's drunk," I said to him beneath my breath. "I tried to keep the booze at bay, but apparently this one does what he wants."

"He's used to getting his way," Austin said quietly to me. "Let's get him to the limousine."

"Are the paparazzi waiting for us?"

"Thankfully, no."

"Then, let's hurry, because tonight has been a disaster."

"Define 'disaster,'" Jackson said as we urged him toward the escalator.

"Trust me, you'll find out in the morning."

And then I realized that the fallout about to come also awaited me, and this incensed me.

Is this how it was going to be with him for the next eight months? If so, what would being with him do to my own career, especially since I was legally bound to him?

I hadn't entered into this agreement thinking I'd be saddled with a drunk, so what did that mean for me? Did I have a way out of this contract? I didn't know. I hadn't read the damned thing, which I fucking should have. But Harper knew the details, and she'd be hearing from me first thing tomorrow about whether or not I was obligated to stay in this fake relationship. At the very least, knowing Harper, I knew she was going to be furious that this had happened. Whatever she was going to say to Mimi in the morning—when this shit show officially became a public circus—was going to be substantial.

Worry about it tomorrow, I thought, meeting Austin's gaze as we held on to Jackson and helped him down the escalator. *Right now, we need to get out of here and into that limo as quickly as possible.*

"Sorry," Jackson said as we continued our descent. "Sorry about that. Didn't mean for that to happen. Didn't mean to get wasted and shit…"

With the alcohol now fully threading through him, he was becoming a weight I wasn't sure I'd be able to hold up even with Austin's help.

"Austin," I said to him, "he's getting too heavy for me."

"We're almost there," he said. "Just one more flight to go, and then we'll get him across the lobby and into the car."

"People photographed us in the restaurant," I said. "When he stood up, he tipped over the damn table and fell on top of it on the floor. There were people videoing us when that happened. You and I both know that's about to go viral, even if I did say aloud that he had food poisoning."

"You did?" he said to me in surprise.

"Of course I did," I said. "I said it for the millions of people who will soon witness Jackson in all his glory on YouTube. I mean, what else could I do? We ate raw oysters—it was the first thing that came into my mind. I decided to blame his behavior on that instead of the booze."

"You might have just saved his ass," he said. "You should get a bonus for that."

"Please suggest one for me."

"I'll give you a bonus," Jackson said. "Because I got it like that. Austin? Get my checkbook for me, OK? Get me my checkbook and...shit. I don't even know where my checkbook is, because who writes checks anymore? But if you can find it for me, I'll write a check to Sienna that's so big, she'll forgive me. Just you watch."

"Here's what you're going to do, Jackson," Austin said in a firm, controlling voice that rendered Jackson silent. "You're going to shut up, pull yourself together, do as I say, and help us get you into the car. Got it?"

"All right..."

When we reached the lobby, Austin turned to me.

"The car is still running," he said as Jackson's head lifted and dipped between us. "There are people outside, but I don't see any paps. Before they arrive in anticipation of your leaving tonight, we need to get this one into that car as fast as possible. Are you with me?"

"Do you really think I'm going to bail on you now?"

"Some might have, but you haven't," he said. "And that speaks volumes for you, Sienna. I'm sorry about this. Obviously this week has been more difficult on him than any of us knew."

When he said that to me, we looked at each other for a moment, and I could sense a kind of shift between us. We were in the process of managing something that never should have happened, and we both knew that we'd never get through it without one another. Right now, to help Jackson through this, I needed to have Austin's back—but to put this nightmare behind us, he also needed mine.

And we both knew it.

"I'm with you," I said. "But how do we do this so it doesn't look like we're dragging him out of here?"

"We're about to create a blur," he said.

"A what?"

"The car is just outside those doors," he said, nodding toward the exit that led to the street. "Here's what I suggest. I'll sweep him over my shoulder while you run ahead of me. When we're outside, hurry to the car and open the back door so I can get him inside. When I do that, I need *you* to round the car and get inside, and then we'll get the hell out of here."

"I got a little bit ahead of the bottle," Jackson slurred.

"You did," Austin said. "Yet again. Jackson, I've told you you can't let this week keep eating away at you. It isn't like you."

"And there I go again," he said, "letting everyone down..."

"Listen to me, Jackson. I'm going to swing you over my shoulder and get you into that limousine, OK?"

"Jesus fucking Christ," Jackson said. "Over your shoulder? Seriously?"

"Seriously. And when I do that, you are going to keep your head down so no one sees your face. Got it?"

"Got it."

"And then we'll get you home. Tomorrow, Mimi is going to have to manage the fallout, but she'll do it, because that's what she does best."

"I've been bad," Jackson said.

Exasperated, Austin looked at me.

"Are you ready?" he asked.

"I'm ready."

"Good. I'll put him over my shoulder while you open the doors for us. Just as planned. Go!"

I hurried toward the doors and opened them as Austin

charged toward me with Jackson slung over his massive right shoulder, and then we were out and into the warm night air. As we rushed across the sidewalk, people looked oddly at us as I ran toward the limousine. I opened the back door just before Austin lowered Jackson to the ground and shoved him inside.

"Now you," he said.

I rounded the car and got inside, Austin shut my door behind me, and then suddenly he was in the front seat and peeling away into traffic.

"Jesus," I said.

"I'm sorry, Sienna," Austin said. "Thank you for your help."

I placed my hand against Jackson's back to see if he was OK, but when I did, he just careened over onto his side and passed out.

As angry as I was with him, I couldn't help but feel for him. This week had been too much for him. First the scandal, then the fallout, and then the scheme to have a fake girlfriend. Despite the damage being with him tonight might have done to my own career, I nevertheless found myself stroking his back as we hurtled across the city, where Jackson had a penthouse apartment on Fifth in a high-rise that overlooked Central Park.

"He's out," I said to Austin.

"I see that," he said. "Now, tell me—how are you?"

"I'm upset," I said. "And angry. And also sad that Jackson's going through all this. Once it became clear to me that he was drinking too much, I tried to stop him, but he wouldn't have it. He just kept slinging back bourbon after bourbon while I encouraged him to eat bread and drink water. When I realized things were only going to get worse, I urged him to bail on dinner and call you to pick us up. Because at that point, Jackson got so loaded so quickly that the people around us started filming it, Austin. Mimi needs to know that."

"I'll call her tonight," he said. "I'll tell her everything. And try not to worry about this, Sienna. Tonight is on him, not you. I plan to make that very clear to Mimi."

"Thank you," I said. "Now, listen—do you need me to help you get Jackson into his apartment?"

"No," he said. "I can do it."

"Are you sure? He's pretty much dead weight right now."

A moment passed before he spoke. "This isn't the first time this has happened, Sienna. I can manage on my own."

What have I gotten myself into?

"All right. Well, while you're taking him inside, I'll just catch a cab and head home."

"That's not happening," he said.

"Sorry?"

"It's in the contract."

"What's in the contract?"

"I've already told you," he said. "I'm also here to protect you. And because of that, I'll be taking you home myself. When we arrive at Jackson's apartment, just wait for me in the car, and when I return, I'll take you home."

I wanted this day behind me, and getting a cab on my own was the quickest way to make that happen. But as Austin looked at me in the rearview mirror, I knew I had to honor my contract. So, I just nodded at him as we roared across the city.

THIRTY MINUTES LATER, after Austin had taken Jackson to his

apartment, he returned to the car, which was double-parked just outside the building's entrance.

"Is he all right?" I asked when Austin stepped behind the wheel, turned off the hazard lights, and shut the door behind him.

"Let's just say he's going to have one hell of a hangover in the morning. But he's in bed and safe, and that's what matters. Thanks again for your help."

"Of course," I said.

He looked over his shoulder and out the rear window, waiting for an opening so he could cut into traffic. As he did, I admired his profile. I thought he had the most beautiful Romanesque nose—it was bold, strong, and masculine, with a prominent bridge that suited him. His lips, now pressed together as he judged the right moment to hit the gas, were full and sensuous, and I wondered what it would be like to kiss him.

And then I wondered why I was so drawn to him.

It wasn't just his looks, although they certainly helped. But because this was a city brimming with attractive men, I knew it had to be something more. What was it? Was it his quiet confidence that got to me? Or was it his clear devotion to Jackson that spoke to me—despite the lows that clearly came with that job? Or was it the way he'd looked at me when he'd massaged my feet and helped me into my shoes? His touch had been as gentle as it had been erotic. It had sent shivers through me, but I still had to wonder—was that because of *him*? Or was it because it had been the first time I'd allowed another man to touch me since I'd left Eric two years ago?

When we cut into traffic, I glanced down at my watch and couldn't believe it was only ten o'clock. My night out with Jackson Cruise had lasted all of two hours. Since

Jackson was such a major celebrity, I knew it would only be a matter of time before somebody in that restaurant sold their video of him going down with that table to a member of the paparazzi. Worse, I knew in my gut that that video would dominate tomorrow's news cycle.

As Austin hooked a left back onto Fifth and we started heading downtown, I felt myself start to cool off as I considered how hard it must be for Jackson not to be able to be himself but have to live his life as a lie.

It had to be hell for him, especially given the divisive culture in which we lived today, with neo-Nazis and white supremacists fearlessly rising up in ways that unnerved me. It broke my heart that if Jackson wanted to continue his career as an action star, he would probably have to hide his true self from the world. It was so unfair that it troubled me.

Please let tomorrow not be as awful as I think it's going to be for him, I thought to myself. *Because when he wakes up to this mess, he's going to feel shaken and vulnerable. I have the privilege of being a straight, white woman. I can handle whatever is said about me tomorrow. But I'm not so sure that Jackson can...*

"Would you like to talk?" Austin asked.

I was so deep in thought that I was startled when he spoke.

"I'm sorry?" I said.

"Would you like to talk? Or would you rather keep thinking about what happened tonight? Because that's what you're doing, Sienna. I can see it on your face. You're worried about Jackson. You're worried about tomorrow's news cycle. Why don't you let me take your mind off all that—even if it's just for a few moments?"

"What would you like to talk about?" I asked.

"Anything," he said. "Given the kind of traffic I'm looking at right now, we're in for at least a twenty-minute drive to get to your place. I'd hate to do it in silence, especially since I think you need a distraction as much as I do. So, let me ask the first question, because it's really important to see where you stand on this particular issue."

"All right," I said as I looked at him in the rearview mirror. "Which issue?"

"Are you're a Yankees or a Mets fan?"

I smiled when he said that, because after the hell of tonight, I knew he was making an effort to lighten the mood.

"Yankees," I said. "I hope that doesn't offend—"

"Hell, no!" he said. "Total Yankees fan here. Been one my entire life."

"Your entire life? Did you grow up here?"

"Born and raised in the Bronx."

"And yet I don't hear an accent," I remarked.

"That's because my grandmother beat it out of me."

"Why would she do that?"

"Because she was born and raised in England and always hated the Bronx accent. Since she and my grandfather lived next door to us when I was growing up, she took it upon herself to become my dialect coach. Apparently she thought that if I didn't speak 'properly,' it would be harder for me to succeed in life."

"Well, Austin, I have to say that's one of the stranger stories I've heard in a while."

"It's pretty messed up," he said with a laugh. "But that's my grandmother. So, how about you? Where are you from?"

"Guess."

"California?"

"More like Dubuque, Iowa."

"Dubuque? So, who scrubbed you of *your* accent?"

"That would be acting classes, where my accent also was stripped from me."

"How did you fall into acting?"

"Long story."

"Give it to me long, or give it to me short."

"Let's go for the short version," I said with a smile.

"Fine by me."

"Ever since I was a kid, I wanted to perform on Broadway, which is the reason I moved to Manhattan. Unfortunately, no work came my way until a friend scored me a meeting with Harper, who took me on as a model, not an actress. She knew I wanted to act, but she also knew that I needed to eat. So, the whole modeling thing happened. When I wasn't modeling, I was studying acting. Seven long years later and with only a few minor roles coming my way, I was about to give up on my dream when last year I landed the lead role in *Lion*. And then, this year, came Cannes. And then the award I received there. And then came Jackson. And now I'm in a limousine with you, driving down Fifth Avenue. My life has officially become surreal, Austin."

"I'm glad you're here, Sienna," he said to me. "I'm glad you're beginning to realize your dreams. Because they don't come easily, do they?"

"No," I said. "They don't."

"Did you eat anything at Per Se tonight?" he asked. "Beyond the oyster?"

"Unfortunately, no. We'd just been served our second course when Jackson upended the table."

"It's only ten thirty," he said. "Are you hungry? Because I have a favorite diner I go to downtown, and I haven't had dinner myself tonight. If you'd like to join me, we could get something to eat."

And there it was in front of me—one seriously dangerous proposition—and one that I couldn't take lightly.

"We could have a burger," he said. "Some fries. What do you say?"

"That I can't do it," I said.

He glanced at me in the rearview mirror and furrowed his brow.

"Why?"

Because of the way you put my shoes on me earlier tonight, Austin. And because of how my body responded to you when you held my feet in your hands. And because I'm beyond attracted to you. No good can come from this—at least for now. I'm owned by Jackson for the next eight months...

"I signed an agreement to be exclusive to Jackson," I said, wishing in view of tonight's fiasco that I hadn't. "As you know, the contract states that when it comes to men, I can only ever be seen out in public with him until the contract has run its course. I need to honor that. I hope you understand."

"I understand," he said.

"It's not that I don't want to, Austin. It's that I can't."

"No, I get it," he said. "But that doesn't mean I can't be disappointed. It's been a long time since I've met someone as interesting as you, Sienna. You're smart, you're quick on your feet, and you walked over coals tonight for Jackson as if the heat barely touched you. I'd like to get to know you better, but if I have to wait..." He paused for a moment and shrugged. "Then I guess I'll have to wait."

"If this city had a drive-thru restaurant and we could park somewhere, I probably could get away with that," I said.

He hesitated before he said, "I think it's best if I get you home."

"How about this?" I said. "If you still find me interesting eight months from now, how about if we have a burger and fries then? Or maybe sooner if I can somehow get out of this contract tomorrow. Trust me, after what happened tonight, I'm going to try to."

When I said that, he looked over his shoulder at me. "Consider it a date," he said. "Just let me know when and where, and trust me on this—I'll be there."

7

AT FIVE-THIRTY THE NEXT MORNING, my cell rang on my bedside table. With a sense of dread, I looked over at my phone to see who was calling, even though I already knew it would be Harper Carmichael.

And it was.

"Hi, Harper," I said meekly.

Please don't filet me right now. I haven't had my coffee yet.

"And hello, Jesus!" she said when I answered the phone. "Are you awake? Because I really need you to be awake for this."

Why did she sound so excited? Ever since I'd gone to bed, I'd been expecting her to rant at me when she read the news and decided to call.

"I'm awake," I said, "but not exactly rested, because for the life of me, I couldn't get to sleep last—"

"Stop!" she said. "Just listen to me."

"Listen to what?" I said.

"Are you sitting down?"

"Actually, I'm lying flat on my back."

"Even better."

"Why are you so worked up?" I asked.

"I don't know, Sienna—maybe because you're trending on Twitter?"

"I'm trending on what?"

"Twitter!" she said.

I sat up in bed, propped a few pillows behind my back, and ran a hand through my hair as I tried to shake off the remnants of what little sleep I'd gotten. "After last night, I can't imagine that's a good thing."

"Parts of it are good, parts of it are pure shit—but apparently that old adage remains true to this day."

"What old adage?"

"Unless you're involved in something truly awful—which you weren't last night, despite how horrible the optics look—there's no such thing as bad press when it comes to this business, as you'll soon find out. I need you in my office at eight. We have to talk."

"At eight?" I said. "Why the rush?"

"Seriously, Sienna? That's your question after your evening of abject ruin and humiliation with Jackson last night?"

When she said that, I closed my eyes and felt my stomach sink. "I tried to stop him from drinking, Harper, but he wouldn't stop. He just kept throwing back one drink after the other. I did my best, but he shut me down at every turn."

"I know the story. Austin relayed it to Mimi. And Mimi just relayed it to me. That sorry little heathen even tried to blame *you* for what happened."

"She tried to blame *me*?" I said, enraged. "How? Why? What the hell did I do? I only tried to stop him, for God's sake!"

"Don't worry about it," she said. " I've already taken her down to her pitted knees. Things got heated between us, as they generally do because of our toxic past, but in the end, I won—as I always do when it comes to her. She'll never be as quick as I am, Sienna. Or as smart. After I let her have it, Mimi reluctantly agreed that what happened last night is in fact on Jackson and not on you."

"Last night was a nightmare, Harper."

"I've seen the videos," she said. "I can only imagine how difficult last night was for you. But you? You handled yourself beautifully. And brava for that, my darling girl, because Jackson put you in a tough spot."

"The videos," I said with a groan. "People were using their cell phones to video us last night. So, let me guess— one or more of those videos are circling now, right? Which is the reason I'm trending on Twitter."

"As I speak, five videos have been published," she said. "All from different viewpoints. And there will likely be more to come. And yes, all of them have gone viral. Your first date with Jackson Cruise has turned out to be one for the record books, especially since Jackson toppled over that goddamned table. And at Per Se, of all places! But tell me this, because I need all the fire I can bring to the table when Mimi lands in my office later this morning."

"What do you want to know?"

"Despite what you said when Jackson went down, he didn't fall over because of food poisoning, did he?"

"No," I said. "I already told you—he got wasted last night. And believe me when I say that I tried my best to stop him. But there was no stopping him, because apparently Jackson Cruise does whatever the hell he wants."

"Trust me, darling, I get it. A-list stars can be one major A-list pain in the ass."

"Do you believe me?"

"Sienna, your American horror story has been caught on

tape, so of course I believe you. And I'm angry that Jackson would even allow himself to go there given how important last night was to him. By doing so, he's cast yet another cloud of negativity around himself, which is terrible when it comes to his career and his image. I can only imagine how furious you are with him."

"On one level I am, but on another, I'm not."

"How can that be?"

"Jackson opened up to me last night," I said. "He comes from a broken family. With each drink he tossed back, he told me things about his parents and his past that were heartbreaking. He hasn't had an easy life, particularly when it comes to his ridiculous family. But despite that, Harper, if Jackson has issues with alcohol, I don't think it's best for me to be associated with him, because if this is what the next eight months look like for me, I want no part of it. Am I able to get out of this contract?"

"I don't think you should, Sienna."

"But I do."

"Look, just be here at eight," she said. "Things are happening that you know nothing about."

"What things?"

"I'll tell you when you get here."

"Is Austin picking me up?"

"No," she said. "He's taking care of Jackson this morning, who apparently has the mother of all hangovers. Just pull yourself together, get some coffee in you, and take a cab—and don't you dare be late!"

∾

By the time I arrived at Harper's office, I'd read the news and seen the videos TMZ and countless other outlets were circulating online, and I was infuriated that I'd been put in this position, especially since my name was now being prominently associated with Jackson's.

For him, the headlines were demeaning.

From TMZ:

IS JACKSON CRUISE CRUISING TOWARD REHAB?

From Page Six:

SOMETHING'S FISHY WITH JACKSON CRUISE—
AND IT'S NOT THE OYSTERS AT PER SE

From the *Times*:

AN ACTION STAR'S STEEP, SUDDEN FALL

And then there were the ones that mentioned me.

From the *Los Angeles Times*:

AFTER WINNING THE PALME D'OR,
WILL HOLLYWOOD SHOW SIENNA JONES THE DOOR?

FROM *VARIETY*:

HOW WILL JACKSONGATE
AFFECT SIENNA JONES'S CHANCES OF WINNING
AN OSCAR?

AND FINALLY, from the *Hollywood Reporter*:

JACKSON CRUISE AND SIENNA JONES—
WHO WILL SURVIVE THE FALLOUT?

ACCORDING TO THE ARTICLE, it wasn't me.

When I rounded the corner and came upon Harper's assistant and my best friend, Julia Jacobs, she looked up at me with those wide, beautiful green eyes of hers—and what I saw in them was enough to stop me in my tracks. Unfortunately for me, those eyes were wider than usual, because they sent a clear message to me: *Girl, you are fucked.*

"Hi, Julia," I said.

"How are you holding up, sweetie?"

I'd known Julia ever since I'd first signed with Harper. She and I were the same age, and we'd become fast friends —and for good reason. She was smart and wickedly funny, and she loved fashion as much as I did. To me, she was this tall, stunning, ultrachic blond goddess of a woman. I adored her.

"I'm doing my best," I said. "You've seen the videos?"

She nodded grimly at me. "Handling him last night couldn't have been easy," she said.

"It was horrible."

"I can only imagine. What do you need from me?"

"Can I call you later?" I asked. "Depending on how today goes, you might need to talk me off the edge."

"I can do that," she said. "I'll always be here for you...just as you've always been there for me."

"I appreciate that, Julia."

"It's what best friends do," she said.

I looked over at Harper's closed door.

"Is Harper ready for me?" I asked.

"Let's just say she's ready for you *and* Mimi."

"This is going to be a shit show, isn't it?"

"I'd be lying if I said it wasn't," she said with a sigh as she stood up. "But with Harper on your side, you'll weather through this, Sienna. Right now, you need to trust in her more than you ever have—because as long as I've known her, Harper's instincts have rarely been proved wrong."

"I'll do that," I said.

"Good," she said as she came around her desk in a gorgeous, bright-yellow dress that hugged close to her ridiculous curves. "Now, let's get you inside. Can I get you some coffee?"

"I'd love a cup, Julia."

"Consider it done," she said, giving me a hug. I hugged her back with everything I had within in me.

"Sienna, you're going to be fine," she said.

"But how do you know that?"

"Because I've seen this happen before," she said, "with plenty of other actors. Just listen to what Harper has to say to you—and go with everything she recommends."

"All right."

She opened Harper's door for me, and I saw Harper inside, pacing in front of her wall of windows before she stopped and turned to me.

"I'll be back with your coffee in a minute," Julia said.

And as I stepped inside at the very moment Harper's eyes met mine, hearing the door click solidly shut behind me.

"NICE DRESS," Harper said as I stepped farther into the room. "And look at you, wearing black in the middle of June. Whose funeral are you attending?"

"My own?"

"Please." She motioned toward her desk, and I sat opposite her. "Tell me your version of what happened last night," she said. "All of it."

I told her everything.

"And Austin can substantiate the latter half of your evening with Jackson should I need to bring him in on this?"

"He could," I said. "But since he works for Jackson, and his job would be on the line if he ratted him out, we need to consider that he might choose not to do so. He's protective of Jackson. They're friends."

"Actually, I disagree about how he'd approach this, because I know Austin is an honorable man. If we have to, we'll bring him into the conversation. But since you brought up the whole working-for-Jackson thing, here's what you need to know about Austin Black, Sienna. He's so good at what he does that he's literally sought after by dozens of celebrities—many of whom would kill to have him working *their* security detail. It isn't *he* who needs Jackson. It's the other way around, because Austin is that well regarded—for the very reasons you witnessed last night."

In more ways than one, I thought when I recalled his massaging my feet before he helped me into my shoes.

At that moment, a knock came at the door.

"Yes, Julia?"

"Coffee for Sienna," she said as she entered the room.

"Thank you, Julia," I said as she handed me a steaming white mug.

"Anything for you, doll."

When she left, I turned to Harper.

"I'm being smeared by the press for somebody else's actions. I need to know whether I can get out of this contract. Because if I can, I want to be out of it today."

"Not so fast," she said. "Here's what I wanted to tell you to your face. Ever since you and Jackson started dominating the entertainment cycle this morning, my phone and my e-mail have been blowing up. Five top directors have already sent in scripts for your consideration. And I have a feeling that if I went over to check my e-mail now, there'd be more."

"But how can that be?" I asked in wonderment. "Last night was a total disaster for me!"

"Maybe when it comes to the masses, yes, but soon they'll just be hooked on another story. But when it comes to *this* business? Not so fast, darling. In an impossible situation, you showed the suits of Hollywood that you can handle yourself with poise. And in that situation, you proved to everyone that you are quick on your feet."

"Then, why is *Variety* questioning my chances of receiving an Oscar nod?"

"Ha!" she said. "Consider that headline nothing more than clickbait, because even *Variety* needs to come up with salacious headlines to get traffic to its site. But to answer

your question about why people are sending you scripts—
it's simple: you're attached to Jackson Cruise. Regardless of
the ass he made of himself last night—and the scrutiny
surrounding his sexuality—he nevertheless remains a
major A-list actor, Sienna. And then there are the videos. In
one, you fiercely confronted the paps and insisted that you
were no one's beard. Whether you know it or not, that was a
brilliant move on your part, because you answered a direct
question about Jackson's sexuality—and you were so angry
and believable in that moment that you literally owned it. In
the second video, you were just as believable when you
questioned aloud whether Jackson had food poisoning. It's
because of how you handled yourself in those two videos
that you are on everyone's radar right now, especially after
your recent win at Cannes. My bet is that everyone who
matters in Hollywood is now acutely aware of that win and
that they don't give a damn about your relationship to a
troubled action star."

"Then, prove it," I said. "If you think other scripts are
waiting for me, check your e-mail now."

"Sienna, I just checked it ten minutes before you
stepped in."

I glanced down at my watch. "And we've been talking for
twenty minutes. Check it, Harper. If any other people have
reached out to you concerning me, I want to know."

"Well, *you're* certainly bossy this morning."

"I don't mean to be. It's just that after seeing those videos
and reading the stories that accompanied them—not to
mention some of the headlines, which called me out by
name—I'm feeling really vulnerable right now."

"To be expected," she said as she leaned toward her
computer. And when she started to click her mouse and

read e-mails I couldn't see, a slow smile began to spread across her face.

"Oh, my," she said with a sense of excitement in her voice. "Spielberg," she said. "And Tarantino, who hasn't made a film in years. And one of the greatest directors of all time—Scorsese. All are reaching out to me because of their interest in you."

"I don't believe you," I said.

"Would you like to look at my screen?"

"Seriously?" I said to her. "Spielberg? Scorsese?"

"And Tarantino." Her eyes brightened when she looked at me. "Despite what happened last night, you're not only trending on Twitter, darling, you're also trending with the titans of Hollywood. All this comes down to your ties to Jackson and how well you handled yourself in the videos that are now circulating. By the end of the day, I see several offers coming your way. Hell, I see you booked to do movies for the next several years. So, what I need to ask you is simple—do you still want to be attached to Jackson Cruise?"

"Hell, no," I said. "That man is a nightmare."

"Look," she said with a sigh. "Jackson Cruise has never been associated with a drinking problem. As. In. Never. As far as I'm concerned, he got loaded last night because this past week finally caught up with him. From a personal perspective, I get it—you want out. But from a career perspective, you actually had the good fortune of being Jackson's date on the very night he hit rock bottom. The press's attention might seem negative to you, but I know how Hollywood works. And obviously, from the scripts I've been sent alone, they're impressed by what they saw in you last night. Many want to work with you now. As for your concerns about being connected with Jackson, don't worry about it, because later this morning,

Mimi and I plan to get him in line. We might have had our little argument, but even she knows that she needs to get through to him before he throws away his career."

I looked at her over my coffee. "Harper, I don't have a way out of this contract even if I wanted to get out of it, do I?"

"Not technically," she admitted. "Although if you were stupid enough to get out of it, I probably could make it happen for you—but just so you don't forget, in the process you'd be forfeiting ten million dollars. Think about *that* for a minute."

That ten million dollars would set me free, I thought ruefully. *Maybe Harper and Mimi can set Jackson straight. Maybe last night was just a one-off. Maybe it won't happen again...*

"All right," I said. "I'll stay in. But you have to do something about his behavior, Harper, because that can't happen again."

A knock came at the door. Harper looked at me as she rose, and as I watched her square her shoulders in the red power suit she was wearing, I saw her eyes narrow before she lifted her chin at me.

"That will be Jackson, Mimi, and Austin," she said to me. "Are you ready for them?"

"Why? Have you just turned into Thor?"

"I prefer Wonder Woman."

"Actually, it's more like the Black Death, because your eyes have just gone completely dark."

"That's only because you've never seen me go to war before—or just how much I get off on it. But you're about to see that now, Sienna, so strap yourself in, sweetie." She put one hand on her hip and turned smartly toward the door. "Julia?" she called out. "Send them in."

AND IN THEY CAME.

First there was Mimi, also dressed in a red power suit. She stopped cold when she saw that her former partner of eight years was also wearing one.

"Seriously?" she said. "Really, Harper?"

"I wore it first," Harper said.

"The hell you did—I was up and dealing with this fiasco at five."

"Ha!" Harper said. "You're such a layabout, Mimi, you *really* are. I was in full makeup and hair and fielding calls at four."

"I call bullshit on that," Mimi said as she glided into the room. Austin came in behind her, and I thought he looked handsome in his black suit. "Because I know you better than that."

"That's the problem," Harper said as I met Austin's eyes and nodded at him while he discreetly rolled his own eyes at me. "You never really knew me at all, darling."

Why do I feel as if I've known him for years? I wondered as Harper and Mimi bickered. *Why did I feel this strange connec-*

tion with him? We've only known each other for two days, for God's sake. What it is about him that continues to draw me to him? This just isn't like me...

"The gossip I could spread about you," Mimi said.

"The horror stories I could tell about *you*."

Before Mimi could retaliate, Harper looked over at the door, where there was no sign of Jackson. "Where is Jackson, Mimi?" Harper said. "Hiding somewhere? Standing on the precipice of a bridge, considering whether to end it all? Or is he just drowning his sorrows at some sordid bar in Hell's Kitchen?"

I saw Mimi shoot Harper down with a searing glance before she called out for Jackson to come inside. And frankly, I couldn't blame Mimi for doing so. Jackson Cruise was likely her biggest client, and I knew for a fact that Mimi couldn't allow Jackson to be mistreated by Harper now. Because if he didn't feel safe here, he could fire Mimi on the spot and walk straight into another agency, one as powerful as CAA's top competitor, ICM.

"Sorry," Jackson said as he entered the room wearing tight-fitting jeans, a navy-blue T-shirt, and dark aviator sunglasses, which he likely was wearing to conceal his bloodshot eyes. "I was talking with Julia."

"Of course you were," Mimi said. "She's a lovely girl, isn't she? So bright. So positive. So filled with a promise that will likely go unfulfilled, because Harper here never promotes anyone. Instead, she just steals away people's dreams. Anyway, how about if you close the door behind you? Then the four of us can sit down and talk about last night and strategize on how we go forward from here."

"The four of us?" Harper said. "Austin is here, Mimi, and he makes five. Since he witnessed a good deal of what happened last night, he also needs a seat at the table."

"Austin has a confidentiality contract he needs to honor with my client," Mimi said. "Sorry, toots. Naturally, Austin is welcome to stay because we adore him. But it'll just be the four of us discussing last night."

"Then sit on that sofa," Harper said, pointing to the one at her right. It faced the sofa opposite it. "This time, I'll sit with my client alone on the other sofa, Mimi."

"As you should. Jackson?" she said. "Come here, love. Sit next to Mimi."

As I stood and looked over at Jackson, intending to say good morning to him, he behaved as if I wasn't even there. In fact, after I smiled at him, he chose not to acknowledge me at all, which infuriated me.

At the very least, you could be polite, Jackson, I thought as I glared at him. *Especially after I saved your ass last night.*

"So," Harper said when I'd sat down next to her and crossed my legs. "Last night certainly caused a stir, didn't it?"

"Jackson was polluted by sour shellfish," Mimi said. "I mean, Sienna herself called it out for what it was. We've all seen the videos by now. He was poisoned by Per Se!"

Seriously, I thought. *She's going to continue to deny what happened last night? Not with me in this room, she wasn't.*

"That's not true," I said.

"Well, of course it's true," Mimi said.

"I'm afraid it isn't. Despite my best efforts to keep Jackson from getting drunk last night, he drank three bourbons in a row before I made him hand over his fourth to me. And only moments after I took that one away from him, he reached for it and downed it. He got shitfaced last night."

I was expecting a reaction from Jackson when I said that, but he didn't give me one. Instead, he just started to rub his left temple in deep, slow circles, likely in an effort to ease his headache.

"But, Sienna..." Mimi tittered.

"Mimi," Jackson warned in a low voice.

"No, no, it's *fine*, Jackson," she said as she patted his knee. "As you know, it's all on video. You weren't drunk last night —Sienna said so herself in the videos that are circulating right now. She said that you were having a reaction to the oyster you'd just eaten. It's on record."

"I only said that as a favor to Jackson," I said.

"*As a favor to Jackson?*" Mimi said in a weirdly high-pitched voice. "As a favor to *Jackson Cruise*, who needs no favors from anyone, least of all from the likes of you? I mean, let's get real here, cookie. A small win at Cannes doesn't put you at *his* level. If anything, *he's* the one doing *you* a favor given all the free press you've received after last night's little misunderstanding." She narrowed her eyes at me. "I can only imagine how well you're benefiting from *that* kind of coverage."

"Sienna thought fast on her feet and helped Jackson," Harper said. "Both you and Jackson should be grateful for it."

"Grateful?" Mimi said. "Oh, Harper, please. The only person who should be grateful in this room is Sienna, not Jackson."

"Stop it!" Jackson said. "Cut the bullshit, Mimi. I have a movie to shoot in a few hours, and I don't want to deal with this crap right now."

When he said that, he removed his sunglasses, and I saw just how red and fatigued his eyes looked. Then he finally looked at me.

"Sienna, I apologize. Mimi is just trying to protect me. It's in her nature to do so, and while she means well, I'm not going to let her rewrite history just so I can save face. Especially since everyone in this room already knows the truth of what went down last night."

He glanced over at Austin, who was standing at the tall windows that overlooked the city.

"On the drive over here, Austin and I talked, and I agree with him," Jackson said. "I owe you an apology, Sienna. I'm sorry. But after the press questioned whether you were my fucking beard—which they did—it upset me, because I worried that's how they were going to start to spin our story. I didn't handle it well, and I started to drink heavily. I want to thank you for trying to protect me and for being quick enough to blame my behavior on the shellfish. I owe you for that. You and Austin did your best to handle me last night. I got plastered, each of you took care of me, and the ramifications are my own."

"I appreciate the apology, Jackson," I said to him. "But before we arrived at Per Se last night, you must have known the paps were going to get into the gutter when it came to you, especially since that was your first official appearance after those unwanted photos of you went viral. You're a professional. You should have prepared yourself for that. Why didn't you?"

"Listen to how she talks to him," Mimi said. "Listen to how she judges him! It's as if she believes she's in a position to even do so!"

"Actually, she is," Harper said. "Sienna has her own career to consider, Mimi. Going forward, she has every right to know whether this will happen again."

"It won't," Jackson said as he turned to face me. "But I get it, Sienna. If you want out of the contract, you'll get no argument from me, and there will be no hard feelings. Mimi can always find somebody else for me. You can keep the money I've already given you, and that will be that."

Harper looked at Jackson and spoke to him in a quiet voice. "Jackson, Sienna has no plans to contest your contract."

He looked at her in surprise.

"She doesn't?"

"She doesn't. Despite last night, she's agreed to continue to give this her best shot, because she does want to help you, for reasons that are personal to her. As you know, she's worked as a model for years. And because of that, many of her friends are gay. She hates how you've been smeared by the press. She wants to help you. But we also want to make sure this won't happen again. Can you promise her that?"

At that, he looked me straight in the eyes and said, "I can. I'm sorry that it happened at all. It won't happen again."

He's telling the truth, I thought as I looked him. *I can hear it in his voice, see it in his eyes...*

"Then, that's enough for me," I said. "I'll continue to support you, Jackson. Hopefully last night was nothing more than an unfortunate blip. And as much as I wish it hadn't happened, I do get it, Jackson. I can't imagine the pressure you're under right now. But if we are to going to try to convince the world that we're falling in love, you and I need to work together to make that happen. Deal?"

"Deal," he said as he stood. "Now, give me a hug, because I really am sorry, Sienna."

When he took me into his arms, I felt his vulnerability pulse through me. I knew he didn't want to share that with anyone in this room, and that made my heart go out to him. Was he capable of pulling himself together? Hopefully he was, because he was a good actor. If he was willing and emotionally able to see this through to the end, I felt we could ride this out.

But still...

"No more drinking," I said in his ear.

"No more drinking."

"Because we need to turn this around for you, right?"

"We do."

"Then let's start over again. Let's make the world believe that you and I are perfect for one another, and hopefully in eight months' time, when we've amicably parted ways, I hope that any speculation about your sexuality will be behind you and that both of us can move forward with our lives."

"I hope for the same," he said.

When we parted, I caught sight of Austin, who was looking intently at me with eyes that were so dark they burned into me.

And unnerved me.

"Austin," Harper said. "Do you have the number to Sienna's cell?"

"Actually, I don't," he said.

"Then you need to have it."

"Why?" Mimi asked. "Austin works for Jackson."

"And also for Sienna, which is in the contract. If Sienna sees anything out of line when it comes to Jackson that might give her concern, she's going to need to reach out to Austin so we can get ahead of things quickly."

"But Sienna can simply reach out to me," Mimi said.

"What if you're with another client?" Harper asked. "Or what if you're in a meeting? Austin is always with Jackson. He's the more logical person for her to call or to text if there's another slip."

"Exchange numbers," Jackson said.

"Jackson, I'll always be there for you," Mimi said.

"I understand that, Mimi, but Harper has a point." He

looked from Austin to me and back again. "Exchange numbers."

We did. And when we did, it didn't escape me that Austin Black now had total access to me in ways he'd never had before.

9
_____

New York City
July

THE NEXT THREE weeks were a whirlwind of events that were so carefully timed and choreographed that they took me out of my body and vaulted me into full-on stardom—which looked very different to me now than the day I'd first agreed to sign that contract with Jackson.

With Harper, Mimi, and Austin working alongside Jackson and me, it took us a full week to get beyond the questions surrounding the videos captured at Per Se—and the questions swirling around Jackson's sexuality—and before noise around each started to settle down and abate.

With Harper and Mimi working the phones to tip off the paparazzi when Jackson would end filming for the day and spend time with me, we were literally photographed all over the city.

As video cameras rolled and cameras flashed, we were

"caught" shopping on Fifth, we were photographed holding hands, looking as if we were falling in love as we strolled through Central Park, and we enjoyed our first public kiss on a sidewalk in the East Village. All of it was designed to provide content for the gossip rags, social media outlets, and thousands of entertainment sites all over the world so the masses could dissect our relationship—and discuss it.

And they did, with a fervor that surprised me. A large part of me was still that girl from Dubuque, Iowa, who had once longed for this kind of life and who couldn't believe she was now living it.

I now understood the full weight of Jackson's international star power. I now had an idea of the kind of microscope he'd been living under for the past thirteen years, ever since his first movie had launched him into the stratosphere. Since public interest in our budding relationship was riding high, entertainment reporters were unrelenting in their coverage of us. Each day, they published fresh stories about Jackson and me to a public insatiable for more.

For me, fashion became a critical part of my life, because everything I wore was quickly sensationalized and scrutinized.

The press chronicled all of it, and since noting every detail of how I presented myself to the world rapidly became a "thing," it drove Harper and me to several discreet shopping sprees at Bergdorf's, Prada, Dior, and a host of other elite outlets in the city to ensure that I looked my best.

My fake relationship with Jackson was heating up to the point that now, when I sat in front of my iMac each morning to read the online entertainment feeds, I saw that people were questioning when Jackson and I would get married, which seemed absurd to me. We'd only been "seeing" each other for less than a month, and already there was speculation about a wedding. But isn't that what people like JLo, Rihanna, and Drake went through whenever they started to see someone new? It was—and I needed to get used to it.

Due to my association with Jackson, single women in particular were fixated on me, and for one reason alone. Tracking showed that they thought if a nobody like me could land one of the world's biggest stars, then at very least there was hope they could find love—but how? Should they wear their hair the way I wore my hair? Should they max out their credit cards and buy the same pair of jeans *I* was just photographed wearing? Since Sienna Jones loved to wear a bold red lip, should they wear one themselves?

Jackson and I weren't just selling ourselves to the world. It soon dawned on me that we were also selling hope to millions of women around the world who wanted to snag a man as hot as he was. And maybe some of them would— but even if they didn't, at the very least, most would come away with a few fashion tips by the time Jackson and I went our separate ways.

And I was OK with that.

Harper and I were also aware of another truth. Due to all the press coverage, my career was exploding.

Already I was scheduled to shoot three movies over the next two years, the first with Martin Scorsese himself. Beyond that, Tarantino had passed on me, but Spielberg hadn't. Next year I'd star in a World War I drama with him. And in the same year, I'd work with Christopher Nolan in one of the twisty, mind-bending thrillers for which he was known.

Throughout this stunt of ours, there were times I'd felt on top of the world, particularly since the acting career I'd always longed for was actually taking shape. But there were other times when I was frightened by the fame, particularly as I watched my private life erode. When Austin drove me home at night after a day of being photographed with Jackson, sometimes I thought I'd never felt more isolated or alone despite how alive, happy, and in love I looked to the world at large.

The irony wasn't lost on me.

"Sienna?" Austin said to me now.

It was evening. I'd just had dinner with Jackson at the Milling Room on the Upper West Side, and Austin was driving me home for the night after the paps had captured Jackson giving me a searing kiss goodnight when we'd dropped him at his apartment.

Over the past three weeks, Austin and I had come to know one another much better, but since I didn't trust myself around him—because I couldn't deny my attraction to him—I'd stonewalled him every time he'd revealed his increasing attraction to me. Often it was just with a telling look. Other times it was with the gentle yet reassuring way he'd touch my arm when the paparazzi became too much and he sensed I was becoming overwhelmed by them.

Like me, he was also struggling with our mutual attraction, which I could feel every time we were near each other. But since I was pretty much owned by Jackson for the next seven months, Austin and I had done our best to be professionals and not allow our chemistry to show. Austin was loyal to Jackson, and he was excellent at his job. I now understood why Harper had said that any A-list celebrity would crave to have Austin and his team as his or her personal security detail. After seeing him in action these past few weeks, I got it.

"What's up?" I said.

He looked at me in the rearview mirror, moved to speak, but then shook his head. "Sorry," he said. "It's nothing."

"Nothing always means something," I said. "What's on your mind?"

"It's not a big deal. Never mind."

"Well, you can't do that to me now," I said, suddenly curious. "What is it?"

"It's just a personal observation."

Personal? I thought. *You and I should go nowhere near anything personal, Austin.*

Still, since I couldn't help myself after being lured with that kind of bait, I naturally charged forward.

"What is it?" I asked.

"Every time I've driven you home this week, you've seemed unhappy."

"I've seemed unhappy?"

"You have. I know you're going through a lot right now. Over the years, I've seen firsthand how isolated Jackson feels at times, but he has me to talk to. I was wondering if you had anyone to talk to, because this business can be tough. You two are seriously putting yourselves out there right now. Every day it gets more and more intense, especially when you're out in public. It can't be easy for you, particularly since you're still relatively new to all this."

Had he been reading my mind? Or could it be that the highs and lows of my life were becoming clear to those in my inner circle? Likely the latter. Obviously I also needed to act for Austin, because this was the last conversation I wanted to have with him. If I opened up to him, it would take our relationship to a more personal level. And if only for the sake of my heart, which I had to protect, I needed to keep our relationship restricted to business. If I didn't, it would just overcomplicate everything.

"I have Harper," I said. "And Julia. We talk every day."

"Are they enough? Do you have anyone else you can talk to?"

"Because of the contract, I can't discuss my relationship with Jackson with anyone who doesn't know about it," I said. "Remember?"

"Right," he said.

"Why the interest, Austin?"

He locked eyes with me in the rearview.

"Can I be frank?"

"Of course you can."

"Are you sure?"

How bad can it be?

"Say what's on your mind."

"You look fucking miserable," he said in a frustrated voice. "And for the past several nights, nothing has changed. I've been watching you, and I'm worried about you."

"Don't be," I said. "I'm tougher than you think I am, Austin—and in more ways than you know, because I've gone through hell to get to where I am today. I can handle this."

"Can you? Because as we've gotten to know one another over these past few weeks, it's hard for me not to worry about you when I see you looking so unhappy. Just a moment ago, when you were lost in thought, you looked like you wanted to jump out of the car and take the first flight out of the States. Are you aware of that?"

"Not exactly..."

"Well, it's true. You did. And since we're being frank here, you also should know something else. Because I can't keep this to myself anymore."

"What can't you keep to yourself?"

"That I can't get you out of my head," he said. "Because of my job, I've tried my best to reveal none of that to you, but

I also know that I haven't always succeeded. Being near you and not telling you how I feel is starting to feel like a fucking lie. And I don't want to keep lying to you anymore."

"Austin," I warned, "we can't go there. We need to keep things professional between us. We talked about this weeks ago, when you asked if I'd like to grab a burger with you. I thought this was settled."

"Back then I didn't know you as well as I do now. But over these past few weeks, look at how well we've come to know one another. Whenever I take you home for the day, we talk. And at this point, we've shared so much with one another that I feel as if I know you. The real you. Yes, we've made an effort to keep things light, but that effort is starting to eat away at me. Tell me it isn't doing the same to you."

Startled by what he was saying, I said nothing.

"Look, Sienna, I know I'm going out on a limb here, but life is too short not to admit that I haven't felt this way toward a woman in years. I'm attracted to you. Beyond that, Jackson will never feel what I feel for you because he's gay. And you know what? I also sense that you're attracted to me. In fact, I *know* you are, because I see it on your face when you steal glances my way whenever we're together. I can see it in your eyes when you think I'm not looking at you because I'm wearing sunglasses. I can't stand all the things that are going unsaid between us, which is why I'm opening up to you now. I want the chance to get to know you better, and I don't want to wait another seven months to do so. There are ways for us to be discreet, and you can trust me on that—especially since I've successfully concealed plenty of Jackson's rendezvous over the years. I can tell you with certainty that if you'd give me a chance and go out on *one* date with me—just one—nobody would know about it."

"You can't guarantee that, Austin," I said. "With so much

attention focused on Jackson and me right now, neither of us knows when or if a photographer will be waiting outside my apartment one night, hoping I'll be entering it with Jackson. And because you can't protect me from that, seeing you isn't a chance I can take."

"I disagree," he said.

"I'm sorry, but I don't."

"Sienna, what I'm proposing is dinner at *my* apartment, not out in public. Compared to Jackson and you, I'm a nobody, for God's sake. I'm a security guard. And because of that, no paps have ever waited for me at my apartment. But since I understand your concern about being exposed, I have a way to get you into my apartment without your ever being seen or followed."

"How?" I asked.

He told me how—and I had to admit it was ingenious.

"I've seen your schedule for tomorrow," he said as we neared my apartment building. "Jackson is shooting all day. You'll be on set with him for a few hours in the morning, but that's it. You're free all evening. Same goes for me. Have dinner with me."

I want to, I thought as I studied his determined profile from the seat behind him. *More than you know, because I'd also like to see if I'm just physically attracted to you or if what I'm feeling is something deeper. But why can't we just wait to find out?*

I stopped myself when I thought that, because I knew that if I did wait, there was every possibility that he could meet somebody else in the meantime. And what if he fell for her? What then? If I didn't agree to this, I might never know if I'd missed out on something great.

Reason with him...

"Austin, the kind of money Jackson is offering me will

change my life. I've been poor for so long that I can't risk that. I need you to understand that."

"So, let me be clear on this," he said. "Are you saying that you're a prisoner in this contract? That you're unable to see friends at their apartment? Because at this point, that's all we are, Sienna—friends."

"If we were found out, it could be interpreted as something else, and Harper, Mimi, and Jackson would have my ass. They might see it as a breach of contract."

"Not if I told them that you were feeling overwhelmed and had come to me seeking advice on how to deal with the paps."

"So, we're to lie to them?"

"How is that a lie? You *are* overwhelmed right now. All of us know it."

I was. It was true. And everyone did know it. Was that the way around this? I thought about it for a moment...and decided that it was.

If you're going to do this, do it with humor to lighten the mood...

"First things first," I said to him.

"What's that?"

"Seriously? Isn't it obvious?"

"Should it be obvious?"

"Oh, come on—naturally I'm wondering if you cook. Because after so many years of having to eat on the cheap... let me tell you a little secret, Austin. These past few weeks with Jackson have spoiled the hell out of me. I mean, who would ever have thought that someone like me would find themselves having dinner at the Four Seasons, for instance? I mean, let's get real here. I spent my entire youth shoveling cow and chicken shit. Before Jackson came into my life, grabbing a pretzel for dinner at some shady street vendor was the way I used to roll."

"That can't be true," he said with a laugh.

"And there you go—laughing at my shame."

"To ease your fears, you should see how well I cook."

"What types of cuisines have you mastered?"

"You name it," he said. "I can do anything."

"Anything?" I said. "With the exception of Meryl Streep, who can do anything?"

He looked over his shoulder and clocked me with a wicked grin. "Me," he said. "Because what I've really mastered is the art of takeout. And when it comes to this city, I know exactly who to call for the best of the best. You want a slice of pizza that will blow you away? I've got you covered. Love Thai? I'll tire you out with the city's best Thai. *Voulez-vous quelque chose de français? Je peux aussi le trouver.*"

"You speak French?" I asked.

"It's a romance language. Naturally I speak French. And Italian. My tongue is talented that way."

He's quick, I thought as desire burned through me. *And funny. And smart.*

"Sienna, whatever you want is at my fingertips. You just need to ask for it."

That's what I'm afraid of, Austin. Your fingertips and where I might want them on my body if I agree to go through this with you...

Still, since I wanted to live my life without regrets, I knew I did have to go through with this, if only to see if something was there. And I mean *really* there. Austin took sexy to levels not many men possessed...at least in my experience. So, either there was something between us or there wasn't. I needed to find out. After so many weeks of sexual tension building between us, it was time to give this a fair shot. If our night fell flat, we'd simply move forward as friends. But if it didn't, and we did connect, we'd need to move forward into the unknown.

"What do you say?" he asked.

That's the thing, I wondered. *Can I handle the unknown?*

"Are you in?"

"I'm thinking."

"If you have to think, then you already have your answer."

Busted.

"OK," I said. "I'm in—provided you choose the menu well."

"But don't you see?" Austin said as he cruised to a stop in front of my apartment building. "The fact that I know how to choose well has just been established."

"How's that?"

"Have a look at my date for tomorrow night, Sienna."

I couldn't help but smile when he said that.

"So, I'll see you tomorrow at the shoot—and then I'll see you tomorrow night for dinner."

It wasn't a question—it was a statement.

Is this really happening? I wondered as he got out of the car and came around to open my door for me. *Please tell me that I haven't made a mistake...*

When he offered me his hand, I took it, stepped out of the car, and emerged into the lights and sounds of the city. And as I did, I not only felt the electricity of his touch, but by standing so close to him on the curb, I could smell the faintest scent of him. He smelled distinct. Masculine. Earthy. And it was all him, because I didn't detect a trace of cologne.

"Good night, Sienna," he said after he'd walked me to my building's entrance.

"Good night, Austin," I said, meeting his gaze with my own. "I'll see you tomorrow."

"And tomorrow night?"

"And tomorrow night."

And hopefully with a fresh face and bright eyes. Because as I entered my building and took the stairs up to my apartment, I already knew that tonight would hold no sleep for me.

10

AND SINCE I knew sleep wouldn't come, the moment I stepped into my apartment, I checked my watch, saw that it was just past nine, and I decided to call the one woman I'd been friends with for so long that I could trust her with anything—Julia Jacobs, who lived nine blocks away from me but in far better digs.

"Julia?" I said when she answered her cell.

"Hey!" she said. "How was your dinner with Jackson tonight?"

"It was good," I said. "He continues to be on point and professional. I think we're at the point where we're becoming friends."

"Well, that's good to hear," she said. "And a relief. So, you're home?"

"Just got here."

"Why do you sound out of breath?"

"Because shit just got real."

"What kind of shit?"

"Unpredictable shit. Potentially life-changing shit."

"Well, shit," she said. "What does that shit even mean?"

"Are you busy right now? Because I seriously need to talk with someone. I wouldn't ask if it wasn't important."

"Busy?" she asked. "Here's how 'busy' I am, Sienna. I'm sitting in my living room watching Ina Garten teach me how to make meatballs the proper way, which apparently means rolling them *lightly* between the palms of your hands so you don't *compress* them. Because if you do that, apparently they get tough, which likely is why *mine* always feel like you're biting into a shoe. So, I'm learning. And by the way, allow me to officially welcome you into my fabulous life as a single woman in Manhattan, which ironically happens to be filled with attractive, single men."

"The right man will come along one day for you, Julia. You're just being careful and selective, as you should be."

"Sienna, I'm three years shy of being thirty. My ovaries are about to go into high alert. And just so we're clear, I'm pretty much on the verge of signing up to Elite Singles. I've already downloaded the app, for God's sake."

"Tell me you haven't signed up," I said in alarm.

"I haven't been able to bring myself to that point—yet," she said.

"You won't do it on my watch," I said. "God only knows what will come your way if you are foolish enough to go there."

"I've heard it can be a freak show," she said.

"Then, listen to the critics. When all this is behind me and Jackson, you and I can start going out again. We can do the circuit like we used to do. Maybe that way, you'll meet an interesting guy."

"Sienna, you're a celebrity now."

"Please don't say that. I'm still just me."

"I know that's how you feel—and I cherish that person. But let's face it—right now you are owned by the world, and we need to acknowledge that. Because of your fake relationship with Jackson, your life has changed forever."

Which is nothing I want to face right now.

"You know what?" I said, wanting to change the subject.

"What's that?"

"Watching the Contessa making meatballs actually sounds kind of relaxing to me."

"After what you've been through these past three weeks, I imagine it would."

"Are you free to come over?" I asked. "For an hour or so, because I need to talk to someone who is sane. And just so you know, that person wouldn't be facing me if I looked into a mirror. I've got wine, vodka, and tequila at the ready. If they don't entice you, we can talk by phone."

"Give me twenty, and I'll be there," she said.

"Really?" I said.

"I'll always have your back, Sienna. I've had it ever since Harper signed you—just as you've always had mine."

"You're the best," I said. "Thanks, lovecat. I really do appreciate it!"

"That's the thing about you, Sienna," she said. "I know that you do. See you soon, OK?"

"Can't wait," I said.

When I hung up the phone, I still felt overwhelmed by everything Austin had said to me in the limousine but better now that I knew my best friend was coming over to guide me through all of it.

TWENTY MINUTES LATER, when Julia took the three flights of stairs that led to my cramped, one-bedroom apartment, I saw the sheen of sweat on her face when she breezed past me without a word and instead went straight into the living room, where an air conditioner hummed in one of the two windows that faced the street.

She was wearing a white tank, cute sandals, and khaki shorts that showed off her best assets: her long, impossibly beautiful legs. She wore her shoulder-length blond hair off her neck in a high ponytail, and despite the fact that she wore no makeup, my girl was a knockout.

"You look hot," I said after locking the door and joining her in the living room.

"Define 'hot' for me."

"You know what I mean. You look great."

"What I am is a sweaty mess."

"At least you make sweat look good. Not many can," I said.

"And look at you," she said, turning to me with narrowed eyes. "Already primed with the compliments. You're either up to something...or you're deep into something."

"To be discussed when the moment isn't so heated," I said.

"Then please, by all means, turn up the air-conditioning," she said. "Because I have a feeling we're going to need it."

"You still look hot," I said as I turned the air-conditioning on high. "I especially love your sandals."

"I'm literally basting in my own juices, Sienna," she said as she lifted her arms above her head and started to turn in front of the cool air. "It's murder out there. I hate being in the city in July. I should be in the Hamptons enjoying the ocean breeze, but since that takes the kind of money I don't have, I'm stuck here."

"And I'm glad you're here," I said. "Because that selfishly means you're near me. Can I get you a drink?"

"Before or after I take a cold shower?"

"Forget about the shower. Just keep turning like a rotisserie in front of the air conditioner, and you'll be fine in no time. What would you like?"

"Is that even a question?"

"Probably not."

"An ice-cold martini, please."

"Coming up!"

When I went into the kitchen to make our drinks, Julia called out to me. "The other day, you mentioned something about moving, which you'll be able to do when you finish your contract with Jackson. Have you given any thought to where you'd like to live?"

I don't know, Julia? Maybe in Austin's arms? But that's still to be determined...

"I'd like to stay in Chelsea," I said. "I love this neighborhood. It's become like a second home to me."

From the freezer, I removed a tray of ice cubes and a bottle of Absolut before grabbing a shaker and two martini glasses from the cupboard above me. With a deft hand, I started to make our drinks.

"I've lived here so long that I've made friends here. The area is safe, and I know exactly where to go for anything I might need—from dry cleaning to my doctor's office to Whole Foods, which is just down the street. What I need is space, because this joint is the size of a mole—which should be lanced, by the way. Whenever I go to your apartment, I feel like I'm at the MET. What you have is huge."

"Look, I just got lucky," she said. "And might I remind you that it took me a full year to land that apartment? Hopefully the same won't be true for you."

"Agreed," I said as I joined her in the living room with our drinks in hand. Julia liked her martini dirty with olives, while I liked mine crisp and clean with just a twist of lemon. She took hers from me, we touched glasses, and we sipped. "To a larger apartment," I said.

"Cheers to that," she said as we sat next to one another on my sorry-looking sofa. It was so old that the cushions had long since been supported by a sheet of plywood. Without it, Julia and I would have collided with one another when we'd sat down. "Now, tell me why I'm here," she said. "Naturally I'm curious."

"How about if you have a few more sips of your drink, and *then* I'll tell you?" I said.

"It's that bad?"

My shoulders slumped. "I'm not sure whether it's good or bad," I said. "But I do know this—I'm in deep."

"Deep into what?"

"Just drink," I said. "And when I feel that you can handle everything that happened to me tonight, I'll tell you all of it. Because I need to bare my heart and soul to someone other than Harper. In a minute or so, you'll see why that person is you."

"WELL, SHIT," Julia said after I told her what Austin had said to me in the car. "I mean—my God! On the surface it all sounds promising, doesn't it? Especially since he's a ridiculously good-looking man. And also smart. *And* a super nice guy. He's kind of the total package. But when you think about the ramifications, what he's proposing sounds way too risky to me, Sienna. With ten million dollars on the line, I wouldn't chance that for the world. My best advice is to turn him down—at least for now."

"I was worried you'd say that," I said. "But I'm not sure I can."

"Of course you can."

"I don't think it'll be that easy."

"Why?"

"Because the moment I first laid eyes on Austin, I was instantly attracted to him, Julia. How often has that happened since you've known me?"

"Never," she said softly. "Ever since Eric cheated on you, you've been so focused on your career that you've allowed nothing and no one to sideline you from it."

"Then, why am I willing to do so now?"

"Because Austin *is* special," she said. "Both of us know that. Each of us agrees with that. But if we take a step back and look at the big picture, things are going really well for you now. It took Harper no time to line up three major movies for you to headline. Your career is literally in the process of blowing up, and let's be frank—it's not just because of your win at Cannes. It's also because you're now seen as Jackson Cruise's new girlfriend. My best advice is to stick to your contract. Don't destroy this moment—you've worked too hard to get here."

"There's a tiny problem when it comes to that," I said.

She furrowed her brow at me. "What problem?"

"I might have told Austin I'd meet him at his place tomorrow night. For dinner. Because that's what he offered —dinner. Not dinner out in public, but dinner in private at his apartment."

"You did not agree to that..."

"I kind of did."

"Sienna, what were you thinking?"

"I don't think it was *me* who was doing the thinking, Julia."

"What does that mean?"

I waved my free hand across my breasts and then between my thighs. "They were the ones doing the thinking for me."

"It *has* been a while," she said.

"Over two years and counting!"

"Were you planning on sleeping with him?"

"God, no—you know me better than that. Good Catholic farm girl and all. By spending a few hours alone with him, I just wanted to see if my attraction to him was just physical or if it was more than that. A part of me thinks it's the latter."

"Why?"

"Because I've gotten to know him over the past few weeks. I like how he thinks. I like what I see and hear. But since we're only ever alone with each other for the short time it takes him to bring me to or from my apartment, I haven't had enough time to figure out if I'm just turned on by his looks or if it's deeper than that. So, I figured that if I did have dinner with him, and if there was no lasting chemistry between us, I'd know that I was just hooked on his looks, and that would be that. I'd be free to move on with my life."

"But what if it turns out to be the other way around?" she asked. "What if the chemistry between you two skyrockets off the charts?"

"Then I'd be fucked."

"And there's your answer," she said. "Don't do it. Don't take the risk. Ten million dollars will change your life, Sienna—and you've only got seven months to go before you're handed that final check. You need to see your fake relationship with Jackson through to the end so you can secure your future, because no man in the world is worth that kind of money. You must know that."

"I get it," I said with disappointment. "And that's why I asked you here tonight. I needed a sounding board I could trust—and that person is you."

"Then, let me say it again—stick to the contract. Forget about Austin."

"You're right," I said. "Ten million dollars *will* change my life. And...you know what?"

"What's that?"

"Getting a new apartment would be pretty great. I hadn't thought about that until you mentioned it."

"You totally need to get out of here," she said, looking around my small living space. "And before you know it, you'll be able to."

"I also can't let Harper down," I said. "She means too much to me. She made this happen between Jackson and me, and just look at all the opportunities that have come my way since." I sat back on the sofa and finished my drink. "What was I thinking?" I said out loud. "I never should have agreed to that dinner. And now I need to cancel it, which is just going to make me look ridiculous in his eyes."

"If you explain your reasons to him, I'm not sure that it will," Julia said. "Austin's a good guy. Tell him that you've since considered the ramifications of meeting alone with him and that you can't risk the chance of being found out. Remind him that you've made a binding agreement with Jackson and that it's not fair to him if you let anything get in the way of that. And there's more: you also need to be true to Harper, who has put her full faith in you. If I were you, I'd ask for a rain check. If he's available when you and Jackson break up, perfect. And if he isn't, tell him that you wish him well."

"He'll probably be with another woman by that point."

"It could happen," she said. "But maybe it won't—neither of us knows."

"I should call him. If I cancelled with a text, I'd look like an asshole."

"Agreed. So, call him now, and decline the invitation. It's not that late. He still might be up. And if he isn't, at least you can leave him a voice message, which is still far better than a text."

She got up from the sofa and took my empty martini glass from my hand.

"Where's your cell?" she asked.

"In my pocket."

"Then, call him while I'm still here with you."

"This sucks," I said as I reached for my phone.

"Actually, losing ten million is what would suck, sweetie. Call him."

When I mustered up the nerve to dial Austin, he answered on the third ring.

"Sienna?" he said. "Is something wrong?"

"No," I said. "I'm sorry—were you in bed, Austin? Did I wake you up?"

"I was just reading. What's up?"

"I can't do dinner," I said. "I've thought about it, and I...I apologize—I just got caught up in the moment when you asked me in the car. I hope you understand that I need to stay true to my contract and that I need to be focused on being Jackson's girlfriend, because I have a feeling I won't be able to if we get to know one another better."

"Because you feel the same way I do?" he asked. "That there's something worth exploring here?"

I looked up at Julia when he said that, and while she couldn't hear what Austin was saying to me, I could nevertheless feel her support raining down on me.

"I do," I said. "But if I need anything from you right now, it's your support. I signed a contract, and by doing so, I gave Jackson, Mimi, and Harper my word, which is my bond. Given the money alone, I owe it to Jackson to see this 'relationship' of ours through to its end. If you're still single and interested seven months from now—when Jackson and I are officially over—maybe we can have that dinner date then. Either at your place or in public. Because I'd like that."

"I don't give up easily, Sienna."

"I need you to, Austin."

A long silence stretched between us before he cleared his throat.

"I should probably go to bed," he said. "As you know, tomorrow is an early shoot. I'll see you on set when you arrive for your press shots with Jackson. In the meantime, don't worry about this. We'll figure it out. Sleep well, OK?"

"I'm sorry, Austin."

"Don't be," he said. "You just got a little freaked out, that's all."

"I did—and I apologize. I didn't mean to lead you on."

"I get it," he said in that deep, soothing voice of his. "And I plan to work on that, OK? You'll see."

"What will I see?"

But he didn't answer. Instead, the line went dead. I looked up at Julia, who was standing in front of me and biting down hard on her lower lip as I shut off my phone.

"He's gone," I said. "He hung up."

She sat down beside me. "Tell me everything I couldn't hear."

I told her.

"Well, then," she said when I'd finished. "This isn't over between you two. He's going to pursue you."

"But you just heard what I said to him, Julia. I couldn't have been more clear with him."

"I agree," she said. "But that doesn't mean he doesn't have his own agenda. I don't know what he has in mind to lure you in, but you need to prepare yourself for him to try to do so, because he's not going to stop now. My best advice is that you stand your ground, Sienna. Be firm with him."

"I will," I said.

"But can you?" she asked. "I know you do feel something for him, and I worry."

"No, I will," I said, meaning it. "I'll be firm with him. I'll be professional, and I won't let Jackson or Harper down. And in time, all this faking-it bullshit will be behind me. If Austin is still interested in me when the contract ends, great. And if he's with someone else by then? Sure, I'll be hugely disappointed, but it is what it is, isn't it? The good news is that I'll be super busy at that point, shooting three movies back to back. And because of that, I'll be sufficiently preoccupied to convince myself I don't care that he met someone else, even though I know I *will* care. Very much so."

Julia hugged me when I said that, and into her shoulder, I said, "He's the first one to catch my eye since Eric, Julia."

"I know he is, sweetie."

"He's the only man I felt was worth trusting again. So, that's something, isn't it?"

"It's progress," she said. "You're healing."

"But why him?" I asked. "What is it about him? I keep asking myself that same question time and again. Over and over again. Why is *he* the one who broke through my walls?"

She pulled away from me when I said that and looked at me closely.

"I don't know why, Sienna," she said. "But I do know this

—by choosing to secure your future, you just made the best decision of your life."

But even when she said that, I still wondered whether I had. Was my life to be measured by money alone? No—it couldn't be. But despite that, I'd just thrown the potential of finding love away, hadn't I?

Yes, I had. And I felt sick about it.

11

THE NEXT MORNING, when I arrived on set at ten thirty in a blocked-off area of West Nineteenth Street, Jackson had just finished a grueling and complicated action scene he'd been shooting since six, which meant that I was right on time.

When I first spotted him in the crowd of supporting actors, extras, writers, cameramen, and the director herself, I thought that Jackson looked bloodied, beaten, and bruised to a pulp—all thanks to the magic of makeup.

Since he'd told me how intense this particular shoot would be, Jackson had already put in a full day's work as far as I was concerned. But since more shoots were scheduled for later in the afternoon and evening, his day was far from over yet.

As I waited for him to catch sight of me, I saw Austin standing across the street, and when our eyes locked, I couldn't deny the fire I felt in my gut. He was wearing a fitted black suit that showed off his muscular frame, his dark hair had been parted on the side and was slicked down with gel, and his chiseled face and piercing blue eyes nearly got the best of me when he finally nodded at me.

To be polite, I nodded back. We did have to work together, after all. And I didn't want to make the situation between us any worse or awkward than it already was.

"Hey," Jackson said when he saw me standing behind one of the three cameras onsite. "How are you, beautiful?"

Since nobody but Harper, Mimi, Austin, and Julia knew about our fake relationship, everyone on the set of *Annihilate Them* was meant to believe what we hoped the world now believed—that our budding relationship was the real thing.

"Give me a kiss," I said as he neared me.

When he did, Jackson swept me into his arms and twirled me around once, and I kissed him with everything I had, noticing as I did so one of the extras taking a photograph of us with her cell. Were others doing the same? Probably, which just underscored how important it was that Jackson and I remain in character whenever we were in public together.

Because I already knew that by the end of the day, that photo just taken of us would likely have been sold to the highest bidder, and it would be trending in my entertainment feeds by morning.

"How was your scene?" I asked.

His face lit up when I said that.

"Intense—and fun as hell. You should have been here for the pyrotechnics alone. They were awesome. We blew shit up!"

"You do all your own stunts, don't you? I think I read that somewhere."

"All of them. In *Quick into Night*, that was me strapped to the side of that plane. That was no stunt double. I wanted to do it because I get off on that kind of shit."

"You're such a jock," I said teasingly.

He laughed when I said that and gave me a kiss on the

cheek—and this time, I knew that particular kiss was the real thing. It was a kiss between two people who had become friends.

Ever since the disaster at Per Se, Jackson had gotten his act together—just as he'd promised to do. And because he had, he and I had grown close in the ensuing weeks. It had been in the limousine—where no one could hear us but Austin—that we started to open up to each other.

I'd told him what it had been like growing up in Dubuque—and how badly I'd wanted to get out so I could see the world. He'd told me what it had been like growing up in the city, how he'd landed his first acting job, and what it had been like when fame first touched him—and what fame felt like now. As time passed and we came to trust one another, we talked about men, from my ruinous relationship with Eric to his dream of one day being able to be open with his sexuality and maybe even find love himself.

"Do you think you'll ever come out?" I'd asked him one night.

"I don't know," he'd said. "I'd like to, but it won't be for a while, Sienna. If ever."

"But that's so sad," I'd said. "You deserve to be who you are and find a man you want to share your life with. Times have changed. Many celebrities have come out, and for the most part, their careers have actually spiked because people have evolved."

When I'd said that, he'd just looked at me.

"Name one action star who has come out of the closet, Sienna. Just one. I'm friends with a few major action stars who are gay, and none of them dare come out. Like me, they understand the ramifications."

I couldn't name one person, which saddened me.

"So, you see?" he'd said. "I'm fucked. The public will

accept an Ellen and a Neil Patrick Harris because they're charming and funny, but since my career has long been defined by this ultrabutch male stereotype, coming out isn't in the cards for me—at least not if I want to continue to have a career, which I do. Because I love what I do. And I'm only thirty-five, for Christ's sake. I want to keep working and creating. So, when it comes to finding real love, I think that's out of the question for me now. Will it come later in life? I don't know. Because I also need to think of my legacy. How will I be remembered when I'm dead? Will it be for the body of work I've created? Or if I came out, would it be for the fact that I lived a lie? I think it would be the latter. And I hate it. Trust me, I wish there was something I could do about it, but there isn't. So, here I sit next to you tonight—a man actively living a lie. But if I want to continue to perform in these kinds of action roles that I love doing, I seriously don't think I have any choice but to do just that."

"I'm so sorry," I'd said.

"Same here."

It was because of the friendship building between us that it became easier to fool the press whenever Jackson kissed me, because now we had genuine chemistry built on truth and mutual affection.

"You look like a bloody mess," I said to him now. "How are we supposed to go out in public with you looking like this?"

"Give me twenty," he said with a wink. "I clean up fast. Mimi's somewhere around here. She said you and I are supposed to have an early lunch at some diner off Twenty-Third Street."

"It's the Malibu Diner," I said. "Julia's been there, and she raved about it. It's all the buzz. It's supposed to be amazing."

For a moment, he looked at me curiously, assessing me, and then he took me into his arms again as he spoke into my ear.

"You're glowing today," he said. "What's up with you?"

Austin, I said to myself. *Obviously I knew he'd be here, Jackson. And since I don't want to disappoint him since I have asked him to wait seven months to have that date with me, I'm trying my best to keep him interested. Thus my skin-tight white jersey dress...*

"I'm just happy," I said quietly as I kissed him on the cheek. "Things are going well right now. With all the interviews I've done lately and the movie projects coming in, I kind of want to pinch myself."

"I get it," he said. "It's an exciting time for you."

"It is. But just so you know, I'm also starving. Let's go to lunch."

"Let me clean up, and Austin can take us."

No pressure there, I thought.

"Look your hottest," I said to him. I didn't need to tell him why. He knew why. Either Harper or Mimi had already alerted the paps that we'd be eating there this afternoon, and the press was probably already lying in wait for us as I spoke.

"Got it," he said. "See you in a few."

When he left, I stood alone as cameramen, extras, and a whole host of crew members busied themselves around me. Taking in the moment, I couldn't help but remember how great it had felt to work on *Lion*, because each day, the sheer jolt of creative energy had been palpable. I longed to be back on a movie set soon, but I'd have to wait until next year before that happened. And when it did, I'd be working with the master himself—Martin Scorsese. And how lucky was I to be able to learn from *that* man?

I was thinking about how that experience would change my life and elevate my craft when I heard my cell ding in my handbag, alerting me to a text message. I withdrew my phone and saw that the text was from Austin, which caused me to pause. Before I read it, I looked over at him and saw that he was talking to Mimi, who was gesticulating dramatically. Then she just threw up her hands and walked away.

I checked the text and read it. "We still could have dinner tonight, you know."

"No, we can't," I typed as fast as I could. "I thought I'd made that clear."

When I sent the message, he pulled his cell out of his pants pocket and read what I'd written, and then we quickly fell into a routine.

"I was joking about the takeout," he wrote back. "*I* plan to cook for you. My grandfather was a chef. He taught me plenty, and I'm an excellent cook. You seriously need to try my bangers and mash."

"Now you're just being obscene."

"Well, it's true. And then there's my beef stroganoff..."

"You're trying to *seduce* me!"

"You know what, Sienna? I think you *need* to be seduced."

"No, I don't. What I need is to keep focused and tend to my contract."

"You certainly were professional when you kissed Jackson a moment ago, that's for fucking sure."

"What does that even mean?"

"For those on the outside? Probably nothing, so good on you and Jackson for your acting skills. But since I happen to be on the inside...shit, Sienna, I could have kissed you way better than that. And I probably would have brought you to your knees in the process, because I'm that good—and I'm that into you."

"Austin, you need to stop."

"I don't want to stop."

"Well, you need to. I explained the reasons why last night. I need you to respect that."

"And you need to respect that ever since I saw you today, I've done my best to conceal my erection, which by the way isn't exactly an easy thing to do."

When I read that text, I looked over at him in shock. He arched a mischievous eyebrow at me and then moved his jacket aside so I could see the massive bulge in his pants.

"Put that away," I wrote.

"Can't," he texted me back. "It doesn't work that way for a man, especially since I'm looking at you in that dress of yours. And just so you know, your nipples have been stiffening ever since we began texting."

I glanced down at my breasts, saw that I clearly was aroused, and cursed my body for betraying me at the very moment when it absolutely couldn't.

"How many times do I have to say that we need to be professional?"

"Professional?" he texted back. "One day you'll see just how *professional* I am when my mouth is pressed against your lips. Because sooner rather than later, that's going to happen, Sienna. One day you'll finally give in to me. You'll throw caution to the wind, and you'll let me kiss you. It's going to happen at some point, so why try fighting it? When I do kiss you and you realize all that you've been missing out on, you'll be begging me to kiss you somewhere else."

He. Did. Not!

"Stop talking dirty to me," I wrote. "It's inappropriate."

"Tell that to your body."

I blushed when I read that, because given the state of my nipples alone, a part of me *was* turned on by this exchange. In frustration, I looked over at him, which was a big fucking mistake—just laying my eyes on him was enough to do me in. I was so physically attracted to him that he was turning me into a wonton sex siren—which wasn't me at all. What the hell was happening to me? I was better than this. I never behaved like this.

Who have I become?

"Jackson will be back soon," he texted. "So, before he comes back, I'll ask you this again. We both know you're free tonight, so why not come to my apartment, and I'll make dinner for you? I learned a lot at my grandfather's side, and I can promise you that I can curl your toes with my talents in the kitchen. And someday soon, I'll be curling your toes in ways that have nothing to do with food."

"Why are you doing this?" I asked. "I signed a contract with Jackson, Austin. I've been poor for so long...you know I can't blow this. Why are you pressing me right now?"

"Maybe because I want to thrust my tongue into your mouth? And also because I'd never put you in harm's way. There are ways to see you without anyone knowing, Sienna. I've got a whole network of ways to be discreet."

"I still can't take that risk. Please stop."

"Can't promise that," he said. "Especially when I see Jackson and you faking it all over town. I won't bullshit you, Sienna. I love Jackson as if he were my brother, but I sure as hell wish I were him right now. That's for fucking sure."

I was about to text him back when I heard Jackson's voice to my left. I turned and saw him talking with one of the writers. He was wearing what he pretty much always wore when we were meant to be seen together in public— tight-fitting Levis and a revealing T-shirt that left little to the imagination. I don't know what Jackson was packing, but looking at him now, I knew he could give Jon Hamm a run for his money. Because Jackson's bulge was off the charts.

Before he could see what I was doing, I shut my phone off so he wouldn't know if or when Austin sent me another text.

"Hey, handsome," I said as he walked toward me.

"And look at you," he said with a grin. "It's, like, ninety degrees out right now. Do you run cold or something?"

"What are you talking about?"

"Your boobs are on high alert, Sienna."

"Don't embarrass me," I said under my breath.

"You might have already done that yourself. What's with the headlights?"

Oh, fucking hell!

I glanced around the street and saw a good-looking man standing alone on the sidewalk. Since I didn't recognize him, he was likely an extra. He looked roughed up with spots of fake blood on his face.

"OK, fine," I said. "I might have found that guy over there attractive."

"Which guy?" he asked.

With discretion, I nodded toward the man, and when Jackson looked over at him, he was just as discreet.

"I saw him earlier," he said in a voice only I was meant to hear. "He's totally hot."

"*You're* the one who's hot," I said as I took him by the arm. "And it's time for us to go to lunch." I looked around me. "Where's Austin? Where's the car? Harper and Mimi aren't going to want us to be late, so we need to get a move on now."

"All we need to do is walk to the curb, and I guarantee

you Austin will be there waiting for us. He never lets me down."

After having been texting furiously with Austin over the past ten minutes, I wished I could say the same. And then I checked myself, realizing that wasn't true. If I were to be honest with myself, parts of me *had* enjoyed our exchange. After two long years of being single, a man I found dangerously attractive had just sexted me into oblivion. And it had felt good, even though I knew it shouldn't have.

So, what the hell was I supposed to do now? How could I possibly control Austin going forward, especially since he was hell-bent on getting me alone so he could feed me his bangers and mash? Or his beef stroganoff, for God's sake? Somehow, I had to get through to him that this wasn't a joke and that he seriously needed to stop behaving like this—but how best to do so?

And then it came to me.

What if I do agree to have dinner with him tonight? I thought. *What if I get him alone in his apartment and corner him? If I did that, I could look him square in the face and tell him that this flirtation bullshit needs to end at once. Maybe that's the best way around this. Maybe he just needs to see how important it is for me to see this through with Jackson. If I agreed to meet him for dinner, I could shut this down...*

As we moved toward the limousine parked at curbside and Austin got out of the car to open the rear door for us, I shot him a withering look and watched his eyes twinkle at me when they met mine. And right then and there, I had my answer.

He needed to be confronted not by phone or by text but right to his face.

LATER, after Jackson and I had been photographed by the paparazzi and had had lunch together—and when Austin picked us up and drove us back to West Nineteenth Street, where Jackson had additional scenes to shoot—I'd thought all of it through and come to my decision.

"Would you like me to take Sienna home?" Austin asked Jackson.

"Of course," he said. "I'm on set now. The rest of your security team is here, so I'll be fine." He got out of the car and shot me a smile. "See you tomorrow, Sienna," he said as he walked away from us. "Lunch was great."

"It was, Jackson," I said. "Until tomorrow. Have a great shoot—and be safe. I worry about these crazy stunts of yours."

"They're nothing to worry about," he said. "I get off on them."

And with a mere smile, he simply walked away.

"Don't move the car, Austin," I said as Jackson faded from sight.

"Why? I need to take you home."

"There's no need for you to take me home. I'm getting out here."

He clocked me in the rearview.

"No, you're not. Sienna, everyone recognizes you now. Making sure you get home safely is part of my job."

"I live three blocks from here, Austin. This is a safe neighborhood. Hell, it's *my* neighborhood. I know it like the back of my hand. I walked here this morning without incident, and I'll be fine walking home. And besides," I said, "since you *are* going to cook for me tonight, you could probably use whatever extra time you have on your hands to make dinner just right. I totally have high expectations when it comes to that, just so you know."

He raised his eyebrows in surprise when I said that.

"I'm cooking for you tonight?"

"You are, unless you've suddenly gotten cold feet."

"My feet don't get cold when I think of you, Sienna. And neither do other parts of my body."

So I saw...

"Good," I said. "So, what time?"

"Why the sudden turnaround?"

"Why does it matter? You wanted this to happen, so it's happening. What time?"

"Eight?"

"Eight works for me. I'll bring the wine—white or red?"

"For what I have in mind, a bottle of sauvignon blanc would be perfect."

"Consider it done. Now, before I leave, I need to make certain that your plan of getting me into your apartment without anyone seeing me or knowing about it will work."

"It's foolproof," he said.

"Nothing's foolproof, Austin. We both know that. If we're going to do this, you can't fuck this up for me. You can't let that happen."

"Sienna, I'd never put you in harm's way," he said. "Trust me on this. I've done exactly this time and again for Jackson. It works."

"It had better work."

"And it will, because I understand how important it is to you. I get it. I'm taking none of this lightly. I'd never put you at risk."

I won't either, Austin, which is why tonight is happening. Because after the way you behaved today, I can't let you do that to me anymore, and we're going to have a long conversation about that. When I'm out of my contract—and if you're still single then—things will be different, and we'll go from there. But

*if you're with someone else...as much as that will disappoint me,
we'll just have to go our separate ways.*

"You remember the pickup plan I laid out to you
before?" he asked.

"I do."

"Be there at seven forty-five. I'll call Max and let him
know the scoop, and then just do what he tells you to do. If
you do, you'll be at my place by eight."

"How can I trust Max not to betray me?"

"Because he's one of my best friends, and I don't take my
friendships lightly. He's a good guy—you'll soon see for
yourself."

"All right," I said, opening the door and stepping out
onto the sidewalk with dark sunglasses covering my eyes.
"Done. And...Austin?" I said before I closed the door.

"What's that, Sienna?"

"I'm a farm girl from Iowa, and I know how to eat. So...
you know? Bring it tonight. Make your grandfather proud.
Go for the nines. Surprise me." He moved to speak, but I
was already closing the door. "See you later," I said.

And then, with a purpose I didn't feel in my gut—
because my gut was twisted in knots—I started to walk
uptown to my apartment, wondering whether I'd done the
right thing or whether I'd just sabotaged myself. Julia would
say that I'd done the latter. But after Austin's behavior with
me today, I knew I needed to be very clear with him, and
that obviously had to be done face-to-face.

12

BEFORE I RETURNED HOME, I stopped by my favorite wine store on West Twenty-First Street to buy a bottle of sauvignon blanc.

As usual, the place was packed and humming with its hip, well-dressed, trendy clientele. With my sunglasses in place and my head slightly lowered, I maneuvered toward the right side of the store, where there was a massive chilled-wine section. When I found the sauvignon blanc section, my choice turned out to be a no-brainer. I went with the brand the store itself recommended with a little card placed in front of a row of bottles: "Choose this one—you'll be happy you did." Since I trusted this store and its owner, Adam Shift, that's the one I went with.

It was when I went to the checkout and smiled at Adam that I heard someone mention my name.

"Is that Sienna Jones?" whispered a woman behind me.

I flushed at the comment and was grateful I hadn't taken off my sunglasses. Although he couldn't see my eyes, I looked at Adam as he looked at me.

I'd been a customer of his for years, and we'd become

friendly. But just how friendly? With me in his store right now, would he sell me out and acknowledge it was me standing before him so his customers would know that celebrities frequented his store? Or would he respect my privacy? I wasn't sure, so I bit my lower lip and waited for what was to come.

"How's it going, Deb?" he asked in a voice just loud enough for those around us to hear. "How are the kids?"

Thank God, I thought. *I had a feeling you were one of the good ones, Adam, and you are.*

"They're driving me crazy, Adam—thus the wine."

"*Deb*?" I heard the woman behind me say. "I could have sworn that was Sienna Jones."

"Who the hell is Sienna Jones?" another woman asked, which would have made me laugh out loud if my heart weren't pounding so quickly against my chest. Countless times over the past several weeks, I'd been recognized when I'd been out and about with Jackson, but this was the first time I'd ever been recognized while out on my own. And never in my right mind did I think it would be so unnerving. I was starting to get recognized, and that carried with it its share of risks, especially given the clandestine evening I had planned later tonight with Austin.

"Oh, come on," the woman said. "I've *told* you who she is. Sienna Jones is Jackson Cruise's new girlfriend. I swear that's her."

"Girlfriend? I heard that Jackson Cruise is gay or something."

"Jackson Cruise isn't gay," the woman said. "I mean, yes, I *saw* the photos of him allegedly kissing that man, but let's get real here. Those photos weren't just blurry, they were also over-the-top photoshopped. Plus, Jackson is being photographed all over the city with Sienna Jones right now.

He's shooting his new movie here. They're totally falling in love right in front of our eyes. Haven't you been paying attention? Obviously you haven't. God, how I wish I were her."

"How are the apartment renovations coming along, Deb?" Adam asked with a slightly arched eyebrow that told me he had my back.

I owe you one mother of a tip, Adam, I thought.

"It's going well—if you don't mind the demo."

"I know how that goes," he said. "Mike and I went through a renovation a few years ago. It was hell."

"I remember when that happened," I said, which was true. "I also remember that you two didn't fight even once, which says plenty when it comes to your marriage."

"He's a keeper!"

"How is Mike?" I asked. "I haven't seen him in a while."

"He's great—just busy. And just so you know, it's seventeen years for us tomorrow, and somehow there isn't a gray hair to be found on my head. Obviously when it comes to him, I chose well."

"Congratulations," I said, not knowing if he was just providing me the distraction I needed. "Seventeen years. I should be giving *you* this bottle of wine."

"Trust me," he said, "I've got all that covered. Tomorrow night, Mike's not going to know what hit him."

"Give him my best, OK?"

"I'll do that, Deb."

I removed my wallet from my handbag.

"How much do I owe you?"

"Forty-seven fifty. And by the way—you chose well when it comes to this bottle," he said, wrapping it in bright-yellow tissue paper and placing it into a shiny red bag. "Graywacke is one of my favorites."

"I chose it because you recommended it," I said. "And trust me—with the kids off from school this summer, their mother needs a glass of wine at the end of the day."

"What's life without wine?" he asked me.

"One not worth living?"

"Agreed," he said as he rang me up. I handed him a hundred, he gave me my change, and I discreetly gave it back to him as I wished him well with Mike tomorrow night. After that, I got the hell out of there before further speculation could arise that it *had* been Sienna Jones who'd been in Adam's store and not somebody named Deb.

As I hustled through the crowds on the sidewalk, I had to wonder. Jackson and I had generated so much press, what *would* happen if people knew that I lived in this neighborhood?

As far as I knew, none of the paps had ever mentioned where I lived—they were so caught up in Jackson's evolving life that I was still only considered his It Girl in our fake relationship.

But I was no idiot, because things were changing.

That woman in the wine store might have been the first to recognize me out on my own, but I knew in my gut that it was just the tipping point. Jackson and I had dominated the press for so many weeks that I knew I'd soon be recognized wherever I went.

And how would that affect my life? How would fame alter it?

Worse, how could Austin promise to protect me tonight? Because right now, after having been recognized back there, I wasn't so sure that he could—which would only compromise everything if we went forward with our date this evening.

LATER THAT EVENING, after meditating for an hour to the soothing the sounds of a babbling fucking brook—accompanied with the kind of liquid courage that could only come in the form of an ice-cold martini—I decided that shutting Austin down in person *was* worth the risk.

Whatever was unfolding between us needed to be handled in private, because with Jackson, Harper, and Mimi always around us, it was almost impossible to talk to Austin alone. Clearly, spending twenty minutes with him in a car wasn't enough time to get through to him.

But tonight I could. Tonight I'd have plenty of time to put our fire on ice.

At least for the interim...

IN FIVE MORE MINUTES, I would leave for Austin's apartment. I was showered, dressed, and ready to go.

I turned in front of my wardrobe's full-length mirror and thought I'd nailed it. I'd decided to go with a little black dress that clung to my curves in ways that were so revealing and alluring that I hoped I looked sexy enough to make Austin want to wait seven months for me. As for the shoes, they were pure Prada, they were hot—and for a man who had once massaged my feet with great care, I hoped to hell they were on point.

Before I left for our date, I went into my bathroom to check my hair and makeup a final time before scrutinizing my face.

I'd chosen to go with nude makeup highlighted by thick mink eyelashes and a bold red lip that complemented my complexion. As for my hair, I'd chosen to wear it in a loose chignon held together with a slender wooden stick. Since I knew from my modeling years that perfume should only ever be an intimate experience, I'd spritzed a trace of Chanel No. 5 in the air before I'd walked through it. Carolina Herrera herself had once said to me before a show of hers that "perfume should never overpower. Instead, it should *em*power. Never forget that."

I hadn't, because she was right.

When I was finished, I put my iPhone, lipstick, and powder into my killer Judith Leiber clutch, and when my massive Dior sunglasses were in place, I left for Whole Foods—of all places—which is where the first part of this crazy evening would begin.

THE MOMENT I stepped out of my apartment building, I felt unusually nervous and exposed.

The sidewalk was busy with people either going home after a late day at work or going out for the evening. Thankfully everyone around me appeared to be normal pedestrians and not the paps, which allowed me to take at least something of a breath, because after the past three weeks, I knew just how aggressive the paparazzi could be. But now? Now it appeared that no one was even remotely interested in me, which felt like a godsend for exactly two seconds before I checked myself.

None of that means shit, I thought as I walked forward. *The paps are snipers. They could be across the street taking photographs of me right now. They could be anywhere.*

Which is why Austin's scheme *had* to work.

Two blocks later, when I entered Whole Foods on West

Twenty-Fourth Street, only a moment passed before a tall bald man with a muscular frame and a kind, youthful face approached me.

"Sienna?" he said in a low voice.

"Max?" I answered.

He nodded once before he extended his right hand to me, which I shook. "Come with me. To the far back of the store. Right now, a car is waiting for you outside the receiving area. When I open the doors, I need you to go to the white Prius parked just outside for you. Keep your head down, go toward the car, get into the back of it—and try your best to be discreet."

While he spoke, we walked swiftly toward the back of the store, which was teeming with customers filling their carts with organic this and organic that. As Max and I came upon an enormous commercial door, with crashing relief I sensed that because everyone seemed to be focused more on the produce than on me, not one of them had recognized me.

He was about to press a red button on the wall to the right of the door when he stopped and turned to me. "Are you ready?" he asked.

"I think so," I said. "The car is right outside? A white Prius?"

"When I press this button and the door opens, you'll find just that waiting for you. Are we good?"

"We're good," I said. "And thank you, Max."

"It was my pleasure, Sienna. Have a wonderful evening with Austin tonight."

When he pressed the button, the door started to rumble up and roll above us, exposing the side street in the process. People were hurrying by on the sidewalk. The industrial smells of the city wafted in to claim us.

"That's the Prius," he said, pointing at the car idling at the loading dock. "Maria is inside waiting for you."

"Who is Maria?" I asked.

"Your driver," he said. "Now, go. Austin said that you needed to be quick about this."

And Austin was right. So, off I went onto the sidewalk. I stepped into the car, I said hello to Maria, I shut the door behind me and fastened my seatbelt, and when Maria found her moment to cut into traffic?

She stepped hard on the gas—and off I went into yet another unknown.

13

AUSTIN LIVED a few blocks uptown from me in a sleek, narrow high-rise on West Thirty-First Street.

When Maria swept the car in front of the building's entrance, a doorman stepped outside and opened my door for me.

"Ms. Jones?" he asked.

"I'm Sienna Jones."

"Welcome to Turnbille."

He offered me his hand, which I took as I stepped out.

"Thank you," I said. "Just let me pay the driver, and you can take me inside."

"That's unnecessary," he said. "Payment has already been taken care of by Mr. Black. My orders are to get you inside as quickly as possible."

Austin is *covering my ass*, I thought with a sense of relief. *He's on top of this...*

Before the doorman shut the car door, I thanked Maria and then followed the doorman into the building, through a lavish lobby lit with warm, low lighting, and then to a bank of elevators far off to my right. When he pressed a button to call for an elevator, the doors to one of them swished open behind me.

"Mr. Black lives on the thirty-sixth floor," he said as I stepped into the car. "Unit thirty-six F. When you leave the elevator, take the hallway to your left. His is a corner unit. It's six doors down."

"Thank you," I said as I selected Austin's floor.

"It was my pleasure," the man said.

And then, as the doors closed, the elevator began its swift ascent.

This is happening too quickly...

As the car rose, I checked myself in the elevator's mirrored doors. This was the first time Austin and I would be alone together for an extended period of time, and because I had my own agenda when it came to tonight, I wanted to look my best for him. I adjusted my hair, straightened my outfit, and applied a fresh swipe of lipstick before the car slowed to a stop and the doors opened.

Living here has to be seriously expensive, I thought as I stepped out of the elevator and into a gorgeous space marked by gleaming pearl marble floors and rich mahogany-covered walls. *But Harper did say that Austin headed one of the most sought-after security details in the industry, so clearly he's making serious bank from Jackson. I can only imagine what he thinks of my sorry apartment.*

But the moment that thought crossed my mind, I knew he *didn't* care. Because I wouldn't be here now if he *had* cared. And that knowledge alone made me feel somehow closer to him—which is the last thing I wanted, given all that was to come.

Feeling vulnerable, alive, overwhelmed, and excited at the prospect of spending time alone with him, I came upon his apartment door and stood there for a moment, collecting myself.

End the flirtation. See if he's willing to wait for you. If he's not, move on.

I took a deep breath before I knocked on the door, and then I lifted the girls before the door opened to reveal Austin himself.

When I saw him, he took my breath away.

I thought he'd be wearing something casual tonight— maybe a pair of khakis matched with a white button-down shirt. But that was not at all what he was wearing.

Instead, he was sporting a black tuxedo that fitted his muscular body to a tee. He hadn't shaved since morning, and his sexy dark stubble—not to mention his piercing blue eyes, which were framed with dark lashes—were lust inducing.

He looked beyond handsome to me, and given the drunk look of desire in his eyes, he also appeared genuinely happy to see me.

I moved to speak, but before I could, he held out his hand to me, and I took it. He led me into the foyer before closing the door behind us.

"You look amazing," he said.

Sidelined by how well he'd dressed for the night, I tried to compose myself when he released my trembling hand.

"Thank you," I said.

"And thank you for choosing that dress. I hope you chose it with me in mind."

I was about to tell him that I hadn't, but why lie? Why deny it? I'd come here looking like this for a reason.

"I did," I said.

"I'm glad you did, Sienna. You look stunning. Thank you for going to all the trouble for me."

"I could say the same to you," I said. "I certainly didn't come here expecting to find you in a tux."

"When you're having dinner with one of the most beautiful women in the world, you wear a tux," he said. "Now, how about a drink? I have champagne chilling in the fridge for dinner, so that's covered. But over the past three weeks of watching over Jackson and you, I also have a pitcher of martinis prepared." He arched an eyebrow at me. "Care to join me with one?"

Austin, you can't get a martini in my hand fast enough...

"I'd love a martini," I said.

"No olives—just a twist, right?"

"You've been paying *that* close attention?"

"I've been paying attention to you ever since we first met."

I wanted to say, "You too?" But I couldn't, and so I didn't.

"That would be perfect," I said. "How do you like yours?"

"Filthy."

God, if you're listening right now, please get me through this!

"The living room is just ahead of us," he said as his hand took hold of mine and led me down a long hallway, through which I saw that Austin had a serious eye for art. A whole host of paintings colored every wall in interesting ways that made me want to linger and look at them.

But I wasn't given the chance to do so.

Instead, as we walked deeper into his apartment, I became aware of several mouth-watering aromas. Dinner was clearly in the making, but what was he cooking? I smelled tarragon, mustard, garlic, and what had to be meat of some sort. It was beef—not pork or chicken.

And there were other notes, such as the starch of roasted potatoes—or was that risotto? I couldn't be sure, but it had to be one or the other. Another undercurrent was the rich, piney smell of rosemary, which I particularly loved.

As we passed the brightly lit kitchen to our right, I caught a glimpse of it and saw that it was gleaming with stainless-steel appliances, a massive island in the center of the room, and shiny granite countertops. It was a true cook's kitchen, which underscored what Austin had said to me earlier.

He took cooking seriously, likely because of his relationship with his grandfather. When we passed the dimly lit dining room, a saw a low bowl filled with gorgeous white roses in the center of a round table that sparkled with white china and tall stemware.

He's totally gone all out tonight, I thought. *And I'm about to disappoint him. I hate that I am, but what choice do I have? Because Julia is right. I've been broke for too many years, and seeing Jackson's contract through to its end will give me the financial security I need. Will Austin agree to wait for me? I hope he will, but if that's too much to ask of him, I'll have to accept it gracefully and just move the hell on.*

When I stepped into the large and impressive living room, I was immediately struck by the two huge windows that offered generous views of the city, which glimmered before us like a dream.

In the center of the room, two retro beige sofas faced each other. Between them stood a glass coffee table, on which flickered a low, off-white candle.

Otherwise, the lights had been dimmed to a romantic glow. And likely because I was in the midst of experiencing sensory overload, only then did I become aware of the music Austin had chosen for us to listen to tonight. It was a soft, moody, contemporary jazz that surreally matched exactly how I felt at that moment: completely unprepared for the next beat and unaware of what was to come next.

"While I make our martinis, you can either have a seat on one of the sofas and relax, or you can take in the view. Whatever you like."

"I'm choosing the view," I said. "Where I live, my view looks nothing like this, as you've already seen."

"One day you'll have a spectacular view of the city, Sienna. But for now, please enjoy mine. Believe me, it took me years and a hell of a lot of hard work before I finally got that view for myself. I'll be right back."

As I walked over to one of the windows and looked out at the city, I thought it looked particularly pretty tonight. After I'd soaked it in, I closed my eyes and listened to the music playing through the surround-sound system, drinking it in and becoming lost in it—until I heard Austin aggressively start to shake our drinks in the kitchen, which brought me back into myself.

I looked over my shoulder as ice and liquid started to smash against each other, and when I turned to look for him, all I saw was the wall that divided us.

He's seducing me, I thought, returning my attention to the city. *But not overtly—he's being more subtle in person than he was in his texts this morning. He's playing me now...*

I'd come here armed for something more aggressive, but if anything, Austin was going out of his way to make sure I was relaxed—not that he'd fully succeeded when it came to that. After all, seeing him in his tuxedo had nearly done me in—could he possibly have looked any hotter? No. And then there was this gorgeous apartment of his. Everything about it was impeccable. No detail had been overlooked. And nothing about it remotely looked like a bachelor pad. If anything, it looked more like a home to me.

His home. A place where he could relax after a long day's work. I looked around the living room and could only imagine how soothing it would be to sit on one of these sofas with a cocktail in hand and relax while admiring the city.

How the hell was this man still single? It stymied me. I couldn't make sense of it. This city was filled with gorgeous, accomplished single women, and Austin was the full package. So, I had to wonder. How could it be that no one had managed to open that package yet?

Maybe some have tried, I thought, turning again back to the city. *Like me, maybe he's just been focusing on his career while waiting for the right person to come along.*

When I considered that, I stopped myself.

Am I that person? Because if I am—

"Are you enjoying the view?" he said from behind me.

I turned to face him when he said that, and when I did, I saw that he was standing at the living room's entrance with two martinis in his hands. The light of the candle on the coffee table reflected off the glasses as well as his eyes, which seemed lit with fire as he crossed the room and offered me my drink.

"I'm glad you came, Sienna," he said. "I know you felt it was a risk. I hope that now you feel it's less of one."

No, Austin, I thought as we touched glasses and sipped our drinks. *Now I feel that the risk is even bigger than I'd imagined. I should have listened to Julia. I never should have let it go this far. I never should have believed I could do this in person. To your face. Because right now...right now I feel too weak to stop the heat that's building between us. After all the trouble you've gone through tonight, I don't know if I can even find the words to say what I was planning to say to you. I had no idea you'd go to so much trouble. I've completely underestimated everything, and now I feel like a goddamn fool to have believed I could just come here and shut down whatever has been escalating between us.*

"What's wrong?" he asked.

"I'm sorry?" I said, looking up at him, startled out of my reverie.

"Your expression just changed. I hope I'm not crossing any lines here, but you just looked overcome by grief."

Had I? I probably had. And for good reason—I now had a clear idea of the man I needed to leave behind. And it was killing me.

He must have known exactly what I was about to say, because before I could say a word, he took my martini from my hand and placed our drinks on the coffee table. When he turned back to me, there was a pulsing sense of need in his eyes, and he held my face in his hands for a long, heated moment before he acted.

"Austin—"

"No," he said. "Don't."

With one swift motion, he pressed the full weight of his body against mine and nailed me against one of the windows. Everything after that happened so quickly that it left my head spinning. When his lips met mine, the kiss we shared was so electric, intense, and erotic, I could feel it pass from my heart straight through to my toes, which curled upward in my heels as I drank him into me.

When I could no longer help but give him a fierce kiss of my own, I did so—and I knew in my gut that whatever happened next would forever change the course of our lives.

14
_____

As we kissed, his lips scorched against my flesh, leaving in their wake what felt to me like fire as my arms reached around the back of his neck and drew him in even closer.

Our tongues collided and danced. Our bodies surged and thrummed. At one point, I felt that the universe was expanding right in front of me—but then I realized what was expanding was Austin, whose crotch was pressed against my left thigh...and my God was the universe ever huge!

As frightened as you are, you know this is right, I thought, shoving aside my initial fears. *Let down your guard. Let go of what's holding you back. At least for tonight. If only for tonight...*

I became unhinged.

"Christ, you're hot," he said roughly against my ear.

"And your name is Austin—as in Texas," I said deliriously. "You practically personify heat."

He clocked me with a humorous smile when I said that, and then—with a wicked grin—he took me into his arms as we flung ourselves headlong into a heated hotbed of desire.

I raked my fingers through his impossibly thick head of

black hair and tugged at the back of it, which only made him growl as he reached down and grabbed a handful of my ass.

"Better than I imagined," he said.

Not to be outdone, I lowered my right hand and took a fistful of his own ass, feeling my knees go a little weak as I did. "And yours is just as tight as I thought it would be."

Undone by desire, we started to flip horizontally across the living room's two windows as we kissed each other with a fervor I'd never felt in my life.

First it was my back pressed against the cool panes of glass, then it was his, and then we continued until we were out of windows and had no choice but to go back in the other direction.

As we pinwheeled across the living room, my heart and my soul seemed to shoot straight into the ether as I wondered what had become of me. Who was I? Where was I? How had this man claimed my body and my mind and turned them into a cylinder of sex unleashed?

At one point, Austin removed the wooden stick holding my hair together, and when he did, my hair fell down around my back in a shiver of soft waves. I shook it out and tossed it back, noting the dangerous look of desire that entered his eyes.

"I want you," he said. "I can't wait, Sienna. To hell with dinner—we can order takeout later if we want. More than anything in the world, I want to make love to you now. Don't deny us this moment."

I looked longingly at him when he said that, thinking about all the ramifications having sex with him would bring, but even as they emerged, they only struck bricks—because I already knew there was no stopping this from happening. As much as I wanted to deny it, all this had been inevitable. It was time to find out if our connection was real.

"Where is your bedroom?" I asked.

His eyes brightened when I said that, likely because he'd thought I had been about to shut him down. But without missing a beat or saying a word, he swept me off my feet and into his arms as if I weighed nothing. And when he did, our lips crashed against each other again as he led us out of the living room and into the hallway...where I smelled dinner cooking.

"Austin—" I said.

"God, you taste good," he said when our lips parted.

"Austin, I think you might want to—"

His mouth stopped me again, this time as it lightly kissed the nape of my neck, which felt so tender and sensuous to me that it was enough to silence me just so I could linger in the sheer amazement of it all. But only for a moment. I quickly came back into myself. With my index finger, I lifted his chin so he had no choice but to look at me.

"Austin," I said.

"I can't wait to have my—"

"*Dinner*," I said to him.

He furrowed his brow at me. "Dinner? Sienna, you're not dinner. You're fucking dessert."

I giggled when he said that, which clearly perplexed him.

"What am I missing here?" he asked.

"Dinner," I said. "I can smell it cooking in the kitchen. Before you take me to your bedroom, I think you should tend to whatever you're cooking. I'd hate for it to burn and set off smoke alarms before we do so ourselves."

"Shit," he said, swinging me toward the kitchen. "I forgot about dinner."

"The only thing that should be cooking in your apartment right now is us," I said in his ear. "Put me down and go take care of the kitchen. I'll be here waiting for you."

"I'm not letting go of you," he said as he strode toward the kitchen. "Not now. You're coming with me."

"But with me in your arms, how are you going to manage?"

"Trust me," he said, "I can manage."

And because he was so strong, he did.

With his right arm curved along the low of my ass, I held tightly to his neck as we entered the kitchen. There, Austin turned off two ovens before deftly slipping into an oven mitt that was lying on the countertop. He opened the oven doors and removed two pans—a delicious-looking beef tenderloin in one of them and sizzling roasted potatoes in the other. He placed each pan on top of a six-burner stove before looking at me.

"That was going to be dinner," he said, "along with a Caesar salad." He arched an eyebrow at me. "Just so you know, I also made a cucumber-infused amuse-bouche."

"That sounds dirty," I said to him.

"It was meant to sound dirty."

"Why am I turned on by you and your culinary ways?" I asked him.

"Probably for the same reason I'm turned on by you and your humor?"

"Well," I said, glancing down at the tenderloin and the potatoes. "They look wonderful, Austin. Even if they are undercooked."

"May they rest in peace," he said before he kissed me again.

Why does he continue to underscore just how funny he is? I thought as we kissed. *Because that alone is beyond sexy...*

As we left the kitchen and he carried me down the hallway toward his bedroom, I felt at once tense with anticipation, overcome with excitement, and thrilled in the moment. I hadn't been with a man since Eric.

And so, I had to wonder—what would it be like to make love to Austin Black?

15

WHEN WE ENTERED Austin's bedroom, he switched on the lights and dimmed them to a soft glow. When I looked around the room, I glimpsed a masculine, stylish interior dominated by two things.

First was the large window at the room's far left, which offered sweeping views of a city that seemed as electric as I felt. Second was the king-size bed along the wall across from me. Made in the arts and crafts style, it was the room's focal point, particularly given its striking brown-leather head-board and the two reading lamps fixed to the wall above it, thus illuminating it.

When Austin put me down in the center of the room, my heart was beating hard against my chest in anticipation of all that was to come, I felt light-headed. With his eyes trained on mine, he shrugged off his jacket, tossed it onto a nearby chair, and started to remove his bow tie. Everything about him was perfect. His chiseled face, his impossibly muscular body, his quiet confidence, his kindness—and the very clear sense that he hungered for me.

He was sexy as hell.

With his tie gone, he leaned forward and gave me a searing kiss that was heated. Fierce. Passionate.

And wanting more.

When we parted, he pressed his forehead against mine for a long moment before he took a step back and started to unbutton his shirt, beginning at the neck and then working his way down. Unable to help myself, I glanced down and saw the broad expanse of his chest as it was slowly revealed to me. Like the rest of him, it was massive, the white T-shirt he wore underneath stretched tightly across it. When the shirt was gone, his stiff, aroused nipples tented the thin material of this T-shirt in ways that were wildly erotic to me. I just stared at the magnificence of him.

"I want to undress you," he said.

I wanted the same.

In response, I simply turned my back to him so he could unzip me. But when he didn't do so at once, it occurred to me that Austin was in no hurry when it came to getting me into his bed. As I stood there, unable to see him but knowing he was taking in every inch of me, my senses became acute.

I could hear him breathing—low, shallow, steady. When I took a deep breath to calm my nerves, I smelled his distinct, masculine scent, which was enough to make me shut my eyes tightly.

How long had it been since I'd smelled a man who needed no cologne to define who he was? I'd been surrounded by male models for so long, it had been too long ago to remember—but I loved it. I appreciated it. Finally Austin came up behind me, and when he did, he wrapped his arms low against the flat of my stomach and pulled me toward him so I could feel his excitement throbbing against my ass.

It was too much. It was sensation overload. When he kissed each of my bare shoulders before stepping away from me and beginning to lower my dress's zipper, I thought for sure I was about to come right then and there.

But I didn't.

As cool air touched my back, a shiver of anticipation shot through me. I looked at the window in front of me and saw in it my own reflection. I looked like a woman undone. My lips were parted. The desire in my eyes was unmistakable. I thought I looked like another person—someone who'd just been set free.

As my dress came off and Austin helped me out of it, I saw in my reflection the pretty lace bra and panties I'd chosen to wear tonight, and I thanked God I'd had the sense to wear them. Before I could turn to Austin and show them to him, his lips were already against the nape of my neck, where they lingered before he slowly, maddeningly started to kiss the length of my spine, stopping just above the curve of my ass.

The stubble on his chin sent waves of heat through me. I felt his hands curve around my inner thighs, which he began to stroke with the light, feathery touch of his fingertips. With his breath hot against my skin, I could feel myself growing wet for him.

Never in my life had I thought it possible to crave a person so much. But I did. And his name was Austin Black.

"Turn to me," he said.

He was still kneeling in front of me. If I turned now, he'd come face-to-face with my sex. It was covered for now, but given the thickness I heard in his voice, I knew it wouldn't be for long.

I turned to him, and when I did, his eyes burned as he looked up at me.

"I want to explore every inch of you," he said.

Unable to stop this now, I simply shrugged at him. "What's stopping you?"

He smiled when I said that, and then he stood. He kicked off his shoes, looked straight into my eyes as he removed his belt, and then pulled his T-shirt over his head, finally revealing to me all that had been hidden beneath. I stared at his naked torso. His chest was thick yet cut, and it sported the faintest dusting of soft, dark hair, which trailed down his corded abs before disappearing into his bulging black pants.

"Who should take off my pants?" he asked. "Me? Or should that be you?"

"That would be me," I said.

"So...what's stopping you?"

I smiled when he said that, and I watched him put his hands on his narrow hips as he waited for me to do to him what he'd just done to me.

When I knelt before him, I took my time, wanting this moment to build. First, I unfastened his pants, the top of which pretty much split into a wide V due to the sheer pressure of his erection. Without looking at him, I kissed the area of flesh just below his belly button, and then I ran my tongue along it as he gasped in surprise. With a wicked grin, I reached up and tugged at his zipper. As I continued to lower it, I could feel the anticipation building between us— especially when I realized that Austin wasn't wearing any underwear. When that became clear to me, I stopped and simply looked up at him.

"Do you always go commando?" I asked.

"Not usually," he said. "But lately I have."

"Why?"

"Let's just say I've been needing the extra room lately."

"So I saw this morning."

With a brazenness I rarely felt—but nevertheless seized —I traced my index finger along the curve of his penis, which inflamed him. I went from the base of his balls to the tip of his head before slowly tracing my way back toward the zipper as my own sex throbbed with desire.

Just as I was about to tug his pants down, I suddenly stopped, stood before him as his eyes widened, and then reached down and grabbed his bulge in my right hand as we kissed. After this morning, I already had a good idea of how long Austin was. But I sure as hell wasn't prepared for just how *thick* he was, which unnerved me.

He's bigger than he looked, I thought as my hand tightened around him and our lips parted. *How am I ever going to take him?*

And then I knew.

The longer this *goes on, the more I'll be open for him when he finally enters me.*

"My bra," I said. "Would you take it off?"

"How about this first?"

He claimed my lips with his own, and I felt his tongue plunge into my mouth as he reached around and gently grabbed the base of my neck so he could pull me closer to him. As we kissed, I felt our souls intertwine.

"Turn around," he said when the kiss ended.

I turned, felt him deftly unfasten my bra, and then watched it sail across the room in a brisk shadow of farewell. With my breasts freed, I leaned my back against his rock-hard chest as his warm hands cupped my breasts. When he pinched my nipples, my head reared back in delight, and I heard a low moan of pleasure escape my lips. I heard him say in my ear, "I've waited too long for this."

Unable to stand it anymore, I swung around, and in one

quick move, I pulled down Austin's pants, allowing his enormous cock to spring free and hang heavily before me. The sight of it alone rendered me speechless, but before I could panic at the thought of how I'd ever be able to take all of him, Austin swept me into his arms and carried me over to his bed. There, he laid me down onto my back as he pulled off my black panties, tossed them aside, and knelt before me.

"You're so beautiful, Sienna," he said to me in a low voice. "Do you even know how beautiful you are? Especially naked?"

When his mouth pressed against my sex and his tongue started to run lightly along my folds before he brushed the stubble on his chin across my clit, I arched my back as rivers of pleasure pulsed through me. As his tongue reached in even deeper, I tried not to cry out, but it felt so good that I couldn't help the cries that escaped me as I gave myself over to him.

His hands smoothed up my torso and met my breasts, kneading them as he continued to go down on me. As I lay there with this beautiful man touching me in ways I hadn't been touched in years, I was aware of the perspiration moistening my skin and the fact that my breathing was quickening.

When his tongue started to flutter against my clit, it sent me out of my body as I my eyes snapped open and I tried to catch my breath. Encouraged, Austin didn't stop. Instead, he just he continued to pleasure me to the point that I felt I was about to come undone.

With my hands stretched out at my sides, I grabbed the soft bedspread and twisted it in my fists as his soft tongue explored me in ways that few men had before him. A rush of heat coursed through my body. I felt my sex begin to surge.

And then, when he hit me with the stubble again, I writhed beneath his touch and came almost at once.

Instead of stopping him, my orgasm only urged Austin to keep doing everything he was doing to me until I literally couldn't take it anymore. I wanted him on top of me. Hell, I wanted him *inside* me. Despite how large he was, I knew I was ready for him.

"Austin," I said breathlessly.

He didn't answer me. Instead, his only response was to continue to flick his tongue over my clit before his started to suck gently on it. My body lavished in the sensations he was giving me, but I wanted more. I *needed* more. I subtly bucked my hips, and he lifted his head and looked at me. When he saw the need in my eyes, he slowly stood and revealed all of himself to me.

And that was all it took, because I became undone as I marveled at him. Austin had been touched by the gods. With his skin slick with sweat and his hair hanging damply over his forehead, he looked otherworldly to me. Seeing him like this—in a moment of pure primal lust—was something I knew I'd never forget.

"Take me," I said to him.

Wordlessly, Austin lowered his body onto mine and kissed me deeply, meaningfully. Ribbons of desire rang out into his bedroom as our bodies connected—skin against skin, heart against heart, lips against lips. When he broke away for air, I bit down on one of his nipples, which only seemed to fuel him.

I was so wet and ready for him that with one mere stroke, he was inside me. But before he began to thrust, he paused to make sure I was ready to take him.

"It's OK," I said to him. "Make love to me."

For the next hour, Austin made love to me three times.

As our bodies collided against one another in rising tides of lust and heat that became our own private ocean of pleasure, each of us came to completion again and again and again. When my final climax shook through me, I knew I had my answer when it came to Austin. What we shared was far more than a mere physical attraction. What we had was real. It was palpable. It was undeniable.

We were meant to be together.

And as I lay there gasping, my breasts heaving, an overwhelming sense of guilt overcame me. Before I left here tonight—and regardless what Austin and I had just experienced together—I knew my initial intentions in coming here tonight couldn't change. I still had to honor the promise I'd made to Jackson...and also to myself. And because of that alone, and despite what had just occurred between Austin and me, I knew I had no choice but to ask him to wait seven months for me. And this terrified me—because I couldn't blame if he didn't.

And I knew very well he might not.

16

AFTER WE'D SHOWERED TOGETHER and toweled off together and I had donned one of Austin's white terry-cloth bathrobes—which dwarfed me but which nevertheless smelled distinctly of him—we left the bathroom for the bedroom, and I asked with a sense of dread if we could speak in the living room.

"We should get some sleep," he said, "don't you think? Both of us have a long day with Jackson tomorrow." He was standing before me in nothing more than his boxer shorts, gently stroking my damp hair with the back of his hand. "We can talk in the morning. Over coffee and breakfast." His eyes twinkled when he said that. "Tonight, dinner might have been a miss, but I certainly can cook for you when we wake up."

"Austin, I need to leave here under the cover of night," I said.

He furrowed his brow at me. "Why? While we were showering, I was thinking you'd sleep here. I can get you home safely in the morning. Nobody will know you were here tonight."

"You can't promise me that."

"Yes, I can. I got you here safely tonight, didn't I? I can get you home safely in the morning. Trust me on this."

"It's not that I don't trust you. Who I *don't* trust are the paparazzi and when they're going to start stalking my apartment. Because one day soon, that's going to happen. We both know it."

"Sienna, look—when it comes to Jackson, you should see the kind of shit I've pulled over the years to keep his sexuality private. He got caught kissing his pilot friend while boarding his plane because he broke protocol by choosing to kiss him in public. That's on him—not me. And Jackson knows it, because otherwise he would have fired me. *He's* the one who fucked up."

"That may be, but I need you to hear me out. After you started to sext me this morning, I came here tonight with every intention of asking you in person to please stop, because I need to not only honor my contract with Jackson but also nail down my own financial security. What we just experienced was amazing—it was fabulous—but it hasn't changed why I agreed to come here."

"I don't get it," he said. "You're a successful model, and you just scored big with *Lion*. You've already got financial security."

"Are you serious?" I said.

"Don't you?"

"Austin, come on. You've seen my apartment. Doesn't that say it all?"

"I like your apartment," he said.

"Then, please, let's exchange mine for yours, because this place is a palace compared to mine. And just so you know, mine happens to be rent-controlled, which is why I'm able to afford living in Chelsea, of all places."

"What am I missing here?"

"That I'm borderline poor—and that I'm no supermodel. When I walk the runway, I earn only the daily going rate—which happens to be shit, by the way. As for *Lion*—which was an independent film with almost no budget—I took the fifty grand they offered me to star in it because the script was excellent, the director was new and exciting, and I thought it might open up new opportunities for me—which it did. Because after my win at Cannes, along came Mimi and Jackson and the deal they offered me. If I stick to it—which I must—one day I'll no longer have to worry about living hand to mouth."

"Things have been *that* hard on you?" he asked.

"Austin, I'm pretty much broke."

"But you received a signing bonus," he said.

"I received two hundred and fifty thousand for the next eight months," I said. "Given my credit-card debt—which I plan to pay off so I can breathe again—and especially how expensive it is to live in this city, that money will go fast. Worse, I will only be paid in full if I honor Jackson's contract straight through to the end. If I don't, I'm fucked. That's why I came here tonight, because I don't think you understand how long things have been dire for me. Did I ever think we'd end up making love tonight? God, no. But we did, and it was wonderful. I don't regret it. But you have to understand that I've been living on the edge for so long that I *need* the money Jackson's offering me."

For a moment, we fell silent. Then I gently placed the palm of my hand against the heat of his bare chest. When I felt his heart pounding hard against it, I could sense his passion, his frustration, his lust, and also his compassion. And when I looked into his eyes, I saw all those emotions laid bare to me.

I spoke quietly to him.

"We can't see each other again," I said. "At least not like this, because I can't risk it. There have been times over the years when I couldn't even afford to eat, so Harper stepped in to take care of me, which was humiliating. But I love her for it. If anything, ever since I moved here, my life has only been scary, lonely, frustrating, and difficult. And because of that, I hope you'll understand that not only do I need the money Jackson's offering me, I also need to *earn* it. I need to do well by him. Because seven months from now, when I cash that check of his and finally can walk away knowing Jackson is going to be fine and that his career is back on track, my constant worries about money will be gone. For the first time in my life, I'll finally be financially free."

"I had no idea," he said.

"Only Harper knows," I said. "And Julia, of course. They are my best friends. They've quietly helped me throughout all of this because they've always believed in me. And because they have, I also can't let them down by screwing this up."

"I'm sorry if I pressed you this morning," he said. "I didn't mean to. I didn't know about any of this."

"Why would you?" I asked. "It's private. I only shared it with you so you'd understand why we *can't* be."

"*Can't* be?" he said. "Sienna, what are you talking about? Neither of us can deny what just happened there," he said, pointing toward his bed. "I've never experienced anything like that with anyone before. Not once. Can you say the same? Unless I've misread everything, I don't think you can."

Every fiber of my being told me that *now* was the moment to adhere to Julia's advice and shut this down between us—to tell him I didn't feel as strongly as he felt. To tell him that whatever he was feeling was on *him*—not me.

But that would be a bold-faced lie. And because I now knew for a fact there was something real and right and beautiful between us, I also knew I could never be that cruel to him. If I lied to him, he'd know it—and that was just something I couldn't accept.

So, I told him the truth.

"What we just shared was magical. You were wonderful. *We* were wonderful. It's just that—"

"I get it," he said in a low voice. "You need to honor your commitment to Jackson, and you need to secure your future."

"I do."

"Then, we'll do our best to work around that."

"But how? Austin, I just told you all the reasons I can't mess this up."

"But don't you see?" he insisted. "You don't have to risk anything."

"Tell me how. Especially now that my heart is on the line."

"You're out of this contract in...what? Seven months?"

"About that, yes."

"Then...I'll wait for you."

It was everything I'd wanted to hear, but after being with him and making love to him, could I really believe that a man this sensitive, thoughtful, and beautiful wouldn't catch someone else's eyes in the ensuing months? And that he might respond in kind? Tonight had been powerful, but had it been powerful enough to see us through to the other side? As much as I wanted to believe we could make it, I also knew I never could be sure.

"I can't ask you to do that," I said.

"Why?"

"Because seven months might as well be a year. In the meantime, you could meet someone new who is worthy of you. You and I both know that could happen. Because shit like that *does* happen, Austin, as we just witnessed."

"Which is exactly why I'm willing to wait for you, Sienna. Because I agree—what just happened between us *is* rare."

"You make the idea of waiting sound so easy," I said.

"It won't be easy," he said. "In fact, it will fucking kill me. But that doesn't mean I'm not willing to wait for you, because for me, you *are* worth waiting for, and if you would just trust in me, I will wait. But I have to ask—why don't you believe that I will?"

And here we go into that part of my life...

"Not too long ago, I got seriously burned in my last relationship."

"By who?"

"His name is Eric."

"How long has it been?"

"Two years."

"What did he do to you?"

When Austin asked me that, I felt a fire of rage burning deep within my belly.

"He cheated on me," I said. "I came home unexpectedly one afternoon after a modeling shoot got called off, and I found him screwing another woman in our own bed. We'd been together for four years at that point. Time and again Eric had told me he was in love with me. That I was it for him—and I'd believed it. I'd believed in *him*. And then I walked into that. And when I did—after feeling so close to him and so loved by him—it shattered me. Hell, it *changed* me."

His face softened. "I'm sorry," he said. "What he did to you must have gutted you."

"It did. I haven't dared to be with another man since."

"Because you think that it might happen again."

"Of course," I said. "Why shouldn't I believe that?"

"And yet you were with me tonight."

"Yes, because I sense that you're different."

"You're right," he said. "I'd never do that when it comes to you."

"Austin, what am I to do three, four, or five months from now if you do fall for another woman, especially when I'm invested in you and waiting for you?"

"I'm not going to be looking."

"Were you looking when you met me?"

That caused him to pause.

"No," he admitted. "But you need to understand that my standards are high when it comes to relationships. I've been single for the past five years for that reason alone. I don't take relationships lightly. And trust me on this, I'm not taking this *moment* lightly."

Austin, I had a wonderful time tonight, I thought. *And I hope you really are there seven months from now. But for my heart and sanity alone, I can't allow myself to bet on that. I can't have my heart broken again. The last time was too much...*

Knowing I had to get out of there, I looked around the bedroom and wondered where he'd tossed my dress and my undergarments when he'd removed them from me. Since the lighting was so dim, I couldn't see where they were.

"I need to go," I said as my throat constricted and my eyes welled with tears. "I need to get out of here now before I completely lose it."

"Listen to yourself, Sienna," he said. "You know this is right."

Overcome with emotion, I blinked through tears as I looked around the bedroom. "I can't see my dress," I said, "or my underwear. Can you please turn up the lights?"

With a frustrated sigh, he did.

"Please don't go like this," he said.

When I spotted my panties, bra, and dress lying in various places around the bedroom, I gathered them up, tossed them onto the bed, and then dropped my bathrobe and quickly changed into them. When I was finished, I slipped into my shoes and walked over to him, giving him a meaningful kiss on the lips that seared through me like a scalding knife. And then—unable to cope with the ridiculous groundswell of emotions I felt—I held his face close in my hands and looked into his eyes until I couldn't any longer. There was too much false hope for us there.

Get out, now. Get out before you get in even deeper than you already are.

"Thank you for tonight," I said as I took a step away from him. "I hope that we can still be friends."

He looked wounded when I said that—and that look alone killed me.

"Sienna, I meant everything I said to you. I will wait for you. I'll have you in my bed again. We'll be together like this again."

I wanted nothing more than to believe that, but it was ridiculous to think that any man would wait so long for me. And why would Austin, after just one night together? Why get my hopes up? Only to potentially have them crushed? I couldn't do that to myself—or to him.

Get out of this while you can...

"Why are your eyes so bright, Sienna?" he asked me.

"You already know why, Austin—when we made love,

my body told you everything you need to know about how I feel for you."

When I turned away from him to leave, tears fell from my eyes and spilled onto my cheeks.

Don't let him see them. Don't you dare let him see them.

With my back to him, I left the bedroom and started to walk down the long hallway, moving swiftly past the living room, the dining room, and the kitchen, finally emerging into the foyer, where I found my clutch on a side table.

"I'm not giving up on us, Sienna," he called after me.

When I reached for the door, I felt the palm of his hand press against the low of my back, and he said my name with a sense of urgency that felt so right that I almost turned to kiss him a final time.

But I didn't—I couldn't. It would ruin me if I did.

I had to get out of there. And so, without answering him, I opened the door and left him behind. Upset that for so many reasons that were out of my hands, we couldn't be, I entered the hallway and hurried toward the bank of elevators. When I found them, I entered the first one that opened for me.

It was only when the doors slid shut and I was in the car alone that I buried my face in my hands and openly began to weep.

17

OVER THE NEXT THREE DAYS, Austin began what apparently was his new mission in life—trying his best to tear down my walls and prove to me he was indeed serious about waiting for me.

Since I knew in my gut there was no stopping this man, I was grateful that at least he was discreet and professional whenever we were around Jackson, Harper, or Mimi. When we were with one or all of them, he never once revealed— with his face or with his eyes—any trace of his desire for me.

But it was there. I knew it was—he showed it to me in a whole host of other ways.

First came the dozen roses that were delivered to my apartment the morning after we'd made love. They were full, lush, and beautiful—and came with a card that simply said, "I meant what I said. I'm not giving up on us, Sienna. And because of that, I also don't want you to see red this morning. –A."

I'd smiled when I'd read that, because the roses he'd sent had been white.

The second day, when Jackson had to shoot during the

evening—which meant that my night was free—Austin texted me late in the afternoon. What he said was as simple as it was mysterious: "Don't cook tonight."

Later, I found out why. The man who'd once proclaimed himself the king of takeout proved he wasn't joking. At seven that evening, a large delivery from Momofuku Ko—a high-end restaurant revered in Manhattan and around the world —arrived at my apartment.

The contents were an embarrassment of riches.

Inside the several white takeout boxes were such things as snapper tartare with shiso and green chili; foie gras with pine nuts and lychee; farfalle with brussels sprouts and Szechuan peppercorns; Muscovy duck with lime pickle and crème fraîche; a soft-boiled egg with potato chips, caviar, and herbs; and even a delicious-looking piece of chocolate cake. When I tried to tip the delivery man, he told me the tip had already been taken care of. His parting words to me were, "Mr. Black hopes you enjoy your meal."

I did—and then some.

On the third day, which was today, Jackson and I had spent the afternoon being photographed feverishly as we enjoyed a day of shopping along Fifth Avenue. When our time together was over, Austin drove me home. And when he did, I could literally feel the tense silence stretching between us—all the words going unsaid in the vacuum of silence I'd created when I'd walked out on him.

Although Austin had driven me home every day since that night, we hadn't shared more than a few pleasantries. Since I didn't want to encourage him to think I believed we ever could be—and especially because I didn't want to lead him on—I hadn't thanked him for the roses or for the fabu-lous dinner he'd sent me, which made me feel like a piece of shit, but what could I do? I knew that if I did thank him, I'd only encourage him to do more and also engage him in conversation when I was trying my best to put distance between us so I could protect my heart—and also his. Still, the guilt I felt for not thanking him was so off the charts it was ridiculous.

We were driving downtown to my apartment when he broke the silence.

"Care to listen to some music?" he asked.

I met his eyes in the rearview.

"What kind of music?"

"I don't know. You know...music."

"Are you planning on playing jazz for me again?"

"I don't like to repeat myself. What would you like to listen to?"

"Maybe a dance station?"

"You like to dance?"

"I love to dance."

"Well, look at that," he said. "After three days of silence, I just learned something new about you."

"I haven't exactly been silent," I said.

"Saying good morning to me doesn't really cut it when it comes to having a conversation, Sienna. But I get it. You just need some time and space to come to terms with your feelings for me, especially after what happened between us the other night, which blew both of us away. And when you finally have your come-to-Jesus moment—which you will at some point—I plan on reassuring you that I will wait however long I need to wait for you. Because you're worth the wait. And I'm not giving up."

And here we go with this *again. If we had to wait only a month before I was out of my contract with Jackson, I'd be all in with you, Austin. But seven months? Seven months is the kind of bet I just can't take with my heart.*

Stick to the plan, I thought. *You're right about this. Julia was right about this. Listen to your gut...*

I looked at him in the rearview.

"If dance isn't your thing, what would you like to listen to?" I asked.

He pressed a button on the radio's console. "Lately, I've been listening to this."

When the first notes sounded, I recognized the song immediately—and knew at once I'd been set up. We weren't on any radio station, because just like that we were suddenly listening to Mariah Carey's "Love Takes Time," which speaks about the dangers of letting love slip away, that Carey hadn't been able to escape the pain, and that there was a hollow in her heart that needed to be healed.

He so had that song ready to go. Fuck my life, already.

It didn't exactly take a doctorate in psychology to know what he was doing—Austin was using Carey's song to speak to me in ways I wasn't allowing him to. And even I had to admit that the song did so in ways that resounded. As I listened to the track—which happened to be a favorite of mine—I closed my eyes while Carey sang about a person who said he didn't care about her and didn't need her, but she knew that deep inside he did.

Switch around the pronouns, and that person clearly was meant to be me.

"Austin..." I said.

"Listen to the words, Sienna."

Take the bitter pill, swallow it, and say nothing, I thought. *Let him make his statement. Don't engage him more than you already have.*

As Carey wailed on about how fucking sad she was, I decided to separate myself from the music by looking out the window to my right. There, I saw a thriving city eager to distract me just when I needed it most.

It was midafternoon, the sun was shining high in the sky, and as the city sped by as we cruised down Fifth, it did so in a series of vignettes.

I saw an elderly couple holding hands as they walked down the sidewalk, a man playing saxophone on a street corner to a small gathering of listeners, and three smiling, whooping boys darting through the crowds on skateboards, their colorful shirts blazing in flashes of red, green, and white.

I looked longingly at it all. The city I'd come to love and call home was as unleashed as ever—it was raw, free, and alive in ways I was feeling isolated from due to my growing celebrity.

With each headline Jackson and I made—and they were countless at this point—I was starting to feel mildly claustrophobic. Just this week alone, there was a noticeable shift in the sheer number of people who recognized me on the street. On Monday, when I went to the dry cleaners, I found myself surrounded by people who wanted to take selfies with me or who wanted my autograph—or both. The experience had been so unnerving that I'd called Harper when I got home. She'd talked me down, but not without warning me that Jackson and I had saturated the media for so many weeks with literally thousands of photos posted of us in newspapers, magazines, and online that the tipping point had obviously come.

Fame was upon me.

At first, I thought what had happened on Monday was a fluke. But it wasn't, because next came the crowd of young women who'd swarmed me at the Sephora off West Nineteenth Street on Tuesday.

The moment I'd walked into the store and made the mistake of taking off my sunglasses without even thinking about the ramifications of doing so, it was clear that just seeing me in person was now enough to cause a minor riot —particularly since the store was filled with teenage girls and women in their twenties, all of whom likely had the hots for Jackson. When I was spotted by a pretty brunette, she blinked twice at me before her jaw dropped and she turned to her friends, saying loud enough for the entire block to hear, "Oh, my God—Sienna Jones is in the fucking store!"

When I was engulfed by dozens of teens and twenty-somethings, I quickly became overwhelmed with a whole host of questions that ranged from what Jackson Cruise was like and if I were in love with him or falling in love with him to what he was like in bed—and could they please take a selfie with me? I felt obliged to do the latter, because I got it —as far as they knew, I *was* dating one of their idols. I also knew what they really wanted from me was a photo taken with them for their Instagram feeds. When I saw several of the girls starting to call their friends to alert them that I was in the store, I left without buying anything—but with the knowledge that I was rapidly becoming an object to be studied, assessed, and obsessed over.

I'd always wanted to be an actress, but in my fight to become one, I hadn't given much thought to the true weight of celebrity, which had been naive of me. At some point soon, I needed to come to terms with this new life of mine. Years ago, Jackson had had to do the same thing. As had so many before us who had watched their own worlds shrink as their privacy was stripped away from them. Because this new life of mine wasn't going away anytime soon—if ever.

"Where are you, Sienna?" Austin asked.

I was so lost in thought that I hadn't realized the song had ended and that we were now riding in silence. For how long? I didn't know. Instead of shutting him down, I just shrugged at him.

"I'm in a place that I need to come to terms with," I said.

"What place is that?"

"A place where my anonymity no longer exists."

"You're becoming famous," he said. "Each time you and Jackson go out, it just gets crazier and crazier. I mean, look at what happened today, for instance. Cartier had to shut its doors to the public when you two were inside. And after word had spread that both of you were at Cartier, a few hundred people had gathered outside to catch a glimpse of you. It was pandemonium. That kind of adjustment can't be easy."

"I'll be fine," I said. "And please don't think I'm complaining, because I'm not. I just need to get used to it. And adapt to it. That's going to take some time."

"I saw Jackson go through it," he said. "There were times when the attention gave him a massive high—but other times, I knew he was struggling with his lack of privacy, especially when it came to how it affected his personal life. But he's told you that."

"He has, and it saddens me. Jackson's a good man. He deserves to have love in his life—we all do. I hate that he feels he can't openly share his life with another man. But I'm working on him."

"What does that mean?"

"I drop little hints here and there."

"Little hints about what?"

"The possibilities of his coming out."

"And he gives you no pushback for that?"

"When I first broach the subject, he doesn't. He'll listen.

But when I go too far, he shuts me down. As he probably will over dinner tonight, because I plan to bring up the subject again in a few hours."

"On the yacht Mimi chartered for you two..."

"The paps will be there to see us getting onto it, but once we're on it alone for our 'romantic' cruise on the Hudson, I'll have Jackson to myself."

"Not completely you won't, Sienna. The staff will be listening."

"I'm a master when it comes to speaking in code, Austin."

"And look at that—that's two things I've learned about you today."

"Very funny."

He clocked me in the rearview.

"In all seriousness, I need to ask if you're being recognized when you're out on your own now. Or are you still able to fly under the radar?"

"Yeah, not so much anymore."

"What does that mean?"

I told him what had happened to me this week.

"Why haven't you told me about any of that?" he asked. "Jesus Christ, Sienna, when you are in situations like that, you need some sort of security around you to assist with crowd control. Because if no one is there for you and things become too much for you to handle, what are you going to do then? What would Jackson and you have done today if my security team and I hadn't been in place to protect both of you? You see how insane it's getting. If you and Jackson had gone out today on your own, you would have been screwed. The same is true for you now."

I looked at Austin—and knew he was right.

"Who do I hire?" I asked. "Can you give me some leads?"

"Sienna, what are you thinking?" he asked. "*You* shouldn't be the one paying. Jackson should be the one who provides you with that kind of service. It sure as hell shouldn't come out of *your* pocket. It should come out of his, because you're helping *him*. Now, listen to me for a moment—"

He stopped short when he said that, and then I heard him curse beneath his breath as he touched the brakes.

"What's the matter?" I asked.

"We've got a problem."

"What kind of problem?"

He pointed toward my apartment building. "That problem."

When I leaned forward and looked through the limousine's front window, what I saw left me feeling deflated and exposed. It wasn't just the paparazzi I saw waiting for me in front of my apartment building—there were a few hundred people waiting right along with them.

18

"I TOLD YOU THIS WOULD HAPPEN," I said as Austin pulled the limousine up next to my building. The moment he did, the paps practically popped off the sidewalk and began taking photographs of me inside the car. Right behind them came a slew of other people—likely Jackson's fans, because they certainly couldn't be fans of mine—who were armed with their smartphones, and eager to take my photograph as they cried out in excitement.

In a matter of moments, our car was surrounded by all of them, which caused such a scene that others passing along the street, their curiosities piqued, joined them to see who was inside the car and what all the fuss was about.

Despite the tinted windows, the paparazzi's flashes were so bright that I knew they were capturing me, so despite how unnerved I felt, I nevertheless did my best to compose myself as I reached for my handbag. Inside were my sunglasses. I removed them and put them on.

"I'll get you inside," Austin said. "It'll be OK."

"I'm not so sure I agree with that," I said. "The paps have finally figured out where I live, which means that getting around my neighborhood just became seriously complicated. I told you the other night that this was inevitable—and here we are, Austin. I just didn't think it would happen so soon. But when it comes to the paps, what I don't understand is that they just took photos of Jackson and me while we were shopping. How many other photographs do they need?"

"Sienna, at this point, they clearly want photos of you by yourself. People are interested in *you*. Things are escalating."

"Then, I guess I'd better adapt."

"Look, right now, a few hundred people are surrounding the car," he said. "Getting you into your apartment is going to be difficult. Do you want me to drive around, call in my team, and then handle the crowd when they arrive? I can do that, Sienna. In fact, I think that we *should* do that."

"There's no time. Austin, I need to get ready for my dinner with Jackson tonight. Harper and Mimi have set things into motion. They've already leaked that Jackson and I will be arriving at the North Cove Marina at eight. I need time to look my best."

"If you want to go in now, it's not going to be easy," he said, looking at me over his shoulder. When our eyes met, I tried my best to keep my features neutral, because after days of pretty much not looking at him at all, I now had no choice but to face him directly. And when I did, the attraction I felt for him was like a meteor glancing brightly across the sky.

"So, how do we handle this?" I asked. "How do I get inside?"

"With this many people?" he said. "You need to ignore the paps, and you also need to ignore your fans."

"They aren't *my* fans, Austin—they're Jackson's fans."

"You don't know that," he said. "But because this situation is now about your safety, don't you dare stop for even one selfie. Don't do it. Just take my hand when I offer it to you and hold onto it, and I'll carve a path through all of them."

"All right," I said. "Let's get this over with."

"Are you ready?"

"As ready as I'll ever be. But I'm scared, Austin," I said as I looked out the window and saw the teeming masses desperate for me to step out. Several people had cupped their hands against the limousine's tinted windows to catch a glimpse of me. The din of excitement was building to a frightening level. "This is ridiculous," I said.

"I can call in my team," he said. "We can wait here for them."

"How long will that take?"

"In this traffic? Maybe forty minutes?"

"Too long," I said. "Get me out of here. Get me past them."

"Are you sure?" he asked. "Because I'm not."

"I have to get ready for tonight. I don't have time to wait."

"Then, sit tight," he said. "I'm going to get out of the car, you'll see me walk around the front of it, and then I'll do my best to get you inside as fast as I can."

"OK," I said.

"Let's do this shit."

When Austin opened the door to leave the car, the sudden roar of anticipation from the crowd stunned me to my core. People were literally screaming out my name. They were shouting it out loud. When Austin shut the door behind him, the noise might have ebbed, but I nevertheless heard him ask the crowd to step back and give him the room he needed to get me safely out of the car. Austin was such a foreboding presence that the crowd did move back a bit—

but not by much. He fought his way through the hordes of people and finally came to my door. I held my breath as he swung it open.

Outside, chaos reigned.

It was as if I were a fucking Kardashian. Austin offered me his hand, which I gratefully took as I grabbed my handbag and swung it over my shoulder. Then I stepped out into staccato rhythms of light that were so bright that they literally blinded me despite the sunglasses I wore.

People started to hurl questions at me—from the paps and from my alleged fans.

"Sienna, are you planning to marry Jackson Cruise?"

"Sienna, can I get a selfie with you?"

"Sienna, you are fucking awesome!"

"Sienna, please turn to your left!"

"Has Jackson proposed to you, Sienna?"

"Sienna, please—just one selfie! It would blow up my Instagram! Please! You don't know what that would mean to me!"

Inch by inch, I moved forward through the hurricane of noise and light as I kept my head down and fought to keep a smile on my face. My heart hammered against my chest. I'd been in situations like this before with Jackson, but never once on my own—and it felt different. It felt dangerous. It felt threatening.

What the hell has happened to my life?

"Step back!" Austin warned them. "You're too close—you know that you legally need to give her room."

"Sienna, I saw you at Sephora!"

"Sienna, what's it like to sleep with Jackson Cruise? Is it everything I dream it is? Tell me it's better!"

"Sienna, how did you and Jackson meet?"

"Sienna, please—this way for the camera!"

"Who the hell is Sienna Jones?" I heard one man ask.

I wanted to laugh out loud at that, but then somebody bumped into me so hard that it almost made me lose my footing. I was wearing four-inch heels, for God's sake. If it weren't for Austin's strong grip, I would have gone down. But together, we strengthened our grip, and as we did—despite the circus that was unfolding around us—I felt the same bond we'd shared when we'd first made love. Right now, I felt not only how protective he was of me—but that he'd literally do anything for me.

"I'm sorry, Sienna! That was an accident! Someone pushed me—I didn't mean to bump into you!"

I held up my free hand to signal that all was fine.

Until it wasn't fine. At that moment, somebody rushed up behind me and ran his hands up my torso until they grasped my breasts and squeezed them hard. Startled, I whirled around to see who it was, and when I did, not only did I see the young man laughing as he backed away from me, his cell phone lifted high to film the moment—but in the process, my hand slipped free of Austin's.

"What's wrong?" Austin asked.

"That man just groped me!" I said.

"Which man?"

"That one," I said, pointing a finger at him. "The one who's laughing. He just grabbed my breasts—and *hard*."

"We've got it on tape, Sienna!" one of the paps called out. To score points, the paps always leaped to a celebrity's defense, because they knew that if they did, whatever star they were trying to help out might remember them later—and allow them more access and less resistance in the future. "That was an assault. We'll get the video to you. Give it to the police so they can arrest him."

"Send me that tape," Austin said to the man who'd

offered it. And then he turned to the man who'd groped me. "You're lucky I can't leave her alone, you sorry motherfucker," he said to him. "Because if I could, I'd beat your ass."

"Fuck you," the guy said. But when he said it, the crowd turned against him. People started to call him out. Others closed in on him. I saw one muscular man in his thirties walk over to him, slap the phone out of his hands, and stomp on it—crushing it—before taking the man by the throat and punching him so hard in the face that he collapsed to the ground.

At the first sight of blood, I felt myself go pale, horrified that this was even happening. I turned to Austin and reached for his hand again as the situation became unhinged. Before this exploded into something neither of us wanted to see, I begged him to get me inside.

"Follow me," he said.

With the crowd distracted, he was able to pull me forward through the thundering sound of clicking cameras as the paparazzi moved in fast to get in front of us and block our entrance to the building. In earnest, they went for it and got their unexpected money shot—my horrified, terrified, deeply disturbed expression.

"Get out of the way now, or I'll move you myself," Austin said to them.

When they parted, their cameras still flashing and snapping, we reached the door. Austin swung it open with force and finally got me inside. As the door shut behind us, I heard people screaming my name in ways I now understood were dangerous, threatening, and terrifying. I'd just been sexually assaulted. All of it had been captured by the paps, and they would spread my assault as far and as wide as they could.

What the hell is next for me? I wondered as my body

began to shake. Austin wrapped his arm around me and started to press me forward. *Because that was just the tipping point. What happens from here? How bad will things become for me? I've still got seven more months of this! What the hell have I signed up for?*

19

"ARE YOU ALL RIGHT?" Austin asked.

He'd led us away from the glass door so the paparazzi couldn't continue to photograph us. We were standing around the corner in the stairwell that led to my third-story walk-up.

"He reached around me and grabbed my breasts," I said. "Who in their right fucking mind *does* something like that?"

"I wish I could have taken him out for you, Sienna, but in that situation, there's no way I could have left your side."

"No, you did the right thing—I would have been lost if you'd gone after him. Besides, he got what was coming—whoever that man was took him down."

"From what I saw, that son of a bitch got a busted nose."

"Now we just need to bust his ass for what he did to me."

"The police will be involved—trust me on that. If they aren't already. Because who knows what's happening outside right now. That crowd turned on him for a reason. For all we know, they might be detaining him until the police arrive. You and I both know that someone called 911."

It was too much to absorb. Standing there in front of Austin, I felt shaken, sexually assaulted, and frightened by the thought of how the press would play this when it hit the entertainment shows and online sites sooner rather than later.

What had just happened to me was the kind of thing that went viral, which meant that interest in me would only grow. Not that I wanted any part of that right now. If ever.

"We should get you inside your apartment."

"But what about your car?" I said. "It's double-parked. They'll tow it."

"Let them," he said. "It's a car. I'll get it later. Besides, my business owns several limousines. And I'm not leaving you alone right now."

In truth, I didn't want to be alone, regardless of the potential ramifications of being alone with Austin. I just nodded at him, and we took the stairs to my apartment. When we stepped inside, it was sweltering.

"Sorry," I said. "I should have left the air-conditioning running, but I try my best to keep my electric bill as low as possible."

"It's not a problem," he said.

He reached for my hand and led me into my living room, where the white roses he'd sent me were standing tall and bright in a vase on the coffee table. I'd kept them—and now he knew for a fact that I had. Being the gentleman he was, he didn't say a word about them. Instead, he asked if I'd like to sit on the sofa.

"I would," I said.

"Then, sit," he said. "You need to relax."

When I tossed my handbag onto the chair across from me and sat down, I watched Austin walk over to the window and turn on my air-conditioning unit. The living room was so small that it would cool off quickly enough, for which I was grateful, because it was hellish in there. When Austin stepped in front of me, his concern for my well-being was etched across his handsome face.

"Can I get you a glass of water?" he asked.

"You can get me something that looks like water."

He smiled when I said that.

"Are you talking about a martini?"

"Are you serious? After *that*? That's absolutely what I'm talking about. There's vodka in the freezer. And there's vermouth—"

"I know my way around a kitchen," he said. "I'll find what I need. You just sit tight. Give me a second, and I'll be back in a flash."

"I hope you'll join me," I said as he walked into the kitchen. "You probably could use a drink yourself."

"I shouldn't, because I'm working—but to hell with it. I'm joining you."

"One martini won't kill you."

"One martini won't."

After he'd made our drinks and returned to the living room, he handed me mine and then asked me where I'd like him to sit.

"You can sit next to me," I said.

That seemed to surprise him.

"Are you sure?"

Right now, I felt so violated after what had happened that I needed to be close to someone. And Austin was it.

"I'm sure."

He sat next to me, and we each sipped our drinks. For a moment, we lapsed into silence as we tried to process the last twenty minutes.

For weeks, Harper and Mimi had stoked the flames with

the paparazzi, and having my photo blasted everywhere with Jackson had finally caught up with me. Was today an anomaly? Or was this only the beginning? I had to believe it was the latter. What I also knew is that if my life were going to turn into this kind of shit show, I needed more security around me. And later, when the time was right, I planned to ask for it. Because as good as Austin was, today he'd had to struggle to keep me safe. He'd become as overwhelmed as I was. If he were going to protect me going forward, he would have to bring on other members of his team to do so.

Deal with it later, I thought. *Austin just did his very best for me, and I don't want him to feel that he didn't. Later today, I'll talk to Harper alone, and I'll tell her exactly how hard he tried to protect me. But she also needs to know that in the environment she and Mimi have created for me, I needed more security. No one should expect Austin to handle what he just endured on his own.*

I turned to him.

"Austin, I want to thank you for getting me through that," I said. "You advised me to wait for your staff to arrive so they could assist us, but I was in such a rush to get ready for tonight that I was naive. I should have listened to you. I'm beyond sorry that I didn't. I hope you'll forgive me."

"Why are you sorry?" he asked. "Sienna, you had no control over what just happened. Going into your contract with Jackson, I bet you had no idea that agreeing to be his fake girlfriend would ever blow up into anything like this."

"Harper warned me as best she could, but to be completely honest with you, I don't think I really heard her. I've been trying so hard for so long to make it in this industry that I think I just went blindly into the contract Mimi and Jackson offered me because I knew the attention would help my career and that the kind of money they were

offering me would benefit me forever. What I don't understand is why I don't hear about these sorts of things
happening to the world's biggest stars. Like Julia Roberts. Or
Meryl Streep. Or Oprah, for God's sake?"

"That's easy to answer," he said. "It's because they don't
have agents aggressively tipping off the paps to their every
move. That's the reason this happened to you today. Harper
and Mimi are giving the paparazzi free and total access to
you and Jackson. The other actors you mentioned have
already made it. They *want* to fly under the radar, and for
the most part, they can do so—unless they're attending an
event or a movie premiere."

"When my contract is over, what does my life look
like then?"

"The life you once lived is officially gone, but you
already know that. You're a celebrity now. You're new and
fresh on the scene, and people are excited by what they see.
At the end of your contract, you're set to shoot three major
films in a row with three A-list directors. If even one of those
films becomes a hit, expect your star to rise. But as long as
Harper isn't feeding you to the paps—like the Kardashians
are, for instance, who actually *want* this kind of craziness in
their lives—things should settle down for you. When the
paps aren't aware of where you're going to be every day, the
feeding frenzy should end. And because of that, you'll live a
more tolerable life, I think."

"May it be," I said.

"It'll get better, Sienna."

"I hope so."

"Once your contract is over and your financial situation
is taken care of, I know it will. And I'll be there for you when
it is, because I get it. I've had time to think about this. The

kind of money you're being offered *is* life changing, so I agree with you—you need to finish your contract without me interfering with any of it. But I'll say this again, Sienna— I'm not giving up on us. I will wait for you, whether you want me to or not."

So much conviction was in his voice when he said that that for the first time, I believed him. First the flowers, then the takeout food from the gods, then the song by Mariah Carey—and then his aggression when it came to protecting me today. Was I wrong about Austin's intentions? Was he really willing to wait seven months for me? I was beginning to believe that he might be—that he was serious—and that caught me off guard.

"Thanks for talking me down," I said. "And for having my back today."

"I'll always have your back, Sienna."

"Austin, I don't mean to doubt you, but you've only known me for a month, and yet you sound so certain about us. I'm trying to understand how that can be, but I can't."

"It's because I'm the kind of guy who knows what he wants. Because what I feel for you, Sienna, is real. It's this."

He leaned forward and kissed me when he said that, and when he did, my body responded with shivers of anticipation at the sudden touch of his lips pressed against mine. When he realized I wasn't going to pull away from him, he leaned in closer and claimed my mouth with a hunger that consumed me to my core. There was longing in his kiss. And need. And in that need was something more, something deeper, something profound. Gently, he took my drink out of my hand and he put both our glasses down on the coffee table. When he kissed me again, as his tongue swept into my mouth and tasted me, it was as if he had become untethered.

"We shouldn't do this," I said.

"Look me in the eyes and tell me you don't want this."

I couldn't, and so I didn't.

As the air conditioner tried to cool off the room, we heated it up. As dangerous as this moment felt to me, it also felt dangerously right. When I didn't answer him, Austin took me into his arms, and we shared the beginnings of a searing kiss—just as my cell rang.

"Don't answer it," he said, his breath hot against me. "They'll leave a message. Don't stop this now."

"But it might be Harper," I said, pulling away from him. "Word might have already gotten out, and she might be calling in to check on me because she's concerned about me. I have to answer it."

"Fuck..." he said.

"I need to."

"No, you're right," he said in disappointment as he pulled away from me and straightened on the couch. I did the same as I reached for my handbag and removed my cell from it. Sure enough, it was Harper. I showed Austin the screen and in frustration, he just nodded.

I answered the call.

"Harper," I said.

"I've just seen the news," she said with concern in her voice. "What I need to know first is whether you are all right."

"I'm OK."

"Where is Austin?"

"He's sitting with me now. He's been trying his best to calm me down, which is no easy task. He deserves a raise after what I've put him through today."

"You sound out of breath."

I am. And as much as I'd like to tell you why, Harper, I can't. You'd have my ass if you knew the real reason I'm out of breath.

"I'm upset," I said, which was far from an outright lie, because I *was* upset by what had happened. "It was terrible, Harper. That son of a bitch grabbed me by my breasts in front of hundreds of people."

"I know he did. And I'm sorry, Sienna. I've seen the photos."

"Where have you seen them?"

"At this point, I'm afraid they're everywhere. Naturally TMZ was the first to post them, because when *aren't* they the first to break this sort of news? Everyone else just followed suit."

I knew this was going to break quickly, but not *this* quickly.

She sighed into the phone. "Listen to me now, because I need you to understand that there's actually a silver lining when it comes to these sorts of unwanted situations."

"There's a silver lining when it comes to being sexually assaulted in public?" I asked incredulously.

"In the wake of the Harvey Weinstein scandal? I'm afraid in this business, there is. Before I called you, Julia came into my office and told me you were trending on Twitter again. I read some of the tweets, and what I can tell you is that the public is fiercely on your side. You have their empathy, their sympathy, and their outrage. People are furious about what happened to you today, especially since our country is in the midst of having a heated discussion about sexual assault, whether it be in the entertainment industry or in Washington—or wherever. And because of that, Sienna, your fans are behind you, and they are furious."

"They aren't my fans," I said. "They're Jackson's fans."

"Call them whatever you want, but these people are

actively protesting what that man did to you. They want him arrested."

"What are the chances of that happening?"

"The TMZ article stated that the man was detained by the crowd and that the police had been called. Have they reached out to you yet?"

"No."

"If there's any truth to the TMZ article, they will soon. You need to be prepared for that."

"What does all this mean for my evening with Jackson tonight?"

"Nothing. If the police reach out to you, tell them you'll meet with them tomorrow morning. Because right now? In this climate? The world is waiting to see how well you handle this situation, and the answer is that it must be met with strength, honesty, and conviction. If you cancel your evening with Jackson, the man who assaulted you will have won. Do you want that?"

"Absolutely not."

"Good, because this is your moment to show the world how strong you are, Sienna. People want to see your resilience, and that's what I need you to bring tonight. I need you to *own* tonight. I want you to show up at the North Cove Marina looking more beautiful than you ever have, because that will send a definitive message to your fans and to the world that you are a fierce woman who is bigger than one man's offensive actions. I know I'm asking a lot from you. I understand that doing what I'm suggesting will be hard on you, but I also know how the public thinks. Tonight, the woman who starred in *Lion* needs to come out looking like a lion. It won't only be masses who will respect you if you do that—it also will be everyone who has been sexually assaulted before you. I can promise you that."

"I get it," I said.

"Sienna, I hope you don't think I'm being insensitive right now, because I feel terrible about what happened to you. I'm just trying to guide you here and give you my best advice. I know that wearing a brave face won't be easy for you tonight, but I also know your determination and your strength. And because of that, I also know you'd regret it if you didn't show up for tonight's event despite what that bastard did to you."

As usual, Harper was right. That's the last thing I wanted.

"Tell Jackson and Mimi that tonight is still on," I said. "I will not bow out now because of that freak. I have several hours before I need to leave, and I'll use that time to pull myself together. Don't worry about me, OK? I'll do everything I can to look my best tonight."

"Reach out to me if you need me," she said.

"I will," I said. "I love you, Harper. Thanks for being there for me."

"My love straight back to you," she said. "In spades, Sienna. I'll be thinking of you. And please thank Austin for doing his best in what turned out to be an impossible situation."

"I've already told him so myself, but I'll also share with him your sentiments."

"Good luck tonight. And remember that I'm just a phone call away. Before I let you go, I want to tell you that Jackson and Mimi are terribly upset by what happened and that they are genuinely concerned about you. Jackson is particularly angry. He's already taken to Twitter to condemn what happened to you today. The five of us will meet tomorrow afternoon to assess the damage and how we should proceed going forward to make sure this doesn't happen to you again."

"I look forward to that meeting, because I expect things to change, Harper. This can't happen again. I can't be ambushed like that again. I just can't."

"I hear you," she said. "All of us are on the same page. We'll work this out."

"Thanks for checking in on me."

"I'm always available to you, my dear girl—don't you ever forget that. Now, go out there with your head held high, and knock them dead tonight. Show the world how strong you are. If you do that, you will let everyone know that sexual assault survivors are *in fact* survivors. Leave them with that, my dear, and you'll not only win today—you'll also own the day."

When I got off the phone, Austin was already on his feet and preparing to leave.

"I should go," he said in a brisk tone that surprised me. I thought he'd stay, particularly after we'd been interrupted by Harper.

"You're leaving?" I asked.

"You need to rest a bit, and then you need to get ready for tonight. Clearly I'm a distraction when it comes to that. I'll be here to pick you up at seven thirty. When I arrive, buzz me through, and in case there are any paps or fans waiting outside for you, we'll deal with them."

"But if they're still there, how are we going to deal with them on our own?"

"We won't be dealing with them alone, because I plan on

bringing one of my men with me. I'll come and get you myself, just as I always do. But as far as I'm concerned, what's happening to you now is more than I can handle on my own. When it comes to you, David is now officially part of your security detail, even if he doesn't know it just yet. You met him a week ago, when things really started to become crazy for Jackson and you. You are at the point where you need serious protection, and David is as good as it gets when it comes to that. He and I will protect you. And if the two of us are not enough, I'll bring in another man. Because I will protect you, Sienna, even if I can't do it by myself."

I knew that his inability to protect me on his own couldn't have been easy for him to admit, but that's what he was doing—and I could tell by the troubled look on his face how ashamed he felt that he couldn't.

"Austin, you were terrific today," I said to him.

He looked hard at me.

"Actually, I wasn't, Sienna. I let you down. I apologize for that. I should have known this day would come, just as you predicted it would. I guess I wanted to keep you to myself for as long as I could before the day came that I couldn't. That was selfish of me. You deserve better than that. I'm sorry I allowed my personal feelings for you to get in the way of your safety, because that should have come first. And that's what matters most to me now. If I don't keep you safe, then what the hell kind of man am I?"

Why does he sound as if he's suddenly shutting us down?

"Austin, we got through today together," I said.

"No, we didn't, Sienna. On my watch, you were sexually assaulted. *I'm* the one to blame for that, and because of that, I need to get my shit together. I need to do right by you and not right by me."

"Wait a minute," I said. "Where is this coming from? We were just kissing a moment ago. What's going on with you?"

He lowered his head for a moment before he looked at me.

"While you were on the phone with Harper, telling her what happened to you this afternoon, I realized that my feelings for you are getting in the way of protecting you. And that's something I can't allow to happen. I need to chill out and get my head on straight. I need take a big fucking step back."

"From me?"

"Emotionally, yes."

"And you decided that over a ten-minute phone call with my agent?"

"*I'm not doing my job!*" he said in frustration. "My job isn't to fall in love with you—even though I am, Sienna, so there's that. Instead, my job to take care of you. I'll be doing that going forward."

He's falling in love with me? I thought in bewilderment. *Yes, we have a connection, but it's so new, never once did I believe it was anything more than that. How could I have missed the signs? Why hadn't I taken this more seriously? Was I so blind to love after what Eric had done to me that I couldn't see it when it was unfolding right in front of me?*

I felt a chill overcome me as the ramifications of what Austin was saying hit—and hit hard.

Am I about to lose you? I thought. *I can't lose you. I'm developing feelings for you. You could be the one, for God's sake!*

I needed to face this head on.

"Austin, you *have* been taking care of me," I said. "You can't feel responsible for today. No one could have predicted what took place."

"*You* did."

Christ!

"Maybe I did, but I also said I didn't think it would happen so soon." I cocked my head at him. "What are you doing right now?"

"The right thing."

"For whom?"

"For you. I can't help how I feel about you, but I sure as hell can man up and put those feelings aside so I can properly protect you. That's all this is about. The way I've behaved has distracted both of us, which I can't allow. Because if I keep getting in your head, if I keep sending you flowers, food, and playing music for you...if I keep distracting you, then I'll have failed you, and that's something I could never bear."

He walked over to me and took my face in his hands. His eyes searched mine, and in them, I could see his anguish as my heart started to quicken and my body began to tremble. I'd asked for this moment—*I'd fucking asked for it so that I could honor my contract with Jackson and secure my future*—and yet now it was the very last thing I wanted. If Austin withdrew himself emotionally from me, would he ever find his way back? Was this it for us?

I didn't know. I couldn't be sure, and because I couldn't, my eyes welled with tears.

"Don't do this," I said.

"Listen to me," he said quietly. "What I have to accept is that there are two outcomes here. Either you will be there in the end for me, or you won't. If you are, I'll be the happiest man in the world. If not, at least I'll know in my heart that I did my job by protecting you during one of the most vulnerable moments of your life. I'll also do so knowing that you've secured your future, which I agree is important. I'll still be waiting for you, Sienna. None of that has changed.

But this back and forth I've engaged you in, this distraction I've created—that ends now."

"I'll wait for you," I said. "I will."

He kissed me when I said that, and he did so with such meaning that it felt like a final kiss—a kiss filled with ribbons of longing and the possibilities of goodbye. A kiss he wanted to remember for the rest of his life. A kiss he might tell his son about one day when he looked back on his life and reminisced about the one who got away. With waves of regret washing over me, I took his face in my own hands and kissed him back with everything I had within me, the sting of this moment lancing through me. I had to turn this around. I had to. But how?

"I mean it," I said when our lips parted and we looked into one another's eyes. "I will wait for you, Austin. I'll do it. I just got scared. I didn't realize how deeply you felt. I've gotten this all wrong."

"Sienna, you're at the point in your life where you can't predict the future, because you don't know what the future is going to bring to your door. You have an incredibly exciting life ahead of you. I can see it. In fact, I've felt the first moments of it, and they've been a whirlwind. When your contract is up, you're set to film three movies in a row. You'll be busier than you'd ever imagined. So, please don't make promises you might not be able to keep, because I also have a heart. I know the risks of waiting—I understand them, and I accept them. I will wait for you. But on my own terms—and with full knowledge that you might not be there for me in the end."

I moved to speak, but he stopped me.

"Get some rest," he said. "I've said enough. I'll see my way out, and then I'll be back at seven thirty to pick you up."

And then, just like that, Austin gave me a chaste kiss on

the cheek. He left the living room, and then I heard the door click shut behind him as he left my apartment.

He was gone. I sat down on my sofa, gutted. As the air conditioner rattled and hummed, I felt that a part of me had just been ripped away. I'd been so focused on Jackson, my future, and just getting through each insane new day that I hadn't once considered that Austin's feelings might be as serious as they were. Never once had it even occurred to me that he was falling in love with me.

But he was.

What had felt like a dance to me had been a pursuit for him. And now, at the very moment he felt I needed to be absolutely focused, he was stepping back so he wouldn't be a distraction.

Would he really wait for me? I felt in my heart that he would. But what about me? He was right when he'd said that my life was blowing up. With each passing day, it only seemed to be getting bigger and bigger. When my contract was up, I was in fact scheduled to shoot three movies back to back, which Austin himself had pointed out to me. By mentioning it, had he quietly been telling me that I was about to become too busy for anything other than my career? That a part of him felt I'd never have time for him?

Overcome with grief, I sank back against my sofa and cried as I hadn't in years. They were great, heaving sobs. And eventually, as time ticked by, they turned into cries of resolve.

Potentially the best thing that had ever happened to me had just left my apartment. I could either let this go now and pretend none of it had ever happened, or I could fight for us.

What do you want?

Now that I know this is real—that he's truly falling in love with me—I want to be with him.

Then, you're going to have to reach him. You're going to have to convince him that you'll be there for him in the end. When he picks you up tonight, you need to be armed and ready to make that happen. Austin might be right that you're unable to predict the future, Sienna, but you sure as hell can choose who will be a part of your future. That's the angle he's missing. And that's the angle you must make him see.

20

BY SEVEN THAT EVENING, I was showered, my hair was blown out in thick brown waves that fell down my back, and my face was on. I looked at myself in the bathroom mirror for a moment, noting the steely determination in my eyes, and then left for my bedroom. There, I went to my wardrobe and removed the dress Mimi had sent over for me to wear tonight. Jackson had paid for it.

It was a sleeveless Alexander McQueen draped-shoulder gown in red crepe with a jeweled neckline and a column silhouette—a statement gown that Mimi had said was perfect for editorial, which essentially meant that when Jackson and I were photographed by the paparazzi tonight before we boarded the yacht, this dress would photograph beautifully.

Before I put it on, I admired it. The hem fell straight to the floor. The red was so red that the color literally popped. And perhaps most dramatic of all, a train in the back would fall over my shoulders and stop at my knees.

The gown had set Jackson back a cool twelve grand. As for the shoes I'd wear tonight, the Jimmy Choo glittery platform slingback sandals that were to die for in red—they had cost him another grand.

Since tonight's illusion was all about looking glamorous as we went on our romantic dinner cruise on the Hudson, Jackson had said that he wanted to pay for everything. And like the gentleman he'd become since our disastrous evening at Per Se several weeks ago, he'd done just that.

When I was dressed, I stood before my wardrobe's full-length mirror and studied myself. Years of modeling had done me proud—the ice packs I'd applied to my eyes earlier had done the trick. After my crying jag over the potential loss of Austin, the swelling and the redness were now gone. Instead of looking like the train wreck I'd been for most of the afternoon, I looked better than I had any reason to look. Because despite how glamorous I appeared right now, my gut was nevertheless in knots.

Soon, Austin would arrive to pick me up. And before we left my apartment, I had a few things to say to him. I had to make him understand that I never would have behaved as I had if I'd for one moment known his true feelings for me.

Because I hadn't known.

I'd thought about it all day, and the conclusion I'd come to time and again was the same. Not for one instant had I believed he was falling in love with me, because if I had, that would have been a game changer. It would have caused me to pause. It would have allowed me to reflect. And to believe that he'd meant it when he'd said that he would wait for me.

Ever since Austin had left me this afternoon, I'd searched my heart about whether I was in love with him. In the end, I'd decided that while I certainly felt strongly about him, I wasn't sure if that feeling was love or lust—but that didn't matter. What mattered was not allowing the *potential* for love to slip away from me. From *us*. Now that I knew how he felt about me, I needed to open my heart to the possibilities of love.

And that was huge for me.

Ever since Eric had cheated on me, I'd refused to entertain any kind of romantic advances. Over the years, suitors had come and gone, but Austin...Austin was different from the others.

When I'd first met him, yes, I'd been attracted to his devastating good looks. But because of the walls I'd built around myself since Eric, I knew there had to be something more to Austin, because he'd put major cracks in those walls —and I couldn't ignore it. It was time for me to get over my past and give myself permission to trust in someone else again. I needed to talk with Austin about that when he arrived—even if it was only for a few minutes, since Jackson would be waiting in the car for me with David.

If Austin is even open to talking...

Even if he didn't say a word, I planned on saying plenty to him. I especially needed to correct him when it came to my future. He was right to say that I couldn't predict it, but he was overlooking that I had every right to choose who would be part of my life in the future, despite what it held for me. I had complete control over *that,* and he needed to hear it from me.

At seven-thirty on the dot, my buzzer rang, and I felt a jolt of nerves shoot through me as I buzzed Austin through. I cracked the door open for him, hurried into my bathroom so I could give myself a final swipe of the bold red lipstick that matched my dress and shoes, and dropped the tube into my clutch as I heard Austin enter my apartment and shut the door behind him.

"Coming!" I called. As I turned off the bathroom lights, I

felt butterflies swirl in my stomach. I moved toward the living room. "Austin, before we go, there's something I need to say to you."

But when I entered the living area, it wasn't Austin who stood waiting for me—it was David. Tall, blond, stoic David. And not Austin, which rattled me, because I knew at once that by sending David to get me, Austin already was putting distance between us. Obviously he'd had time to do some thinking on his own, because earlier he'd said that *he* would be the one to retrieve me. And then I wondered. Was Austin even here tonight? Or had he removed himself completely from the equation? Was I now to be protected by other men?

"I'm sorry, David," I said, walking toward him. He was a handsome man in his midthirties with a strong nose, solid jaw, and eyes that were preternaturally green. He was wearing a fitted black suit that complimented his muscular physique. "Austin said he'd pick me up tonight. I thought you were him."

"Austin's in the car with Jackson, Miss Jones. He sent me up."

So, he is here. He just didn't want to be alone with me.

"It's Sienna," I said, trying not to let my disappointment show.

"Sienna it is. Look, before we leave, I wanted to tell you how sorry I am about what happened to you today."

"I appreciate that," I said to him.

"I also want you to know that I'm now officially part of your security detail, so we'll get you through these next several months. We'll do our best to protect you. If we feel that two men aren't enough, then we'll bring in another man. And so forth. We'll have your back."

Why isn't he saying Austin's name? Why isn't it "Austin and I will protect you"? What's going on here?

"David, does that 'we' include Austin?"

"I'm not sure," he said. "He's sorting that out now, because Jackson also needs protection. He said that he'll decide in the morning whether he'll be leading Jackson's team or yours."

I couldn't believe it. Did Austin really believe he couldn't do his best to protect me if he felt that he was distracting me? Clearly he did—and that frustrated the hell out of me.

"We should go," I said. "Jackson hates waiting for me. Is anyone lurking outside my building?"

"We're clear," he said. "The paparazzi will be waiting for you and Jackson at the marina, as expected."

"Can't wait for that," I said sarcastically.

"I've seen you in action, Sienna. You'll be fine."

"I'm not so sure about that," I said. "Especially given the questions they're about to hurl my way, David. Today, I was groped in public at the very moment the nation is discussing sexual assault. And those people? They're going to be all over that."

WHEN WE LEFT MY APARTMENT, the sun had already dipped below the skyline, but it was still light outside. Given the dramatic way I was dressed, several people on the sidewalk recognized me before David hastily opened the limousine's back door so I could step inside. As I did so, I heard a few people call out my name as I sat next Jackson, who looked at me in concern as David shut my door and got into the front seat next to Austin, who was driving. I looked at him in the rearview mirror, hoping to catch his gaze, but he was wearing sunglasses, so I couldn't tell where he was looking.

Jackson took my hand and squeezed it. "Are you OK?" he asked.

"I'm good," I said.

"Define 'good' for me."

"Look, today was rough, but Austin got me through it. That's what matters."

"You were groped by a stranger, Sienna," Austin said. "We did our best, but to be honest, today didn't go well at all."

"I'm alive and breathing, aren't I?" I snapped at him.

"Whoa..." Jackson said.

Sienna, you can't let your frustration show. Get it together.

"I'm sorry," I said. "Everyone, please meet Evil Sienna. She'll go away after a moment or two—I promise."

"You have every reason to be upset," Jackson said.

I do, Jackson. And for a whole shitload of reasons I can't even tell you.

"I saw the photos of what that man did to you," he said. "I'm sorry for all of it. You deserve better than that."

"Let's not talk about it," I said as Austin eased into traffic. "Because if we do, we'll have to stop at a bar so I can get a drink."

"I'd buy you one," Jackson said.

I smiled at him when he said that, because I knew he would. "I appreciate that, Jackson, especially since I know you aren't joking." I looked forward. "I guess the one thing I would like to know is whether that son of a bitch has been arrested. Because nobody's told me if that's the case. Austin, do you know if he was? And if you do know, then why don't I know?"

Apparently I couldn't help myself. I was so angry with him for not coming up to my apartment to get me—thus blowing any chance I might have had to talk with him alone

—I couldn't keep the anger I felt out of my voice. He heard it, and he lifted his face to the rearview.

"Harper didn't call you?"

"She called me once today, when you were talking me down in my apartment. Should I have heard from her again?"

"Yes," he said. "You should have heard from her. She told me that she was going to call you. The crowd came through for you. They detained him. The police now have him under arrest."

"Good to know," I said.

"I thought you *did* know," he said.

"I didn't. But...whatever. What's going to happen to him?"

"That'll be up to a judge, but he'll pay. We'll make sure of it. Everything was caught on video."

"I'm surprised Harper didn't call you," Jackson remarked.

I removed my cell from my clutch and switched it on. "Maybe she did," I said. "When Austin left, I was so undone by everything that happened today that I crashed on the sofa for a couple of hours. I might have missed her call." I checked my messages, and sure enough, there was one from Harper. "She called," I said as I listened to her message. "And it was about him. Sorry, I didn't think to check it earlier. That's on me, everyone."

"Sienna, are you sure you want to go through with tonight? We don't have to," Jackson said.

I was being unprofessional. I needed to get myself in line —and fast. I took a breath, settled down, and patted Jackson's knee.

"I've got to go," I said. "If I don't, that will send a clear message to the world that I've allowed that man to beat me down, which is something I won't have—and not just for me. I need to stand up and be strong so I can send out a clear message to every woman out there that all of us are united, and that all of us refuse to let men like him continue to get away with sexual assault. I can't let him win, Jackson."

"He won't win," Jackson said. "We'll see to it. And when you take him to court, *I'll* throw money at the best attorney we can find."

"You're the best," I said.

"Change of subject?" he proposed.

I could tell by the light tone of his voice that he sensed I didn't want to talk about any of this, so I gave him an affectionate smile.

"Did I mention that you're the best?" I asked.

"You might have..."

"I'd love a change of subject," I said as I took his hand in mine.

"I can do that. Now, look, if this means anything to you, I've never seen you looking quite as beautiful as you do tonight. The dress you're wearing is seriously off the charts."

"Thank you," I said. "And by the way, thanks for paying for it."

"My pleasure."

"My shoes are pretty killer," I said as I showed them to him.

"Not to mention your legs."

"You like my legs?"

"You've got some serious legs on you, Jones."

"How do the boobs look?"

He admired them for a moment.

"Let's just say that if I were straight, I'd totally do you."

"Best news of the day."

When a silence passed between us, I rested my head on his shoulder, glad that we had become friends.

"Thanks for saying all the right things, Jackson," I said after a moment.

"I mean everything, Sienna."

"I know you do—that's why it's so easy to be fake in love with you."

"Now, there's a compliment," he said.

"You deserve it."

"Feeling better?" he asked.

"Much." I lifted my head off his shoulder and turned to him. "But enough about me, because look at *you* in your black suit! You're even wearing a tie that matches the color of my dress. You look pretty hot tonight, Mr. Cruise, if I do say so myself."

"I'm a T-shirt-and-jeans kind of guy," he said. "Trust me, I had some help."

"Mimi?"

When I said that, his face flushed.

"No, not Mimi," he said. "Somebody else."

Was it the pilot he'd been caught kissing? The man whose name I didn't know but who Jackson said he might be in love with? Or was it some other man? By not giving me a name, I knew it had to be one or the other.

I wouldn't press him about that now. But I would on the yacht.

"Whatever the case," I said to him. "You look like the movie star you are. Lucky me that I get to have you at my side tonight."

"You're a good friend, Sienna."

"I'm about to become an even better one."

He furrowed his brow at me. "What does that mean?" he asked.

I gave him a quick peck on the cheek.

"You'll see…"

MANHATTAN'S NORTH Cove Marina was located along the Hudson at 250 Vesey Street, not far from One World Trade Center, which soared tall in the sky behind it. With the fiery setting sun glinting off its countless windows, at that moment the building looked especially alive to me, as if it were fiercely making its presence known for all the world to see.

After the horror of 9/11, it had become this city's exclamation point.

When Austin dropped the car at the Brookfield Curbside Valet on Liberty Street, the rest of us put on our sunglasses and got out of the car. On the pavement, I lifted my hair up and over my shoulders and then I adjusted my gown as I waited for Austin to turn to catch a glimpse of me —to see why Jackson had complimented me in the car—but he didn't.

Or at least I thought he didn't.

Given the dark aviator sunglasses covering his eyes, if he *had* sized me up, he'd sure as hell been subtle in doing so, which disappointed the hell out of me. Because I hadn't dressed just for Jackson tonight—I'd also dressed for Austin, who was behaving as if I barely existed.

I will *get through to you*, I thought. *We will talk, Austin, despite whatever guard you're throwing up to make sure that won't happen.*

Together, the four of us walked the short distance to the marina, where the paps would be waiting for us. But before that happened, in our brief moment of anonymity, I took in the sights while I could.

The marina was lovely, filled with many public spaces to sit and relax, a boardwalk on which to stroll, restaurants in which to dine, and a mix of boats bobbing at their docks amid the salty smells of the Hudson's muddy waters.

Some of the crafts were small, but overwhelmingly, the others were huge and impressive, a blatant show of luxury, money, and power by people who lived lives I'd never lived. Everything I'd experienced since I'd been with Jackson had been so foreign to me that I still marveled at how ridiculously over the top the superrich lived. As close to it as I was because of Jackson's high-flying lifestyle, I still felt like the girl from Dubuque, Iowa. I was an outsider who'd been given the privilege of looking in before I'd eventually be cast out.

And so I had to wonder—what would my life be like when the contract ended and Jackson was no longer part of my life, at least in a fake romance kind of way? I wasn't sure, because Austin had been partly right: when it came to predicting my future, I didn't know if I would have a successful career. I didn't know how big or small it would become. Harper had set me up for success by nailing down those movies for me, but what if they weren't successful? Or what if they were *huge* successes? That was the unknown I faced going forward—and it had nothing to do with choosing whom I wanted in my life.

And that's what Austin needs to understand.

"Penny for your thoughts," Jackson said as he reached for my hand.

Just a penny? I thought. *Considering the shit I'm going through with Austin, today's rate is more like a million, Jackson...*

Austin was walking in front of us while David had the

rear. As we passed dozens of people on the boardwalk, several glanced our way—likely because of the way we were dressed—but so far, people were either being respectful, or somehow we were flying under the radar. I knew that wouldn't last for long, so I enjoyed it while I could.

I didn't want to tell Jackson that I'd been thinking what my life looked like without him in it, so I deflected.

"I was actually wondering which one of those beastly yachts is ours."

"I'm not sure," he said. "Austin, do you know?"

"It's that one over there," he said, pointing ahead of us. "See the paps standing near it? They might as well be our compass."

"I see them," I said. "But it appears they haven't seen us yet. Shouldn't someone be here to greet us?"

"A man is coming our way now," Austin said. "Do you see him? The older gentleman in the white captain's suit? He just spotted us. What I need you two to do for me now is get ready for the pending onslaught."

"Sienna, before that happens, take a moment and look at the yacht before we board it," Jackson said. "Because that motherfucker is insane."

It was.

"It's huge," he said.

"It's a goddamned mountain," I agreed. "But look how pretty it is."

"Forget how pretty it is," he said. "When you and I are photographed in front of it, people are going to think I'm overcompensating for something."

I laughed when he said that and ribbed him. "Oh, they will not. They've been lusting after that infamous package of yours for years, and you know it. I mean, on an IMAX screen alone, your package is, like...what? Fifty by seventy feet or

something? Imagine the moist panties and the host of erec-
tions you've left in your wake over the years. Don't give it
another thought."

"Fifty by seventy feet," he said. "Why do I feel weirdly
aroused right now?"

"And why do *I* feel weirdly aroused?" I admitted. "What
are we? A couple of size queens?"

"We're nothing of the sort," Jackson said quickly. Maybe
a little too quickly.

I giggled and squeezed his hand as I admired the yacht
Mimi had secured for us. From what Harper had told me, it
was 120 feet long, it was called the *Nameless*, and while its
underbelly was black, the top of it was bright white and
glowed in the waves of swirling lights that shone upon it.
There appeared to be four main decks, and on the top one
sat a shiny black helicopter.

Who even owns something like this? I wondered.

As we neared the boat, I heard one woman we passed
say to her friend, "Holy mother of God—that's Jackson
Cruise!"

"Hold my hand tightly," Jackson said to me. "Don't let go
of it. Tonight isn't going to be what you experienced earlier
today. I promise you that, Sienna. I've got you, and so do
Austin and David."

"It *is* him!" I heard the woman say as we moved past her.
"And that's Sienna Jones!"

When our cover was blown, people on the boardwalk
started to pull out their cell phones and point them at us as
recognition struck. I felt a chill rush through me, the sting of
what had happened to me only hours ago, and I couldn't
help but wonder if something just as awful would happen to
me again. With Austin, David, and Jackson surrounding me,
I thought it was unlikely. But I worried. What had happened

earlier was still too fresh. I could still feel that man's hands on my breasts even now as we walked toward the yacht. What he'd done to me was something that wouldn't be leaving me simply and easily. The man had assaulted me, and by doing so, I knew that he hadn't just become an unwanted part of my life, but by doing what he'd done to me, that he'd also given me a voice that I must publicly use against him and people like him.

Please get me through this, I thought.

"We move forward," Austin said. "Our endgame is the paps. You'll give them one minute to photograph you, and when I think it's enough, we'll get both of you safely onto the yacht."

"Agreed," Jackson said.

But the swarms of people surrounding us didn't give a damn what Austin had in mind. They swooped in, got in front of us, and started to either take photos of us or film us as we came upon the yacht's captain. He was a groomed, sharp-looking man in his midsixties with white hair and a white, closely cropped beard. As he shook hands with Austin, he reminded me of CNN's Wolf Blitzer.

"Captain Ward?" Austin asked.

"Yes, that's me."

"Austin Black."

"Good to meet you, Austin," the captain said as people continued to press closer to Jackson and me.

Riddled with anxiety, I did my best to fake my feelings. I wore a face that said I was happy, in love, and eager for my dinner date with Jackson, knowing full well that the majority of the photos being taken of us now would soon be shared on social media.

Power through this, I thought. *Don't you dare let them see for a moment how you really feel...*

"What do you need from me right now?" the captain asked Austin.

"If you'd lead us to the paparazzi, Jackson and Sienna will pause for photographs. We will give them only a moment, because we aren't going to allow them to press Sienna about what happened to her today. She will smile at Jackson's side, but she will not answer them. When I nod at you, I need you to get us onto that yacht."

Who's to say I won't answer them, Austin? I wondered.

"Done," the man said. "Follow me before this turns into something none of us want. We're not far from the yacht."

"We need to make this quick and dirty," Austin said.

"I'll make that happen," the captain said.

When we came upon the paps, Jackson and I were overcome by flashing lights. Smiling, we stood as one before the questions began in earnest, all of which were focused on me.

"Sienna, what is your response to what happened to you today?"

"Sienna, the man who accosted you has been arrested. What do you have to say to him?"

"Sienna, you were sexually assaulted today. Would you please share with the world how you're feeling now?"

That was exactly the kind of question I'd been seeking, so I chose to address the reporter. I turned to her.

"As anyone who has been sexually assaulted, today has been difficult. To get through it, I drew on the strength of all of the brave women and men who have recently come out to share with the world their own experiences. Did I ever think this would happen to me? Never. Did any of those who came before me think it would ever happen to them? Not once. But it did, and I stand united with them in love and in solidarity. What happened to me today will not define me, but it will inform me, and I promise you that it will strengthen me. I thank God for the women and men who have come forward with their stories of sexual assault. They have selfishly put their reputations on the line in an effort to shed light on an ugly truth that must be told. I want to give my profound thanks to them for getting me through today, because they did. My promise to them and to you is this— my voice joins theirs. And together? As more voices rise up to be heard? We will create change."

When I said that, the cameras flashed rapidly as Jackson gripped my hand in a show of support.

"Sienna, please...turn to the left. Let the world see how beautiful and strong you are tonight."

I rather liked that question, so I did turn to my left. And I did so with Jackson at my side. With every turn we were asked to take, I made certain that Jackson turned with me until I saw Austin catch Jackson's eye.

And that was that.

Jackson held up a hand, we thanked everyone, and with the captain leading the way, we boarded the yacht together —with Austin and David joining us for the ride.

21

___

FOR THE NEXT HOUR, Jackson and I explored the yacht together, eventually finding ourselves on the third deck, which offered the best views of Manhattan.

It was twilight. With Jackson at my side, I stood at the railing and allowed the cool breeze to wash over me as the yacht traveled upriver. It was a welcome relief after what had been a searing day in the city—in more ways than one. With my dress fluttering around me and my hair lifting off my shoulders, for the first time that day I felt a sense of calm. Seeing Manhattan ablaze in lights like this was as heady as it was amazing.

"You're quiet," Jackson said to me.

"Am I?" I said. "I'm sorry. I'm just enjoying the show right now. Look at how beautiful the city is like this. And there's no noise. No photographers. Nobody shouting questions at us. I get to enjoy tonight and this yacht with my friend—which is you, Jackson. Together we get to admire a city I've come to love from a perspective I've never seen before. It's kind of perfect."

"I'm glad you're enjoying yourself, Sienna. You deserve it after today."

I looked over at him as I wrapped an arm around his waist.

"How about you?" I asked. "How are you holding up?"

"Me?" he asked with a shrug. "I'm OK."

"Just OK?"

"Yeah...I mean, the shoot is going well. You've been great throughout all of this. And the noise surrounding my sexuality seems to have ended. I guess this whole fake-relationship thing worked. Good for me."

When he said that last part, it sounded almost sarcastic to me.

"Are you happy about that?" I asked.

He looked out at the water. "In some ways I am. In others, I'm not."

"Jackson, if you need someone to confide in, I'm always here for you. And I'd never betray you."

"That's the thing about you, Sienna," he said as he looked at me. "I know you wouldn't."

I took hold of his arm and squeezed it. "Look, how about if we have a martini together and chill out in those chairs behind us. We're alone now—it's just the two of us. We can talk freely here. Dinner will be different. There will be waiters around us."

"And less privacy?"

"Exactly," I said.

"I'm down for a martini," he said.

"Good, because I'd love to have one."

"Let me use the phone to order them," he said as we left the rail and moved toward the two deck chairs that had been set out for us. Between them was a table, on which was the phone to call the staff. He took my hand and helped me into my seat before he picked up the receiver and ordered our drinks. "Five minutes," he said as he hung up the phone. "Let's enjoy the view in the meantime."

OVER THE NEXT HOUR, Jackson and I sipped our martinis and enjoyed each other's company. Before I went there with him, I wanted him to feel relaxed and safe with me, so we just started to talk about everything and anything.

He shared more of his Hollywood stories with me, which ranged from the downright racy to the outrageously hilarious. He was curious about what it was like to be a model, so I shared a few priceless stories of my own, including the time I'd been ambushed with an unexpected waxing before a Victoria's Secret show—and that it hadn't been just me. It had been all the models. When we'd arrived before the show, we'd been asked to disrobe and lie on yoga mats scattered around a large and otherwise empty room. And then, before I knew it, women in white surgical jackets arrived, and it became a waxing free-for-all.

"Imagine the screams!" I said to him. "I felt like I was in a Fellini movie."

"I can't believe they sprang that on all of you," he said with a laugh. "And with zero privacy."

"In the modeling world, you get used to the no-privacy thing," I said. "Naked bodies everywhere. But the group waxing thing? The suddenly no-hair-down-there thing? That shit was just bizarre. Some of the girls had done the show before, so it was nothing new to them. But since that was my first and last show, it sure as hell was new to me."

"Women get the raw end of the stick," he said as he finished his drink. "I mean, I'm down with keeping everything groomed down there, but to rip it out with hot wax? That just sounds like torture to me."

"It *is* torture," I said. "And you're kind to admit that men do have it easier. Men, for instance, don't have Aunt Flow visiting them every month. They don't have to push out a child. Or feed that child when it's hungry. Or go through menopause later in life." I finished my own drink. "The list is endless."

"Shall we salute to the bravery of your kind with another drink?"

"Please, let's."

My aim wasn't to get Jackson drunk—I already knew what *that* looked like. Instead, my aim was to get him to a point where he'd be willing to let down his formidable guard and be open with me. If I could get him there, then I could set into motion something that might offer Jackson everything he was denying himself.

Love.

When the waiter left us with our second round of martinis, we touched glasses and took a quick sip. I waited until I was certain we were alone before I spoke.

"So...who dressed you tonight?" I asked. "You wouldn't say in the car, but whoever it was nailed it. You seriously look good."

"You think?"

"I know."

"And you also know it was another man, don't you?"

"Am I that obvious?" I asked.

"In the most endearing of ways, yes. But it's OK. I was weighing out whether to talk to you about him tonight, anyway. To be honest, I've got no one to talk to when it comes to this. If I said anything to Mimi, she'd just warn me away from him and tell me to think about my career.

Austin's instinct would be to protect me—in whatever form that might take, which is unpredictable. What I need is someone who's just willing to listen to me."

"I think you found your girl, Jackson."

"I know I have—and I appreciate it more than you know, Sienna. Because I'm really struggling right now."

"You are?" I asked in surprise.

"Yeah," he said. "I am."

"Jackson, I'm so sorry. You should have come to me sooner. You should never feel that you are isolated. Who's the guy?" I asked.

"His name is Ash," he said.

"Is he the man you kissed on the plane?"

"Yes. We've been seeing each other on the sly for about eight months now. When it comes to Austin...I know you don't know this about him, but he's kind of brilliant when it comes to doing things undercover."

"A side of him I've never seen," I said.

"It's true. He got Ash into my apartment today. It was the first time we'd seen each other since that kiss of ours went public. And guess what?"

"What?"

"Seeing him again confirmed everything I was trying *not* to feel before we had to separate because of my career. But being with him today, just when I thought I was about to lose him? Fuck it. I'm in love with him, Sienna, and it took the possibility of losing him for me to even realize that I was. I need some guidance here. Have you ever been in a situation even remotely like this before?"

As realization struck, it occurred to me that I was in that exact situation right now. I closed my eyes as my heartbeat quickened.

I've been in denial, I thought. *After what Eric did to me, I never wanted to put myself in the position of being hurt again. And because of that, I didn't want to recognize what was right in front of me. And that's love. I've tried my best to call it a million other things, but somehow I've fallen in love with Austin. I can try to convince myself that it's something else, but that's what it is. That's what I've been feeling: love.*

In earnest, I turned to Jackson.

"If you were to look back on your relationship with Ash, how long were you seeing him before you think you fell in love with him?"

"I don't believe in love at first sight," he said. "That's for fucking sure. But when it came to Ash, I don't know why, but it didn't take me long to feel just that. Looking back, I think we had been seeing one another for only a month or so when I first started to have those feelings for him."

"Only a month?"

"About that," he said. "I know it sounds ridiculous to feel that way after such a brief period of time, but I fell in love with him quickly. He's that great. He's that smart, kind, sexy, funny, loving—everything. Being with him has been powerful."

What the hell have I been doing?

"Look, Sienna—I've been with a lot of men in my life, but there's something about Ash that's special. He gets me. He's exactly the kind of person I want to spend the rest of my life with, but I can't. And I hate that I can't. I've tried my best to fake it through this 'relationship' of ours, but it's getting harder and harder to do. You want to know why?"

I already knew why, but I wanted to hear him say it himself. "Why?" I asked.

"It's because I feel like a fucking fraud," he said, his eyes becoming bright. "Ash is it for me—he's the one—and yet because of my fame and my career, I can't allow him fully into my life. I'm angry about that. And it's breaking my heart that I can't."

I reached out and held his free hand.

"Have you told him that?"

"I did. We made love this afternoon. And when we did, I told him I was in love with him. That's when things got emotional between us...but in a good way. We held each other, just soaked each other in. But when he wanted to talk about our future, that's where I disappointed him."

"How?"

"Ash has been out of the closet since he was nineteen. He understands why he feels I can't come out, but in the end, he also said that if I don't, what's the point of putting ourselves through this? Was he just someone to be put away? To be seen in quiet and on the side? I told him he wasn't, so what now? He's given me one month to get my shit together. He said that for the sake of his own heart, he'd have to walk away, because it would be the right thing to do for both of us."

"Let me ask you a question," I said.

"Please, ask away. I need whatever kind of insight I can get from you."

"What does your life look like without him in it?" I asked. "If you broke up right now, what does it *feel* like without him in it?"

"Fucking bleak," he said. "What if you were in my situation, Sienna? What would your life look like if you were in my shoes?"

"The same," I said.

Because it already does.

"Right?" he said.

"Jackson, I need you to listen to me now."

"I know what you're going to say."

"You probably do, but are you going to listen to me or not?"

"I'll listen."

"Good, because ever since I learned that you're gay and that there was this mystery man on the side, I've been thinking about your situation. I've turned it over in my head time and again, and I still come down to one thing."

"What's that?" he asked.

"What if you did come out? What if you owned who you are? What if you set an example for people who are struggling with the same issues you're struggling with? What if you skewered the stereotypes that continue to plague gay men? Everyone views you as this butch alpha male, which you are. The fact that you're gay changes none of that, because that *is* who you are. I mean, you strap yourself to fucking *planes*, Jackson. Show me how many straight men would get off on that in ways that you've told me *you* do! You once told me that you didn't want to come out because you feared it would harm your legacy. But here's what I think you've missed—what if your legacy is greater than the movies you've made? What if it's also about being a role model and a badass game changer?"

He didn't answer me—and for the first time since I'd been talking to him about his sexuality, he also didn't shut me down, which was a gold-star win for me. So, I just seized the moment and charged forward.

"Listen to me now. What if your legacy isn't what you originally thought it was? What if you were put on this earth to become a celebrity for a reason? What if your life is to be remembered not just for the movies you've made but also for becoming a trailblazer? Someone people look up to? Someone who has saved other people's lives because they look up to you? Have you considered any of that?"

He looked shell-shocked when I said that.

"No," he said. "Not like that."

"Fair enough," I said. "Because I get it—this is over-whelming for you. So, my best advice is that you rethink the kind of legacy you *could* leave behind as opposed to the false, unspoken legacy you were thinking of leaving behind before Ash came into your life. Is that what you want? Is hiding behind a curtain how you want to leave this earth? And then there's Ash. Since you're in love with him, you must also consider that you might never find a man like him again. I heard the love and conviction in your voice when you told me all the reasons why you love him, Jackson. I felt all of it to my core. What we both know at this point in our lives is that men like Ash don't come around often, do they? No, they don't. Men like them are fucking *rare*. And just so you know, here's some breaking news I've only shared with Julia, who is my best friend—but since I can see you and I becoming great, lifelong friends, I'll come clean with you. I'm in the same situation you're in right now."

When I revealed that to him, his eyes widened.

"You are? With whom?"

"It's still fresh and personal," I said. "Unlike you, his name is not something I'm ready to share with anyone just yet. But when I am, I'll share it with you first in honor of how open, honest, and trusting you've been with me tonight. I've got a lot on my mind right now, but our conversation tonight made one thing very clear to me. I'm also in love with someone...someone I've been pushing away from me because I'm contractually bound to you. If I can, I plan to correct that. So, please...wish me well with that."

"Sienna, I had no idea."

"Before our conversation tonight, neither did I, Jackson. But after listening to what you're going through, I knew that in a similar way, I'm going through the same thing. I'm in love with someone who is actively distancing himself from me right now because I keep throwing up walls. I need to fix that...although I'm not sure how."

"We can talk about it if you want," he said.

"Tonight isn't about me," I said. "Tonight needs to be about you, because you're the one who's been handed a deadline. We both know that you have two choices: either you come out and allow Ash to be part of your life, or you continue to focus on your career and lose him in the process. You have worked hard to get where you are at this point in your life. I understand your fear. But I will always champion real love first, which I believe is what you feel for him. Is it?"

"Yes," he said, "it is."

"And you're certain he feels the same for you?"

"I know he does."

"If you were to come out, where do you see each other ten years from now?"

"That's easy," he said. "I've already thought about it. I see us building a wonderful home together, traveling the world together, having children together through a surrogate, and enjoying our lives with one another."

"Where is your career in that answer, Jackson?"

That stopped him. When he didn't answer me—when he looked as if he were at a loss for words—I had to wonder if he'd finally heard me.

22

THE NEXT MORNING, after a fitful sleep in which I obsessed over how I could get Austin alone so I could tell him how I felt about him, David picked me up at eleven sharp to drive me to CAA. There, I was to meet with Harper, Mimi, Jackson, and Austin to discuss what plans Austin had for me going forward when it came to my security detail.

Would he completely remove himself from my life so he would no longer be a "distraction" to me? I was betting on it.

But I wasn't about to go down without a fight.

I wanted to look my best when I walked into Harper's office, so I'd spent my morning going all out to make certain that happened. Before I made coffee, I washed my face in the bathroom sink and applied a facial masque that would shrink my pores and hydrate my skin.

While the masque set, I'd made coffee and went to my computer to see how the press had covered my evening with Jackson. While a few stories covered the statement I'd made about being sexually assaulted, too many other stories salaciously showed photo and photo of me being groped, with no mention of the statement I'd made before we'd boarded the yacht. Disgusted and disappointed, I turned off my computer, rinsed off the masque, and selected a whole host of potent elixirs to get my skin looking as fresh and as radiant as possible.

They worked.

In the shower, I'd used an exfoliating scrub over my entire body. For my hair, I'd gone with Aveda's strongest conditioner—their Deep Remedy line. The result? Soft, incredibly shiny hair that I decided to flatiron and wear in a high ponytail.

Since I didn't want to look like I wasn't trying too hard, I kept my makeup fresh and natural, with the exception of my eyes. Since something needed to pop, I applied mink eyelashes to them, which was just enough to create a bit of drama. The whole point of my look was city chic, so I chose a pair of Prada cropped shantung pants in black, a white jersey top that clung to my curves, and a classic pair of black patent-leather pumps.

At just about the time David would arrive to pick me up, I stood before my wardrobe's mirror and assessed myself, turning this way and that. I checked my face and my hair— and then my ass and my tits. I'd chosen not to wear a bra, and right now, with my nipples on full show...

I also wasn't regretting it.

～

"SIENNA," Julia said in greeting when I approached her desk. She stood to give me a hug. "Good lord, you look amazing."

"There's a reason why—and you and I need to talk soon so I can *tell* you why. I've been so busy these past several days that I haven't had a moment to call you, and I apologize for that. I would have told you what I've been needing to tell you sooner if I could have."

"What are you talking about?" she asked.

"To be revealed—sooner rather than later. You're not going to be happy with me, so plan on my plying you with enough vodka to make sure you see things from my point of view."

"Why are you talking in code?" she asked. And then, as it hit her, I watched her eyes widen in disbelief. "This isn't about what I think it's about, is it?" she asked under her breath. "Tell me this isn't about Austin. What have you done?"

"I don't know. I might have fallen in love with him or something."

"Fallen in love?"

"Or something."

"Have you slept with him?"

"Kind of did that, too."

"Sienna, what were you thinking?" she asked in a hushed tone. "We talked about this."

"We did," I said, my own voice low. "What you don't know is that he aggressively came after me. I tried my best to shut him down, and then, when he got me alone, my lady parts got the best of me. And here's the irony: now he's shutting *me* down because he doesn't want to be a distraction when it comes to keeping me safe. My life is a mess right now, Julia—and that's just a taste of the things we need to talk about. Is Harper ready to see me?"

"First, when am *I* going to see *you*?"

"You're in charge of my schedule," I said. "Choose a night that I'm free, and I'll either come to you, or you can come to me."

In frustration, she sat down at her computer, pulled up

my schedule, and then looked up at me. "Turns out you're free tonight."

"OK. So, will it be my slum digs or your fab apartment?"

"With the paps going bonkers over you now, it would be easier if I came to you."

"How does eight o'clock sound?"

"Fine," she said. "Do you need me to bring anything?"

"Maybe a bottle of the Goose," I said. "And please, feel free to buy the biggest bottle you can find."

"I can't believe you allowed this to happen," she said, standing up and coming around her desk to bring me to Harper's office. "And I'm not going to lie to you—I'm disappointed in you."

"Julia, I'm in love," I said. "Try not to be disappointed, because you know I must be feeling something pretty substantial for that to have happened."

"Especially after Eric," she said as she looked at me. "I get it. But don't you dare let this get in the way of your future, Sienna."

"I don't plan to. I promise you that. Now, look," I said, "we'll discuss everything tonight. But right now I have to focus on being my best when I walk into Harper's office. Are the boys here yet?"

"All of them are in there," she said, "including Mimi."

I hoisted up my boobs, and when I did so, Julia looked nakedly at them.

"You're not wearing a bra."

"I'm not."

"Well, that's pretty racy."

"Sometimes one needs to be. But don't worry—I plan to play it cool." I arched an eyebrow at her. "Shall we?"

~

"Sienna!" Harper said when Julia opened the door for me. I stepped into Harper's lavish office. With a quick glance around the room, I saw that Jackson and Mimi had taken the sofa to the right, while Austin was sitting in a chair that had been centered at the end of the two sofas. He was facing me. I looked straight at him as Harper came over to me, and as I did, I saw his gaze sweep over my body as she embraced me. Austin totally clocked my breasts before he glanced away again.

Was that lust I just saw in your eyes, Austin? I believe it was...

"How are you, love?" Harper said in my ear. "Yesterday was pure hell for you. I've been beyond worried about you."

"I'm good," I said, hugging her back. I felt her love for me in her embrace, and I made sure she felt my own for her. "I'm really happy to see you," I said.

She held my hands and took a step away from me. "You look stunning," she said. "I don't know how you're doing it, but coming in here looking like this gives me hope that you really are weathering the storm. You've always been strong, my love. And tough. I'll forever admire you for that—and particularly for the statement you made to the press last night. It was heartfelt, meaningful, and spoke to the moment. I'm proud of you."

"As am I," Mimi said as she stood and came over to me. "Sienna knows that she needs to be tough if she's going to be in this business. And just look at her now—stronger than ever. Sienna, you look like the star that you are. After everything you went through yesterday, here you arrive looking flawless. Those pants!" she said. "Sublime slender sticks! And then there's your top, which is screaming red-light district to me right now. *So* hot. *So* beyond! I love it!"

"Stop coming on to my client, Mimi," Harper said. "It's grotesque."

"I am not coming on to Sienna, Harper. Like you, I'm merely admiring her."

"Like a cat admires a bowl of milk?"

"Please," she said as she stood before her former lover. "As you well know, Harper, women chase *me*. It's never been the other way around."

"And yet some regret it."

"That's on you, darling. Now beg off."

In her bright-white power suit, Mimi practically charged at me. As we exchanged a quick hug and she showered me with more compliments, I heard Harper clear her throat before Mimi and I broke away from each other.

"I mean it," Mimi said. "You look fantastic."

"Thank you," I said. "I appreciate that, Mimi."

"What you've accomplished is no small feat, Sienna," she said. "I mean, just look at the blizzard you and Jackson have endured since all this began. I don't know how you two have kept it together, but you have—and it's worked. The heat is off Jackson, and you're about to become the star you've always wanted to become. I call that a win-win!"

"Sienna is already a star, Mimi," Harper said, her arms crossed. "Now, it's my job to turn her into an icon."

"An *icon*?" I said.

"We'll get you there, my dear—just you watch."

"You know what, Harper?" Mimi said.

"Do I dare ask, Mimi?"

"You should, because I agree. Like Jackson, Sienna's got that 'it' thing going for her. She's a riddle packaged in a mystery. Jackson and I have discussed it ourselves. That said, what I *still* can't understand for the life of me is why it's taken you so long to bring her to this moment. But you finally did, so good on you, I guess."

Before Harper could let her have it, Mimi said, "Sienna, I wanted to tell you personally that we all appreciate everything you've done for Jackson, just as I'm sure that *you* appreciate everything Jackson has done for your career, which is substantial. We feel that way, don't we, Jackson?"

"Mimi, Sienna was on the verge of hitting it big before she even entered my life," Jackson said with a frustrated sigh from the sofa. "So, let's get that straight, OK? She's helped me more than I've helped her."

Mimi's eyes nearly crossed before she said, "Of course!"

"And we've since become friends, Mimi," Jackson said. "Close friends."

"An added benefit if there ever was one," she said. "Wouldn't you agree, Sienna? I mean, my goodness! To be friends with Jackson Cruise!"

"We have become friends, Mimi, and our friendship is real. What Jackson and I have come to feel for one another goes beyond our careers. We might fake our relationship for the masses, but in the meantime, we've since developed a deep friendship that I cherish."

"Well, how positively uplifting!" she said. "And so rewarding. And may I say, how completely unexpected!"

"Quit it with the showbiz, Mimi," Harper said. "Sienna's telling the truth."

"Harper, why do you always feel that I'm being disingenuous?"

"Maybe because I know you? But...whatever. Let's just leave it there, because Jackson has a shoot later today, and time is short. We need to nail down what Austin has in mind when it comes to firming up Sienna's security detail, which is necessary. So, why don't you take your seat next to Jackson, Sienna and I will sit down across from you, and we'll all turn to Austin for his advice?"

When we did, Harper looked at Austin.

"What are you recommending?" she asked.

The moment she said that, my stomach tensed, even though I already knew what he'd decided. He was going to put even more distance between us.

"What I recommend is that I continue to lead Jackson's detail," he said. "When it's Jackson and Sienna out together, I'll bring in other men to assist me in protecting them."

"Who do you have in mind?" Jackson asked.

"David and Brian," he said. "If I feel we need more, I'll also bring in Adam."

"So, you have David and Brian in mind for Sienna?" Mimi asked.

"When it comes to protecting Sienna, David will take over the lead for me, and he'll be joined by Brian, who everyone but Sienna knows is a former Navy SEAL. He's an absolute professional. He and David will see to Sienna's safety until the contract ends. They are among the very best of my team, and I know with certainty they'll protect Sienna going forward." At that moment, he finally looked at me. "Because that's as important to me as it is to everyone else in this room."

As I looked into his eyes, I sensed that he *did* feel this was the best he could do for me. He wanted to keep us apart so I wouldn't be distracted by him—and him by me—while two other men I felt nothing for protected me. To be fair to him, his decision was practical on paper—but it still frustrated the hell out of me, if only because I wasn't sure that was all there was to it. Was his insistence to throw up walls between us just about my safety? Or was it also about protecting his own heart—especially since he didn't know how I felt about him? Did he feel that at the end of this, I'd be too big a star to even consider having a life with him? If that were the case, I wanted to scream at the very idea of it.

Jackson nodded at Austin. "Thanks, Austin," he said.

"My pleasure. I hope everyone believes this is the best direction to take."

"I appreciate the thought you've put into this," Jackson said. "But I have other ideas, and we'll follow through with those."

Surprised, we all turned our gazes toward Jackson.

"Sorry?" Austin said.

"Austin, I don't mean any disrespect when it comes to my own personal assessment of the situation, but because of Sienna's relationship with me, she continues to be fresh meat for the masses—which all of us saw yesterday. And because of that, I can't allow her not to have the best team possible. She was sexually assaulted, for Christ's sake! So, here's what I want: you and David will protect her while Adam and Brian will see to me. When Sienna and I are out in public together, I expect the four of you to be out in force for each of us, because everyone in this room knows that things have become far more insane than any of us imagined when we first went into this. I don't mean to challenge you, Austin, but I will do my best by Sienna, and that means having you leading her team."

A moment passed before Austin said, "OK."

"Thanks for understanding," Jackson said as he turned to me. "How do you feel, Sienna?"

Fucking conflicted, Jackson. But frankly also kind of relieved that I might have an opportunity to get Austin alone.

"That I'll feel safe," I said. "When it comes to my security, you, Mimi, and Austin always have had my back. I'm glad that's going to continue. Thank you, Jackson."

"Anything for you, Sienna." He clapped his hands as he stood. "So, are we good here?"

"We're good," Harper and Mimi said at once.

"I'm good," I said.

"Austin?" Jackson said. "Are you good with this?"

"Sure," he said. "You're the boss, Jackson. David and I will make it work." He glanced over at me, and in his eyes I could feel how conflicted he felt. "We'll keep you safe, Sienna. I can promise you that."

23

LATER THAT EVENING—RIGHT on time, as usual, because Julia was never late—she showed up at my apartment with a brown paper sack in her hand, which she thrust at me when I opened the door to greet her.

"I got the Goose," she said as I took the sack from her. "You make the martinis. We'll drink one in silence. I'll stare at you in ways that will make you feel uncomfortable. We'll have another drink. And then we'll talk."

"Why do you want to make me feel uncomfortable?" I asked as she walked past me and moved into the living room.

"I think you already know."

I did. She'd now had several hours to come to the conclusion that I'd likely kept Austin a secret from her on purpose, which wasn't the case at all. Naturally I'd planned to tell her everything at some point, but with my life so heavily scheduled, I hadn't found the necessary time to do so until this morning.

I shut and locked the door and then hurried in behind her.

"Julia, before you get angrier than you already are, you have to understand that all this just recently happened. I only slept with Austin four days ago, for God's sake! What happened to me yesterday was a nightmare in more ways than you'll ever know, because being publicly groped was only part of *that* hellish day. The moment I saw you this morning, I told you as much as I could. If you think I've been keeping this from you, I haven't. I'm still trying to process it myself."

With folded arms, she turned to look at me. It was so warm outside that she was wearing a pair of white classic cady shorts, a yellow tank top, and a pretty pair of sandals. Her blond hair was held up in a tight chignon to keep it off her neck and shoulders.

"How could you have fallen in love with him so quickly?" she asked.

"I don't know, but it's happened—I can tell you that."

"Maybe it's just hormones," she said. "Or the fact that you haven't been laid since you were with Eric."

"Well, that's a bit harsh," I said. "And unless I'm wrong here, I thought you knew me better than that. I was attracted to Austin the first time I set eyes on him, which we discussed the last time you were here. What you don't know is what's happened since."

"All right," she said, sinking into my sofa and curling her legs beneath her. "Make the martinis. We'll have a drink, and you can tell me everything I don't know."

"Are you going to stare at me in judgment?"

"I was only joking about that," she said. "But since I care about you, it's still your job to convince me that this is really happening."

After I made the martinis, I gave her hers, sat next to her on the couch, and filled her in on everything I hadn't told her that morning. When I was finished, she looked at me for a moment before she nodded at the roses on the coffee table.

"Are those from him?" she asked.

"They are."

"Well," she said. "I have to say that they're beautiful."

"They are."

"But how do you know if it's love and not lust?" she asked.

"Because I've been in love before—with Eric. Ironically, I used to lust after the likes of Jackson Cruise when I was just a fan of his and not his friend. I know the difference, Julia—and it's profound."

"Well," she said with a sigh as she put her empty martini glass down on the coffee table. "Maybe a lot of this is just on me, Sienna, because I don't think I've ever been in love."

"Never?" I said in surprise. "What about Michael?"

"Look, Michael was a great guy. But did he or any of my other boyfriends rock my world the way Austin clearly has rocked yours? Did any of them catch me off guard and set me on my ass the way Austin and Eric did to you? No. You and I were friends when you met Eric. I remember how taken you were with him. I remember how much in love you were with him, how excited you were just to be with him. And then how crushed you were when he decided to throw it all away by sleeping with that bitch. I've never experienced anything close to what you've experienced in your life, so who am I to judge what love feels like when I don't think I've ever felt it myself?"

I sensed we were about to go somewhere deeper into our friendship than we'd ever gone before, so I nodded at her empty glass.

"Another martini, doctor?" I asked.

"Consider me premed. But, yes—another martini would be great."

When I returned with our drinks, this time we touched glasses when I sat next to her.

"So, you're in love," she said.

It wasn't a question—it was a statement.

"I am."

"What does it feel like?" she asked. "How do you even know?"

"Those are two very different questions, so let's start with the second one, because it leads into the first."

"OK."

"How did I know that I'd fallen in love with Austin? It wasn't when we made love, although that was off the charts. It wasn't when he sent me the flowers or the food or when he played that Mariah Carey song for me—although all those things certainly contributed to how I now feel about him. I think I didn't realize how deeply I felt for him for a few reasons. First is what Eric did to me, which made me create a wall around myself that I wanted no one to get through. Second, I've been so busy with Jackson that I haven't had time to process my feelings for Austin—until I was forced to."

"When did that happen?"

I told her about the conversation I'd had with Jackson on the yacht and how he'd realized he'd fallen in love with Ash the moment Ash had told him that he was prepared to leave Jackson if he couldn't fully be there for him.

"That's when it hit me," I said. "The same day Austin told me he was falling in love with me, he also said he was going to distance himself from me, which he has...for reasons I've already told you."

"The whole not-wanting-to-be-a-distraction thing," she said.

"That's right. When Jackson's own story pulled my true feelings for Austin out of me, it was like light bulbs going off all around me. At that moment, the idea of losing him was such a massive punch to my gut that I couldn't ignore it. If I'd felt nothing for him, I could easily have just walked away from him. But after listening to Jackson's story—and listening to my own heart—I realized I couldn't. I knew then that I was in love with Austin. So, to answer your first question about what love feels like—what I felt when I thought I might lose him was so profound that I felt gutted. There's something about him that makes him singularly special, and I saw it right then and there, just as he was about remove himself from my life—which he's already done as much as he could. I was in love with him before I even knew I was in love with him. And because he's doing his best to shut me out of his life right now, I somehow need to find a way to tell him what I feel for him."

"And yet you can't with David around?"

"That's right. Because if I did, there's a chance it would get back to Mimi and Jackson, and that might put my contract at risk. I need to get Austin alone. But with David in the picture, I'm not sure I can."

"Austin said he'd wait for you," she said. "Why doubt him?"

"Because seven months might as well be a lifetime. Austin is a catch, Julia—you know that. Why should I believe for one moment that another woman won't come along who will catch his eye? He's a single man. He has his needs. Somehow I have to get in front of this and tell him how I feel before it's too late."

"How will you do that?" she asked.

"I don't know," I said, "but I will. You know how persistent I can be. I'll find that crack in his door, and when I do, I plan to bust straight through it."

"A door..." Julia said, almost to herself. "That's exactly what you two need."

Confused, I just looked at her.

"What are you talking about?"

"We need to get you two alone behind a closed door."

"And how is that going to happen with David hovering around us? Please, do your best to enlighten me."

"Harper's day is filled with meetings—you know that. And most of them take place away from her office. Especially when she has one of her three-hour lunches with a client or a studio head, which happens at least two or three times a week."

"But what does that have to do with Austin and me?"

"Sweetie, cookie, baby—just settle down and listen to Julia, OK? You're in a fake relationship with Jackson, right?"

"Obviously, although I have come to adore him."

"Fine. In fact, good! But how about if I set up a fake meeting between Harper and Austin? Only when Austin arrives, he won't know she's at one of her three-hour lunches. I'll let him inside, get him some coffee, and ask him to sit down and relax because Harper's running late. That's when you'll arrive. And that's when I shut the door behind you two. Whoops! Look at that—you two, alone together. What are you two going to talk about? I don't know...maybe about how you feel about him."

"Who are you?" I asked. "What kind of sorcery do you wield that I never knew about?"

"I might be loveless, but I've always been crafty, Sienna. I just don't always show it, which is crafty of me, wouldn't you say?"

"What you're proposing is actually kind of brilliant," I said. "But it's also risky, don't you think?"

"Actually, no. I mean, who's going to spill the beans, even when Austin figures out that he was set up? You? No. Austin? He wouldn't do that to you. Me? Ditto. Harper? She'll be clueless."

"He'll be pissed at me for this."

"Maybe he will, but what matters more to you: his momentary anger or telling him how you feel about him?"

"You already know the answer."

"Good. So, shall I set up the meeting?"

"I have to do something, Julia. I need to get in front of this."

"Then, I guess I'm setting up the meeting."

"Now I feel like I'm going to barf."

"Don't you dare!" she said. "That bottle of Goose set me back sixty bucks. You are *so* not going to barf."

"Do you think it'll work?" I asked her.

She shrugged at me. "I don't know, but what do you have to lose?"

"Nothing," I said.

"Then, I say we give this a try. I say that we get Austin alone with you so you can tell him you're in love with him. This is our best chance for that to happen. As for me, Harper's schedule is so predictable, I already know I can make this work. But for the rest of it to work?" She tossed back the rest of her martini before she looked at me. "That's up to you, sugar. So, bring it. Work it. Make him believe it. Because if you don't, I don't know what lies ahead for you when it comes to him. And that concerns me."

24

New York City
August

UNFORTUNATELY, Julia's plan didn't work. The day before the meeting, Austin had reached out to Harper himself to see if he could reschedule. Since there was in fact no meeting, Harper had gone to Julia, asking why it had been scheduled in the first place. Crafty Julia told me she'd simply said that she must have misheard Harper in one of their morning meetings.

"I thought you'd asked me to set up a meeting between Austin and you," she'd said. "Sorry about that, Harper."

"Not a problem," Harper had said. "I throw so many things at you each morning, it's a wonder you can even keep up."

And that was fucking that.

Over the next four weeks, as my repeated attempts to get Austin alone failed time and again, my frustration kept growing as he continued to put distance between us. Whenever he spoke to me, it was only about business, and David was always within earshot. Whenever he took me home—as he was today after my lunch with Jackson—David was with us, because just getting into my apartment these days was nothing short of a nightmare. The paparazzi was always there, and then there were Jackson's fans, who continued to show up to catch a glimpse of the woman who'd somehow snagged one of the world's most eligible bachelors.

From the back seat, I studied Austin's profile as we drove down Fifth toward my apartment, and I wondered. Did he ever steal glances at me? Since he always wore sunglasses, I never really knew. Did he feel the ache that I felt? Or did he have the ability to put his feeling aside and not let them interfere with his job? Most of the time I was able to conceal how I felt, but other times I felt so desperate that I just couldn't. I was only human, and during those times when he was forced to talk to me, sometimes I looked right at him so he could see how distraught I felt. Not that it had made any difference between us—he'd reacted to none of it.

"Austin," David asked, "would you mind doing me a favor, buddy?"

"Sure," Austin said. "What's up?"

"Sharon just sent me a text," he said, referring to his wife. "If it's OK with Sienna, would you mind stopping at Symphony Cleaners between Thirty-Fifth and Thirty-Sixth? It's right on the way, and it would save me a trip."

"We should probably get Sienna—"

"That's fine by me," I blurted out, realizing with a sense of shock that with David out of the car, I was finally about to have my moment alone with Austin. "Stop at the cleaners, Austin. Let's help David out."

"Thanks, Sienna."

Thank you, David!

"No problem," I said. As I looked at Austin in the rearview, I could literally feel his eyes burning into mine, despite his sunglasses. "I'm in for the night, anyway. There's no hurry to get me home."

As we continued down Fifth, my mind raced.

What would I say to him?

The truth...

What if he gave me pushback?

Push back yourself...

What if he tried to shut me down?

Don't allow him to, because you've just been given a gift, and you need to use that gift to make Austin aware of exactly how you feel. He doesn't know that you're in love with him. Now's your chance to tell him to his face that you are—so, do it. And you'd better convince him.

As we came upon Symphony Cleaners, I saw a line of people standing outside the store, waiting to get in.

"This could take a while," Austin said to David. "We should take Sienna home, and then I'll bring you back."

"Austin, we're here," I said. "Pull the car over, and let David out. He's watched over me for the past four weeks, and he's done a terrific job. It's time for me to pay a kindness to him, regardless of how small it is. I insist."

With a barely audible sigh, Austin pulled the car over. As he came to a stop, he switched on the hazard lights—which I thought was ironic, since this particular hazard was about to come his way.

"Be back as soon as I can," David said.

And then he was out of the car, and Austin and I were alone.

"Take off your sunglasses," I said to him. "Look at me."

"Why?"

"Because I need you to."

"Sienna—"

"Take of your goddamned sunglasses," I said. "Be a man. Look at me, for God's sake. This has gone on long enough. I can't stand it anymore. I'm at my wit's end when it comes to you."

He sat still for a moment, and then he just shook his head, removed his glasses, and looked at me in the rearview.

"I'm in love with you," I said.

That jolted him into a motionless pause.

"You're in love with me?" he asked after a moment.

"I am," I said. "I'm in love with you. And I can't stand us like this. I hate this distance you've been putting between us. Because I *am* in love with you, Austin. I can't get you out of my head. I think about you all the time. I want you to hold me again. To kiss me again. Make *love* to me again. I just want to *be* with you again...but you're making that impossible, which is killing me. You said you were falling in love with me. If that's no longer the case, then please just tell me now. I'll get over it in time, and then we can just work together without—"

"I *am* in love with you!" he shouted, slamming his fists against the steering wheel and then turning around to face me. Startled, I just looked back at him. His eyes weren't just heated and wild—they were also filled with longing and frustration.

"Do you think any of this has been easy for me?" he asked. "It hasn't! Not being able to touch you, to talk to you, and to take you into my arms and make love to you has fucked me up! But, Sienna, come on! Understand this: because of me—and me alone—you were sexually assaulted, and I can't allow that to happen again. You have to allow me to be at my best."

"I did not get assaulted because of you!" I shouted.

"Yes, you did!" he countered. "I wasn't enough for you. I failed you in that moment. And when we got into your apartment and I heard you tell Harper on the phone what had happened to you, I swore to God that I'd never let that happen to you again. So, yes, I've put distance between us. But I also told you that I'd be there waiting for you at the end of your contract. Did you think that was just some kind of a joke? Do you think I'd just casually say that? That's not who I am. I meant what I said. As each day passes, I say good riddance to it, because it means that soon we'll be able to be together again. Not being with you has been hell for me, but what can I do? You're no idiot. You see for yourself how crazy your life has become. And because of that, you need to be present and in the moment so you can also protect *yourself*. You can't afford to be distracted right now, Sienna, and neither can I. Your safety relies on each of us being mindful when you're out in public."

"Well, guess what?" I said. "The opposite has happened, Austin. Ever since you shut me down, I've never been more distracted or preoccupied in my life."

"I told you I'd wait for you—what else do you need to hear from me?"

"Maybe I don't want to hear anything," I said, leaning toward him. "Maybe what I need is this."

When I moved in to kiss him, he hesitated before our lips collided against each other and finally—finally!—we became one again. And when that happened—when we allowed ourselves to become unleashed—my heart soared. As his tongue thrust into my mouth with force and meaning, I felt his heart touch my own in ways that underscored his deep hunger and need for me. As he continued to kiss me with a passion I'd never felt before, he claimed me in waves of such pent-up desire that it was overwhelming—but in the best of ways.

He is *in love with me*, I thought. *I can feel it. I know it. He's right where I am...but with walls built higher than my own.*

He twisted himself around in his seat, took my face in his hands, and kissed me as if he'd never kissed me before. But this kiss was different from the others we'd shared. This kiss spoke volumes about longing, need, and love. Tears welled in my eyes that this period in our lives was finally behind us, and I gave everything I had back to him. As we continued to kiss, I stroked my fingers through his thick black hair and tugged on the back of it. I pressed the palm of my hand against his rock-solid chest and felt his heart hammering against it. When I broke away from him, I said in his ear, "I'm in love with you, Austin Black. After my last relationship, never in a million years did I ever think I'd be here again, but I am. And I'm grateful for it, because I never expected to find love again. Or even to be open to love again, which I am—and it's with you. All I think about is you. You need to know that."

He kissed me when I said that, and then he looked quickly over his shoulder and searched for David on the street. I also looked, and since there was no sign of him, he'd obviously made it into the store. He could be back with us at any moment.

"Sienna, listen to me now."

"What's to listen to?" I asked. "It's done. We both know how we feel. We both know we're in love. And because this horror show is finally behind us, we can be together again."

"No," he said quietly to me. "The only thing that's changed today is that we've acknowledged our feelings for one another."

Bewildered, I just looked at him.

"What does that mean?" I asked.

"You have another six months to go before you part from Jackson. And because of everything you've endured since you signed that contract with him, you *deserve* the ten million dollars Jackson is offering you. And I'll be damned if I'm going to get in the way of that."

"What are you saying?"

"Things between us need to remain the same."

"No," I said. "Austin, I need to be able to see you. I need to be with you. You have the tools to make that happen. If we continue on like this, I think I'll go insane."

"Listen to me," he said. "You need your financial freedom, and because of that, neither of us can risk blowing it. We need to wait out the next six months knowing that we'll be there for one another in the end."

"But you can't shut down on me again," I said. "Please don't start acting like I don't exist. It hurts me when you do that. It *kills* me when you do that. If you go back to behaving as if I didn't exist, I don't think my heart will be able to take it—especially now. Especially after that kiss. And particularly since we both know how we feel about each other."

He looked out the side window again, I followed his gaze —and this time we saw David leaving the store.

"Here comes David," he said. "Now, listen to me. Believe in me. I've told you how I feel. That's not going to change. If you love me, wait for me. Because I can promise you this: six months from now I will absolutely be waiting for you."

Given my fake relationship with Jackson—because of which I'd seen my life completely change over the course of two months—I was old enough to know that life could change within a matter of days, let alone six months.

And because of that, if Austin and I could not enjoy any kind of intimacy for half a year—I called that a long card.

He was going to shut down on me again. And so I had to wonder once again: would Austin and I ever come together? Or were we just a pair of fools to believe we could ride out this storm?

After connecting so physically and emotionally with him only moments ago, he'd just drawn another line in the sand, and it took everything I had within me not to weep as David entered the car with his wife's dry cleaning. The moment David's door clicked shut, Austin plunged the car into traffic and sped toward my apartment.

When they got me home safely and I took the three flights of stairs to my apartment, my tears overflowed when I sat down on the edge of my sofa. They came hard, they were gut-wrenching—and Christ, did they ever hurt.

25

OVER THE FOLLOWING WEEK, I had to draw upon every acting class I'd ever taken just to get through each day. My life had literally become an act, and it was exhausting to keep looking happy for the masses when all I wanted to do was stay home, shut out the world, and get my head on straight.

But there was no time for that.

As Austin receded from me once again, Jackson and I were kept busy with a slew of events throughout the week. With the exception of last Friday, when Jackson had meetings to attend, I'd been out with him every night—and not just for dinner.

On Saturday, we went to a movie premiere, which meant handling the insanity of the red carpet. On Sunday, we found ourselves at a fundraising event held by Jennifer and Alexander Wenn, who were Manhattan royalty due to their philanthropy, and the sprawling conglomerate they owned, Wenn Enterprises.

And then came Monday, when Jackson and I had to do a photo shoot with *People* magazine, which was doing a profile on Jackson's life. Since I was part of his life, I'd also been interviewed and asked repeatedly about our love for each other—which nearly killed me, since I was in love with another man.

Jackson and I had posed together for a whole host of photos. When I'd asked the photographer if I could see what she'd shot, she'd graciously shown me several of her favorites, and right then and there it occurred to me that one day I might indeed win an Oscar, because these photos told the story of a couple in love.

As the days passed, it became clear to me that if I were going to be sane by the time my contract ended with Jackson, I was going to have to shut down my emotions and put my love for Austin aside. That was a tall order, but if I didn't do as Austin was doing, I'd just continue to be a wreck. He'd made his case and his position clear, so I needed to suck it up, be stronger, and trust that he *would* be there for me in the end.

But none of it was easy. If anything, it was hell.

As the week progressed, Jackson and I went to another party on Tuesday, a gala on Wednesday, and then last night, a major human rights benefit. Harper had offered me up to address the crowd with a speech that would focus on equality.

Yesterday afternoon, she, Julia, and I had crafted my speech, which allowed me to address core issues I believed in. And when it was time to attend the event, I was finally allowed to be the real me. The real Sienna. The one who wasn't lying to the world and faking it. When I took to the stage, I seized the moment to speak about sexual assault, race relations, my love for the LGBTQ community, and—most importantly—the equality that only love could bring.

After so many months of not being me, Harper's genius was to allow me to be me—and on a global stage. She knew

I needed that. She'd sensed it—and as usual, she'd come through for me.

And now, as I woke to a new day, I found myself still glowing from the event itself.

Naturally, Jackson had been in the crowd to support me and cheer me on when I hit the right notes. And in those moments when I caught glimpses of him seated in the front row, my one hope when I spoke about gay rights was that he'd feel the power of my words—and the conviction behind them—especially since I'd come to the conclusion that Jackson would never come out, which saddened me.

On the yacht, he'd said that Ash had given him a month to come out or he'd leave him. That day had passed five days ago. And while Jackson hadn't said a word to me about whether Ash had left him or not, I had to believe that after the *People* interview, which had focused so much on our own relationship, that Jackson had decided to remain in the closet. Part of me understood the reasons why, particularly when it came to his career, but a larger part of me didn't understand at all.

He'd told me that he was in love with Ash. Did his career mean so much to him that he'd never allow love into his life? The man was worth hundreds of millions of dollars, for God's sake! How much more money or fame did he need before he grabbed hold of that love—and not the fake love we shared? For somebody who exuded such a strong presence onscreen, Jackson himself wasn't that strong, and that disappointed me. He'd told me that he saw Ash and himself raising a family together. Building a life together. Growing old together.

But in the end, his fear of coming out had clearly gotten the best of him—which I planned to bring up later today when we had lunch together. If I could somehow manage to get through to him before Ash shut the door tightly between them—provided he already hadn't—I would.

After washing my face, brushing my teeth, and grabbing a cup of coffee, I went to my computer and started to read the stories that had been written about last night's event. And when I did, I was somewhat relieved. For the first time since I'd been with Jackson, these stories were about me—not us. This gave me hope that when Jackson and I did go our separate ways, I might be able to come out of this with an identity of my own.

When it was time to get ready for Austin and David to pick me to take me to Jackson, I put my computer to sleep. Today would be a quieter day. Jackson and I were only meant to have lunch at another hot spot called Le Coucou—the sound of which was not lost on me—before he returned to shoot more scenes for *Annihilate Them*.

When I'd finished my coffee, I chose an outfit for the day and was about to step into the shower when I heard my cell ring out in the living room.

Answer it or let it go into voice mail?

As if the latter were an option. I walked naked into the living room and saw that it was Julia calling.

"Give me a second," I said when I answered the phone. "I was just getting into the shower, and I'm naked."

"Oh, you're more than that, honey," she said. "You've been exposed."

"What does that mean?" I asked. "And why do you sound out of breath?"

"I don't know—maybe because some major fucking news just broke?"

"What news?"

"Best if you see it for yourself," she said. "Go to your computer, and bring up Google News. The story went live ten minutes ago—and because of it, it's chaos here at the office. People might as well be walking straight into walls. And then there's Harper and Mimi, who were blindsided by it and are now discussing God only knows what in Harper's office."

"What are you talking about?" I asked, hurriedly retrieving my bathrobe and slipping into it.

"Sienna, just sit in front of your computer, and do as I asked."

"But I was just online," I protested.

"How long ago?"

"Twenty minutes ago?"

"As I said, the story broke ten minutes ago. And the universe is on fire because of it. There are so many phones ringing around me right now that I'd better start answering them. But before you left for the day, I knew I had to warn you about this. So, get to your computer, because shit is getting real in ways none of us saw coming. Especially for you—because a lot of this happens to *involve* you."

"If it involves me, then why hasn't Harper called me?"

"Oh, she'll be calling you at some point soon, but right now she's in crisis-management mode with Mimi."

"Is this about the speech I gave last night?" I said as I started for my bedroom. "Did I say something wrong? Because that's not what I read this morning. People responded well to what I had to say. Has that changed? Have I offended someone?"

"Oh, for God's sake—just get in front of your fucking computer, Sienna!"

"I'm now sitting in front of my computer," I said, "and I'm bringing up Google News. The page is loading. And I'm skimming...and...*Oh. My. God!* Jackson did it! He came out! Holy shit! It's right there on the front page. And he did so through *People* magazine! He must have been planning this! And stop the presses, but who's the hot guy on the cover with him? Is that who I think it is?"

"That would be a certain Ash Walker," Julia said. "Otherwise known as the man Jackson has been seeing on the sly for nearly a year—a.k.a. the pilot with the pretty pout."

"He's so handsome," I said. As I looked at the cover of *People*, my heart swelled. The headline was as straightforward as it was simple:

I'M GAY, AND I'M IN LOVE!

WHEN I READ THOSE WORDS, I blinked twice at them. He'd done it. My friend had finally done it!

"Have you passed out, or are you still there?" Julia asked.

"I'm still here. I'm just in shock."

"Shock," Julia said with a grim laugh. "You should *see* this place right now. CAA has officially become a zoo of zombies. Pale, blank faces parading around in Prada wherever you look. If nobody knows what the hell to do here at CAA, just imagine what's happening to the rest of the world right now. Women are probably throwing themselves off bridges and buildings and headlong into bayous. But the gays? Oh, the gays are on fire! Because with Jackson coming out—an A-list action star stating his love for another man in a major magazine—that's a game changer, kiddo."

"Look at how happy Jackson looks," I said as I gazed at the magazine's cover. "I can't believe this. I thought he'd never go there. I'm so happy he did." And then it hit me. "Wait a minute," I said. "I was interviewed by *People* this week with Jackson. He and I took photographs together. I gushed to the reporter in that interview about how in love we were. In some of the photographs, we were even asked to pose romantically together. Why the hell didn't he *tell* me about any of this?"

"Don't worry," she said. "I've read the entire article, and it's clear Jackson knew exactly what he was doing, as did the reporter. My guess is that for him to give *People* that kind of an exclusive—which will sell millions of magazines—he reached an agreement with the editor before he told them anything."

"What kind of an agreement?"

"Remember when Jackson took last Friday off?"

"Vaguely..."

"Well, he did. And I think he was interviewed by the magazine then. I think he offered them an exclusive if his terms were met. And those terms clearly included being fair to you, because in this article, you come off extremely well. Touching and supportive, a friend standing up for a friend who didn't dare go public with his sexuality. In the article, Jackson says it was you who ultimately encouraged him to do it."

"He said that?" I asked.

"He did. Jackson took care of you, cookie. And by the way, the photos of you two that were supposed to look romantic? In the story's context, now they only look supportive. And whatever mushy, lovey-dovey stuff you had to say about Jackson, none of that's in the interview. Which once again makes me believe that Jackson cut a deal with *People* before giving them the scoop. And by the way, they chose your words well. They've turned you into an advocate for the gay community."

"Now I'm just going to cry," I said, feeling my face flush.

"I'm so happy for him! And you say Mimi knew nothing about this?"

"No, which is why she and Harper are in a frantic craze right now. They're huddled in Harper's office, trying to figure out how best to go forward. Jackson just up and did this on his own—likely because he knew Mimi would have given him pushback. Anyway, I'm calling for another reason."

"What other reason?" I said.

"If it's chaos here, imagine the kind of chaos that's waiting outside your front door as we speak. Harper and Mimi want you and Jackson to be here at two. Austin will send four of his men to protect Jackson while he, David, and two of his other men will come get you. So...listen to me," she said in a voice charged with concern. "I'm worried about you right now. If you think your life was insane even a week ago, with this story going viral—and with Twitter and Facebook exploding because of it—you will be mobbed when you leave your apartment. And it will probably be worse than ever."

"Julia, those reporters are going to hammer me," I said. "What am I supposed to say to them? This entire time, we've been lying to them—and also to the world. They're going to be pissed that we tried to con them. What am I supposed to say to them?"

"Harper will tell you what to say when she calls you, but here's how I see it. The paps have already read the interview, in which Jackson addresses the reasons behind his fake relationship with you. When you read the interview for yourself, you'll see that he thanks you profusely for standing by him until he got up the courage to come out. Given the careful way he framed your relationship, I don't see any negative publicity coming your way. If anything, I see only good things for you. The magazine has portrayed you as a gracious woman who was willing to put her career on hold so she could stand by her friend while she urged him to tell his truth to the world."

"Is there any mention of the contract?" I asked.

"None. Jackson said that what you did for him was out of love and concern. Now, as for how you handle the paps, every photo that will be taken of you is going to tell its own story, and *you* have the power of owning that story."

"How?"

"By being happy for him," she said. "I say you leave your apartment beaming that Jackson has finally claimed who he is, that he's told the world who he's really in love with, and that he's no longer afraid of being ashamed of it—or shamed *for* it. Those are emotions you already feel. So? Wear those emotions on your sleeve. Use them to your benefit. Don't look shell-shocked. You need to look as if you were in the know all along. In the meantime, wait for Harper's call. Know that I love you—and that in the end, this will turn out just fine for you."

"Will it?" I asked.

"I think it will."

"There are no guarantees, Julia," I said.

"There were no guarantees when you signed that contract, Sienna."

"True enough."

"I've given you my best advice. Harper might have a completely different strategy. Take what you want from each, and do what feels right for you."

"Thanks for calling, Julia. Your concern means the world to me."

"What was I supposed to do, hang my best friend out to dry? Think again, lady. Now, please, try your best to get through today. Know that I'll be there for you in spirit. I'll be thinking about you and hoping the best for you. Whenever you can call and talk, you call me, OK? Regardless of the time."

"OK," I said.

"I love you, Sienna."

"I love you too, Julia."

When she ended the call, I literally felt the thundering weight of silence as it fell upon my shoulders.

26

WHEN I GOT off the phone, I read the *People* article twice in its entirety. When I was finished, a part of me felt relieved by how sensitive and how well written it was—and also by how well Jackson had played his hand in an effort to protect me.

One thing he said in particular touched me: "Sienna graciously, bravely, and thanklessly offered to be in a fake relationship with me not only so she could buffer me from the media speculation surrounding my sexuality but also so I could have the necessary time to come to terms with how coming out would affect my career. When I told her I was also concerned that coming out might hurt my legacy, she's the one who suggested that maybe whatever legacy I left behind was far greater than the movies I've made. She changed my way of thinking. She made me see that maybe I'd been put on this planet to be an example for young people struggling to come out as I have. Over these past few months, Sienna Jones has worked hard to help me see that who I am as a person is far larger than the persona people view onscreen."

All of that was true, and the fact that he'd said so in the interview made me smile.

But still, I had to wonder how the paparazzi would handle me today. Would they call me a liar? Why not? I was one. Would they say I'd been a good friend to Jackson? Why not? Because I've been one. Or would it be a mix of both?

Their job was to get a reaction out of me, so I felt that at the very least, it would be a mix of both. And because of that, I felt nervous as hell.

What am I about to step into?

I didn't know, but I did know this: when I left my apartment, I had to look my very best, because the photos that were about to be taken of me would go global before I knew it, and Julia was right—each of them would tell their own story about how I truly felt inside. And that was the thing. While I was elated for Jackson, I was scared for myself.

I was searching through my wardrobe for something better to wear today when Harper called at ten.

"How are you?" she asked when I answered.

"Shaken," I said. "Jackson told me nothing about this. But just so we're clear, you need to know that I'm not angry with him, because I *am* the one who pressed for him to come out, and I'm glad that he has. That said, I am concerned that when Austin picks me up this afternoon, you and I both know the paparazzi will go after me. Tell me how to survive that situation—what do I say to them, and thus to the world, particularly since I've been living a lie for months, which everyone knows by now—or they'll know soon enough. After this, I'm not sure how I'll be met by the paps...or by the masses. I need you to guide me through this, Harper."

"Mimi and I talked about just that this morning, and believe it or not, we agreed on a strategy."

"You two actually agreed on something?"

"Let's just say that today has been peppered with surprises."

"What did you decide?" I asked.

"When you leave your apartment with Austin and his team at your side, Mimi and I think you need to behave as if you *knew* this was going to happen and that you are proud that you were able to be there for Jackson and help him feel it was safe to come out. The good news is that this story is going to be less about you and far more about Jackson. His coming out is going to be the story that dominates the media, Sienna, not you—which is a good thing."

"I'm still attached to it," I said, "in a major way."

"You are," she agreed. "But because of the sensitive way Jackson treated you in the interview, I believe you will come out of this looking like the supportive friend of someone in need. Jackson did right by you, because it's clear that whatever arrangement he made with *People* also included protecting you."

Julia had said the same.

"As for the paparazzi, when you leave your apartment, you have two choices: say nothing, or say something. Since Mimi and I believe you need to own this story, our best advice to you is that you say something. When confronted, say that you did this to help Jackson work through a difficult time in his life. Nobody knows about the contract you signed with him, and nobody will ever know about it, so don't worry about that biting you in the ass, because it won't. So, if anyone says anything negative to you, I say you shoot them down by saying how happy you are that Jackson finally did this for himself. That that's been your intent all along. How does that sound?"

Once again, that was pretty much what Julia had

suggested, and because I respected Harper and her so much, I couldn't ignore that it was good advice.

"Actually, that sounds good," I said. "But I have another question for you."

"What's that?"

"My contract," I said. "Jackson nullified it with that interview. He and I are no longer a couple. Instead, he and *Ash* are a couple. What does that mean for me?"

"It means that you're free," she said. "It means that the contract is officially over as of today."

"Seriously?" I said. "I'm out of it?"

"Of course. Mimi and Jackson have already signed off. You've met your obligations, and Jackson himself has insisted that despite this not having lasted the full eight months, you nevertheless will be paid the full ten million when you arrive for our meeting this afternoon. But never mind about that now. You need to get ready for Austin and his team to pick you up. They'll be there in a matter of hours, and you need to be camera-ready for the world. Wear that chic summery suit of yours that I love so much."

"The Dior one?"

"Yes, the white one. And remember, my darling girl, look beyond happy and thrilled when you leave your apartment. Make everyone believe you have been in on this from the beginning, if only so you could give Jackson time to come to a critical life decision. Can you do that?"

"I totally can do that."

"Good. Now, go and get ready. Be the Sienna I know you can be. I'll see you at two."

27

LATER, once I was showered, dressed, and ready for the cameras, I stood before my wardrobe's mirror and assessed myself. My makeup was light and fresh. The Dior suit Harper wanted me to wear had been a gift from the company when I wore it for them during my modeling days. But since the suit was so formal, I'd decided to soften it by wearing my hair down and flowing down my back in soft waves.

It was a good look. But as time passed, my nerves started getting the better of me.

What's going to happen when I step outside? What are they going to say to me? Are they going to feed me to the dogs, or will they be kind to me?

Once again, I knew I needed to be prepared for both.

And then there was Austin. I was now officially out of my contract with Jackson. Had anyone told Austin that was the case? Or had he surmised it on his own? And because of that, what was going through *his* head right now? Was he going to be as eager to see me as I was to see him?

When my buzzer went off at one thirty, I rang David

through and took a deep breath to collect myself for all that was to come. But as hard as I tried to convince myself that I was ready for whatever came my way, who the hell was I kidding? I wasn't prepared for any of it. When the knock came at my door and I opened it, I was almost paralyzed with fear.

And then I felt paralyzed in other ways, because it wasn't David who'd come for me. Instead, it was Austin. My lips parted as I took in all six foot six of him in his perfectly fitted black business suit. I saw the intensity in his eyes. I tried to speak, but I was so shocked that he was standing before me that words wouldn't come.

"May I come inside?" he asked.

I stepped away from the door. He entered my apartment, shut the door behind him, and got straight to it.

"Your contract," he said. "Have you talked with Harper? Are you officially out of it now?"

"Yes," I said. "I talked with Harper earlier, and because of Jackson's interview with *People*, it's now considered null and void. Apparently when we meet them at two, I'll be paid in full, and—"

"That's all I needed to know," he said. He came toward me with a heated look of desire in his eyes and took me into his arms, pressing my back against the door.

His lips collided against mine, and I felt his need for me surge through me, feeling faint as I realized it was stronger than I'd ever imagined it would be. What I felt in his kiss was a love that was searing and real, unlike anything I'd ever experienced before. In that kiss was such an overwhelming sense of relief, truth, and hunger that my world fell away as his hands smoothed up my body and caressed me before cupping my breasts.

Gently, he squeezed them and then brushed his thumbs

across my taut nipples, causing my head to rear back in ecstasy. With my neck thus exposed to him, he began to kiss it—to the point that I felt certain I was about to come right then and there.

This is happening, I thought. *Finally, we can be one again...*

With his body pressed hard against mine, I could feel the swell of his erection pulsing against my thigh, and it made me catch my breath in a mixture of excitement and raw delight.

When I reached down to take him in my hand, I felt his girth and his impossible length, and as I did so, he claimed my lips with his own as I felt his love for me roar through me, shake me, stun me. Impulsively, I jumped up and clasped my legs tightly around his waist. I felt his hands curve around my ass so he could support me, and we kissed for what seemed like an eternity before he started to move toward my bedroom.

"What are you doing?" I asked. "Austin, we need to leave."

"No, we don't," he said.

"Look, more than anything I want to make love to you, but Harper, Jackson, and Mimi are expecting us."

His blue eyes flashed with mischief at me.

"Actually, the meeting's been pushed back until eight," he said.

"Come again?"

He laughed when I said that.

"Sienna, you are seriously about to come again...and again and again."

"No. Well...I mean, yes. Of course I mean yes. But why has our meeting been pushed back until eight?"

"After the *People* interview, it didn't take a genius to know that you'd already asked Harper if you were still contractually bound to Jackson. After Jackson told the world that he was in love with Ash, I knew your contract with him had to be dead. Did I know it for sure? No, which is why I asked you when I came in. Still, since it only made sense that it was, I called Harper before I came here and told her that it would be safer for you if the paps believed you weren't going anywhere today. I told her it would be safer for all involved if we met this evening. She agreed and made the necessary calls, and everyone said it was the right choice for you and Jackson. I told her I'd call you myself and tell you about the changes. So, here I am—telling you that your meeting is now at eight—just as I'm about to make love to you."

He eased me down onto my bed.

"Being separated from each other is now officially over," he said as he positioned his body above mine. "And now that I know you'll receive your full payment from Jackson, we can be together again. But just so you're clear on this, Sienna, I *would* have waited for you. That wasn't bullshit on my part."

Hearing the conviction in his voice, I knew it wasn't, and so, as I lay on my back looking up at him, I felt thrilled, elated, happy, and in love as I stroked my fingers through his impossibly thick hair.

"Make love to me, Austin," I said. "I've waited too long for this moment. I need to have you inside me again."

He glanced down at me.

"As much as I'd like to tear off your clothes right now, it's probably best if I didn't, because you're going to need that suit to be as fresh as it is now before we leave here. So, how about if you get undressed for me while I watch?"

"Will you do the same for me?"

"If you want."

"Oh, I want," I said. When I was off the bed and standing

before him, I slowly began to remove my suit, finally draping it over a nearby chair.

"Christ, you're beautiful," he said when I was naked.

"Even like this?" I asked. "Even with the sunlight pouring through the windows?"

"I can see all of you now," he said, "in ways I hadn't been able to see before. I'm the luckiest fucking man on earth."

I stood in front of him. "Your turn," I said. "Take off your suit, Austin."

"I was thinking that maybe you'd help me out of it."

"Is that what you want?"

"It's exactly what I want."

"Then, stand up," I said.

Wordlessly, he stood in front of me. I stepped so close to him that only a whisper of lust separated us. But for me, it might as well have been a scream, because I was so hot for him right now, that's exactly what my body felt.

Despite how tall I was, Austin literally towered over me. I was so unnerved that we were going to make love again after being apart for so long that strangely it felt as if this were going to be our first time together.

As I removed his jacket and then started to tug at his black tie, my hands began to tremble in anticipation. When I focused my attention on his shirt, I started at his throat and undid each button, his massive chest—concealed once again by a white T-shirt—slowly revealing itself to me.

"Why are you going so slowly?" he asked in that deep voice of his.

"I don't know," I said as I worked my way down toward his bulging crotch. "Maybe because some things shouldn't be rushed? I'm burning all of this into my memory, because at this moment, finally free to be with the man who owns my heart, I want to remember all of it—right down to my taking off your underwear." I arched an eyebrow at him. "Provided you *are* wearing underwear..."

"I kind of went back to that."

When I leaned down to pull off his pants and saw his tented briefs, I was on my knees, lusting at what was straining against the thin fabric. With a quick, strategic pull of his briefs, I reared back as his weighty cock sprang free in front of me.

Before he could do anything, I took him into my mouth, rolling my tongue along the great expanse of his thick shaft, and this time he allowed me to take all of him down my throat. And when I did, I heard him suck in a surprised rush of air as I cupped his balls in my hand and began to massage them.

But he didn't give me long to do so.

Before I could finish having my way with him, Austin— ever the alpha male who clearly wanted to run this show to meet my needs—withdrew himself from my mouth and asked me to stand.

Turned on by the need in his voice, I stood before him. We were so close to one another that the tips of my nipples brushed against his bare chest—which nearly made me come undone as a jolt of electricity took hold of me at the very moment he claimed my mouth with his own.

"I'm in love with you," he said roughly when our lips parted and we stood face-to-face. "I don't know what it is about us—and frankly, I don't care. What matters is that what I feel is real. It's right. And I know in my soul that this is where I want to be for the rest of my life. With you. With me making love to you. With you by my side forever. You and I are going to be in love for the rest of our lives. I can feel it," he said. "Can you?"

"I can," I said. And I could.

Swiftly, he scooped me into his muscular arms, laid me down onto my bed, and then skillfully hovered just above me, our bodies not touching save for our lips as he kissed me with a passion that underscored just how deeply in love he was with me, which overwhelmed me.

Out of the blue—and in ways I'd never seen coming this morning—this was really happening to me. Despite all the doubts I'd had when it came to us, Austin was here with me. Somehow we were together again, and I was nothing short of grateful that I was being allowed to experience this kind of love again.

As he lowered his body a notch, my nipples grazed against his skin again, and I felt his cock lower against the tip of my sex. Just as I thought he was about to enter me, we looked into each other eyes for a moment before he slowly began to work his way down my body. He covered my torso with kisses before his mouth pressed against my sex, and his tongue plunged into it.

He thinks he needs to prepare me for him, but this time he doesn't. I'm already open and ready for him...

Still, I gave myself over to him.

His tongue licked, tasted, and fluttered against my folds before he moved to my clit and swiped the stubble on his chin over it, which nearly did me in. He kissed me there, and then I felt his fingers reach up to tweak my nipples just as his tongue moved deeper inside me in ways that were so sexy that I gasped as waves of ecstasy overcame me. Only when he was certain I was open and wet enough to accept all of him did he enter me.

And when he did—when I felt so full and tight with him inside me—I looked up into the safety of his eyes, and my body naturally relaxed as he began to move in slow, rhythmic strokes that became more intense at my nod to him that this was good, this was perfect. When I was ready for more, I encouraged him with thrusts of my own.

"What do you need from me right now?" he asked me.

"I want to come."

With a fierceness that I'd never before felt, Austin dipped his head to my right nipple, bit down hard on it, and then shoved himself completely inside me, which sent me out of my body and straight into the ether as I cried out in pleasure. I placed my hands against his sweaty, muscular chest as my body shook with my climax, which cascaded through my body in wild ripples.

But Austin didn't stop there. Instead, he intensified the moment, driving in and out of me, fucking me, kissing me, smoothing his tight body over mine until I came again.

It was too much. This was far beyond what we'd experienced the first time we'd made love. This was something different. This was charged with unrest, lust—and the understanding that we'd fallen in love.

As he rammed into me, I thought about what sex would be like with him going forward. Was this just a primer of what was to come? Was he giving me a mere sampling of what to expect from him?

Convinced it was the latter, I felt in my soul that this man was only beginning to reveal how well he could claim my body. And I responded to all of it as we moved about the bed.

At one point, I found myself straddling him, riding him as he lay on his back with his hands behind his head and watching me with encouraging eyes. Later, when he flipped me onto by side and came up behind me, he thrust tirelessly into me as he kissed the nape of my neck and gently caressed my breasts. And then it occurred to me that Austin himself had yet to come. How was that even possible? Was he supernatural? Or was he just that good?

I didn't know. And I seriously didn't care, because when he turned me onto my back, I could see on his face just how much he was enjoying himself.

I reached out my hand and placed it against his right pec, and when I pinched his own nipple, intense waves of pleasure appeared on his face, and his eyes became hooded as he drove into me. I wanted him to come, so I bucked hard against him just as my own orgasm started to build again. Together, we looked into one another's eyes just as release started to overcome each of us. And as it did, our bodies shuddered as we cried out in ways that underscored our love for one another. It was real. It was undeniable.

And when it was over—when he swung his arms around me, turned me onto my side, and held me close to him as he came up behind me and told me again that he loved me...

I thanked God that we were here.

EPILOGUE

San Miguel de Allende, Mexico
Two months later

AFTER NEARLY TWO months in San Miguel de Allende—a gorgeous, majestic city in the mountains of Mexico—Austin and I spent a final night out on the town before our return to New York.

Our first stop was the rooftop bar of the famed Rosewood hotel, where we enjoyed cocktails, tapas, and the colorful mix of languages that surrounded us, while taking in dramatic, sweeping views of the sunset and the city we'd come to love during our seven-week stay. When it was time for dinner, we took the elevator to the first floor, which housed the hotel's five-star restaurant, 1826.

There, in a large, warmly lit room that could have served as a romantic movie set, we sat at a table for two, where we shared a bottle of champagne, an amuse bouche tinged with frothy flavors of the sea, a first course of tuna tartare, and a host of other mouth-watering delights, all of which made for a fitting end to our time in San Miguel.

After dinner, we walked hand-in-hand from the hotel into the busy, cobblestoned streets, which teemed with people as this city—much like Manhattan—was one that never slept.

When we reached the city's central Jardín, we stopped and shared a bittersweet final look at La Parroquia—the towering parish church that dominated the Jardín with massive pink spires that stretched high into the sky.

"Would you like to take a cab home?" Austin asked. "Or would you rather walk?"

That was no small question, since San Miguel was located in a deep valley surrounded by hills and mountains. The walk home was so steep, it was ridiculous.

"If you're up for it, let's walk," I said. "I want to savor every last moment of our remaining time here."

"I don't want to go back to New York," he said as we left the Jardín and began the uphill walk home.

"Neither do I. This place is a hidden jewel, and experiencing it with you has been one of the highlights of my life."

When I said that to him, he wrapped his arm around my waist and pulled me close. "I love you, Sienna."

"I love you, Austin."

"You know what?" he said.

"What's that?"

"We're pretty lucky."

"We are," I agreed. "In so many ways. But I'm curious. Which ways are you referring to now?"

"I'm not sure where to begin."

"Anywhere is fine."

"Then I'll start with how well Jackson, Harper, and Mimi took the news that we'd fallen in love with each other."

"I can see them now," I said. "Six eyes turning into the size of saucers as they looked at us in disbelief."

"Once the shock wore off, they seemed genuinely happy for us—especially since none of them ever had a clue about our feelings for each other. The fact that we were able to keep our feelings from them proved that we'd done our best to honor your contract with Jackson. I think they respected that."

"Harper told me herself that she did. She said that I was a better actress than I had any reason to be."

"Jackson's been good to us," he said.

"Jackson's the best."

"I'm going to miss spending time at his home here."

"I couldn't agree more. After the *People* story hit, Jackson's the one who told us to get out of the States and let him deal with the fallout of his coming out on his own. It was beyond kind of him to send us here."

"And he was right to do so, because since we arrived, no one has bothered you."

"That's because people don't know me here."

"Whatever the reason, spending nearly two months in his house with you has been something I'll never forget, Sienna. I've enjoyed living with you. Waking up with you. Spending each day with you. Cooking for you. Going shopping with you at the mercado. And especially having complete and total access to you in the bedroom."

"I think that's been my favorite part," I said.

"Just so you know, I'm making love to you tonight."

"You don't say, Mr. Black?

"I do say. And you have no idea what I'm going to do to you."

"What else can you do to me that you already haven't done to me?"

"Plenty," he said. "You'll see."

THE NEXT MORNING, I woke to find a note on Austin's pillow. After wiping my eyes, I picked it up and read it.

I WAS GOING to make breakfast for us, but we're out of eggs. I'm going down to the mercado *to grab a few things.*

I'LL BE BACK in a flash.

—A.

I SAT up in bed and wondered when he'd left. I couldn't be sure, but when I got out of bed to use the bathroom and caught sight of my reflection in the mirror, I knew that I needed to shower before he got a good look at the fright wig my hair had become. Last night, he'd torn me up—and right now? With lipstick and mascara smeared across my face? I needed to go into full repair mode.

Five minutes later, I was in the shower when I heard Austin call out to me that he was home.

Crisis averted, I thought as I scrubbed my face.

"I'm in the shower," I said. "Give me ten minutes, OK?"

"No problem—I'm going to make omelets. How hungry are you?"

"After what you did to me last night? Famished!"

"I've got your back, babe."

You've always had it, I thought with a deep sense of love and gratitude. *Thank God for you, Austin.*

When I got out of the shower, I put on a white terrycloth bathrobe, ran a comb through my damp hair, and brushed my teeth before I applied one type of moisturizer to my face, and another type to my body. When I was finished, I looked at myself in the mirror—and smiled in relief.

From monster to human. Congrats!

When I joined Austin in the kitchen, I realized that I must have slept through his own shower, because it was clear that he'd already had one. He was freshly shaven, his dark hair was parted on the side and slicked through with gel, he was wearing a pair of black Nike running pants that hugged his ass in all the right ways, and he wore a black, V-necked T-shirt that looked so sexy on him, I wanted to say to hell with breakfast and just haul him back into bed with me.

"Look at you," I said as I walked over and kissed him on the lips. "So handsome."

"Handsome?" he said.

"And hot."

He reached for my hands. "When a guy like me has the good fortune of being with a woman like you, he takes none of it for granted."

I blushed when he said that and then I glanced over at the countertop, where there were eggs, cheese, onions, and all sorts of colorful peppers.

"I love your omelets," I said.

"Which is why I'm making them for you. Today, we leave on the highest of notes."

"Do you need help with the prep?"

"I love to cook with you at my side," he said. "How about if I take the onions, and you dice the peppers?"

"Done and done." I shot him a mischievous look. "Hand me the big blade, big boy."

"I'm assuming you mean the butcher knife?"

"You can take that however you want to take it."

He laughed when I said that, and then handed me the knife I wanted.

"You need to get some food in you," he said. "We can talk about the other blade later if you want."

"Oh, I think I'll probably want to do that," I said. "It's only eight o'clock. And we don't leave here until three..."

"Then let's be efficient," he said. "Start chopping."

I saluted him.

"Yes, sir."

AFTER A DELICIOUS BREAKFAST, Austin asked if I'd like to check out the view from the third-story terrace.

"I want to see it one last time," he said.

"Same here," I said. "Let's go."

When he reached for my hand, our fingers intertwined as we started for the staircase that led to the third-story terrace. With each step we took, his grip tightened against mine in a show of love that was so palpable, I couldn't believe for the life of me that I was I was here again—that I was in love again—but I was. And this time love felt different. Years ago, when I fell in love with Eric, love had felt sweet. But love with Austin? This love felt charged and alive, as deep as it was profound. It was the real thing—a lasting thing. I started thinking about what our future together would look like when we returned home just as we stepped out onto the terrace.

And when we did, it wasn't the views of the city that

captured my attention. Instead, everywhere I looked were vases filled with red roses.

"Oh, my God," I said. "What have you done?"

"It's our last day here," he said. "I wanted to make it special."

"Well, you've certainly accomplished that," I said as I admired the flowers. "They're stunning. How did you ever manage to get all of this up here? Did you do this while I was in the shower?"

"I did," he said. "I can be very productive when I need to be." He took hold of my hand. "I need to talk to you," he said.

"All right..."

"Last night, after you fell asleep, I thought about a lot of things. I thought about leaving here. I thought about not living with you. I thought about how hard that would be for me, and also hopefully for you. What I'm going to ask you is something I've never asked another woman."

My breath caught when he said that, and I just blinked at him. Was he about to propose to me? As my mind started to race, he started to speak.

"Sienna, I know that when we return to Manhattan, you want to find a new apartment for yourself, but I have another idea."

"What idea?"

"What if you were to live with me?" he asked. "You've seen my apartment—it's huge. There's plenty of room for each of us. And together, we can change whatever things you don't like so we can make that apartment *our* home, because that matters to me. I want our home to be a reflection of us. So, what do you say? I now know what it's like to live with you, and because of that, I don't want to live without you. I don't want this to end. Will you live with me?"

My heart slowed a bit when he said that, because this wasn't about a marriage proposal—it was about us living together. That I could handle. Still, before I answered him, I needed to be sure that I wanted the same. So, I gently eased away from him and moved to the balcony that overlooked the city. As I looked out at all of the colors that defined San Miguel, I realized that after living with Austin these past seven weeks, waking up without him next to me would be hell. It wouldn't feel right. We'd grown too close.

Then live with him...

I turned to look at him as a breeze caught hold of my hair and lifted it off my shoulders, as if it were meant to take a weight off me.

"Of course, I'll live with you," I said.

"You will?"

"I love you, Austin. I also don't want this to end."

"I'm glad to hear that," he said. "Because neither do I."

And with that, he stood before me and dropped to one knee. Shocked, I just looked at him, knowing what was coming next but not quite believing it.

"Sienna," he said. "I have another question for you..."

Choked with emotion and with my eyes brimming bright with tears, I tried my best to steady myself as he took hold of my left hand.

This can't be happening to me, I thought. *It can't!*

But it was, and I felt my body literally trembling in the face of it. I looked down at him, and saw in his eyes not only his love for me, but also his need to have me completely to himself.

"Yes?" I said to him.

He let go of my hand, reached into his pants pocket, and removed a small black velvet box, which he held out to me before he opened it. And when he did? I pressed my free hand to my mouth, because inside was a massive diamond solitaire engagement ring that glinted against the sun, and set fire to my eyes as this moment claimed each of us.

"Marry me," he said. "Give me the chance to make you the happiest woman in the world. I want to build a life with you. I want to grow old with you. I want to have children with you. And I want to experience a lifetime of happiness with you. Will you marry me?" he asked. "Will you be my wife?"

As I looked at him kneeling in front of me with his heart on his sleeve, I knew that he and I were right together. That we were *meant* to be with one another. So, why deny it? Why throw up walls where there should be no walls? What I knew in that moment is that all I ever wanted was Austin. Always and forever.

I extended my left hand to him, and when I did, I smiled at him.

"Put a ring on it, Austin," I said. "I'd be honored to be your wife. You're the best thing that's ever happened to me. I want to spend the rest of my life with you."

When Austin slipped the ring onto my ring finger, I admired it for a moment, I felt the weight of what that ring meant for us as a couple, and then he suddenly lifted me off my feet and kissed me hard on the lips before he carried me down to our bedroom and made love to me again. And when he did?

He left no part of me untouched or unloved.

And the following year? When I won the Academy Award for Best Actress for my role in *Lion*? As happy as I was at that moment, I was happier still that Austin Black—a man who, in reflection, I now realized I'd fallen hard for during that long ago evening when he'd helped me into my shoes—had come into my life for a reason. With him forever and always at my side, I knew in my heart that together we could bear the full force of life's blunt winds, its glorious surprises, its many disappointments, and also its ridiculous highs.

Soulmates did exist—and Austin was forever mine.

AFTERWORD

Thank you for reading *Faking It*! I hope you enjoyed it. Look for *Making It* and *Killing It* to appear wherever e-books are sold in 2018.

Can't wait for my next book? More are on the way, and finding out when is easy! Join me on Facebook here, and especially join my SPAM-free email blast here. By joining my email blast, you'll never miss another book—or the opportunity to receive a free ARC to review a book before it goes live to the public.

I love to hear from my readers! If you have any questions or comments, please reach out to me at mailto:christinarossauthor@gmail.com. I hope to hear from you soon!

If you would leave a review of this or any of my books, I'd appreciate it. Reviews are critical to every writer. Please leave even the shortest of reviews. And thank you for doing so!

XO,
   Christina